DATE DUE

12-31-93			
MAY 29 1995			
8V 428762		8114195	
MAR 1 7 2000		547151 7	
MAY 25 2003			
GAYLORD			PRINTED IN U.S.A.

MISSING PIECES

**A Chronicle
of Living
with a Disability**

MISSING PIECES:
A Chronicle
of Living
with a Disability

Irving Kenneth Zola

Temple University Press

Philadelphia

Temple University Press, Philadelphia 19122
© 1982 by Temple University. All rights reserved
Published 1982
Printed in the United States of America

Library of Congress Cataloging in Publication Data
Zola, Irving Kenneth, 1935–
   Missing pieces.
   1. Handicapped—Institutional care—Netherlands
—Case studies.   2. Zola, Irving Kenneth, 1935–
3. Physically handicapped—United States—Biography.
I. Title.
HV1559.N4Z64   362.4'385'09492   81-13628
ISBN 0-87722-232-0   AACR2

To Willem Metz—physician, scholar, researcher, friend and humanitarian, and to all who live and work in Het Dorp

Acknowledgments

Acknowledging my indebtedness is exceedingly difficult. Because this is such a personal document, I am first of all indebted to all those people and experiences that enabled me to get to "this place" in my life. Then there are the residents of Het Dorp who shared parts of their lives and experiences and set me on a path of reflection down which I am still travelling. To three people who commented extensively on this manuscript, I owe special thanks. Mara Sanadi saw me and it through its earliest draft. Dr. Bonnie Leonard and Dr. Una Maclean not only helped sharpen the revisions but supported my efforts to stay with the book when publishers were rejecting it. In that regard, I want to particularly appreciate Michael Ames, my editor at Temple University Press. After thirty-five others had said "No," "Maybe," and "Wait," he answered with a resounding "Yes!"

I would like to thank the editors of several journals for allowing me to use material that first appeared in their pages. Portions of Chapter 9 have appeared in "When Getting into the Field Means Getting into Oneself," *The New England Sociologist* 1, no. 2 (Summer 1979): 21–30. Portions of Chapter 10 have appeared in "A Story Difficult to Hear and Tell," *The Exceptional Parent* 9, no. 3 (June 1979): D3–D8. Reprinted with permission of *The Exceptional Parent* magazine; copyright © 1979. Portions of Chapter 10 have also appeared in "Communication Barriers between 'the Able-Bodied' and 'the Handicapped,' " *Archives of Physical Medicine and Rehabilitation* 62, no. 8 (August 1981): 355–359. Portions of Chapter 11 will also appear in a forthcoming issue of *Archives of Physical Medicine and Rehabilitation*.

Finally, there are all my friends and colleagues, particularly those at the Netherlands Institute of Preventive Medicine in Leiden, the Department of Sociology at Brandeis, Greenhouse, Inc., and the Boston Self-Help Center, who helped me overcome my personal reticence to make this account and commentary public. If you the reader get half as much from reading this book as I did from writing up my experiences, then all my efforts will have been worthwhile.

Contents

PART ONE

BEFORE

Prologue

Overcoming Is Only the Start

Any span of the [life] cycle lived without vigorous meaning at the beginning, in the middle, or at the end, endangers the sense of life, and meaning of death in all whose life stages are intertwined.

Erik Erikson

I am by professional training both a social observer and a psychological counselor. Yet for over two decades I have succeeded in hiding a piece of myself from my own view. Given the obviousness of my physical handicap this has taken some doing.

Between the ages of fifteen and twenty, I suffered two major traumas—first polio and then four years later an automobile accident. Each resulted in a year's confinement and each was severely debilitating. With polio I lost all major functions and was originally paralyzed from the neck down. But over a two-year period, there was a gradual return of sensation, motion, and strength. I was left, however, with considerable weakness and nerve loss scattered throughout my body, but particularly in my stomach, back, and right leg.

The accident, which resulted in several cuts, bruises, and a shattered right femur, became a very different experience. With polio, I was in a hospital ward, separated from my family but surrounded by fellow patients engaged in a similar struggle for recovery. With my shattered femur, I was at home, alone in my bedroom and isolated from the rest of the world. Enclosed in a cast from my right foot to my chest, I felt far more immobile and helpless than with my polio. There was no day-by-day progress to watch and participate in. But when my cast was finally removed nine months later, I got up and walked almost as well as before the accident. A long thin scar and an implanted but fairly unobtrusive steel plate were the major physical reminders of the experience.

As a result of these two "medical incidents," I wear a long leg brace and a steel-reinforced back support, and I use a cane. My children, when very young, described me as walking funny. To the rest of the world I limped. To me, all of it was just something that got in the way, another difficulty to be over-come. For twenty years I devoted more psychological and physical energy to this task than I realized. But overcoming is not the same as integrating. And this is one of the bittersweet lessons recorded in this book.

1971–72 was my sabbatical year and I was spending it as a consultant-in-residence to the Netherlands Institute of Preven-tive Medicine in Leiden. Trying to speak Dutch was difficult enough (at the end of a year my Dutch friends noted how much my German had improved!) but hearing them use my language in unaccustomed ways was more disturbing. A particular shock came from their pronunciation of the word for a handicapped person, someone we Americans call an invalid. My Dutch friends, however, enunciated it in accord with its derivation—from the word "valid." To them this was the only natural way to refer to a reality—the difference between healthy people and the handicapped lay in the latter's invalidity. Every time I heard it—and given my work at a medical institution that was often—it made me shudder. The pain stirred was very deep but I put it aside until what I thought was a series of chance events catalyzed me to greater probing.

Through one of my colleagues at the Institute, Dr. Willem Metz, I was invited to see Het Dorp, a 65-acre village specifically designed to house four hundred severely disabled adult Nether-landers. It became the setting for this chronicle and the stimulus for the search for my missing piece, my physical handicap. I approached Het Dorp as I do many things, exploring and un-committed. I went first as a tourist and a professional for a day in January 1972 but waited five months before returning for a week as a resident visitor. I subsequently came again for three days in August 1974, and again for a weekend in June 1976.

Visit was the appropriate word for what I initially set out to do in an aditional week at Het Dorp. I was not fully conscious of what drew me back, but I certainly did not plan to engage in a research project, let alone publish anything based on my story. As is my practice, I expected to take notes but without a specific purpose in mind. To get a feel for Het Dorp, I would rely pretty much on an experiential approach. I decided that for a week I would resume the role of a functional paraplegic. From my personal medical experiences, I was quite confident of my ability to handle the ordinary problems of being physically restricted. So for a week, back into a wheelchair I went. I did everything from that position. I traveled, ate, washed, shaved, and at the end of each day hoisted myself wearily into bed. All I hoped to gain was greater awareness of the physical existence of the residents and perhaps some greater ease of communication with them. I expected to live in a resident room but since I spoke almost no Dutch I anticipated that most of my contacts would be with the administration. In short, I figured that this "patient experience" would provide but an added dimension. Unexpectedly, this "extra" became practically "the all."

Time collapsed during these seven days. Phases of acceptance that in previous circumstances had taken weeks and months, here took minutes and hours. I became so quickly involved in a network of relationships that I occasionally felt part of a speeded-up movie. Though unrelated to the timing of my visit, two events of great symbolic importance took place during this week. The first was the Gala, the big social happening of the year where residents and staff performed, drank, and celebrated. The second event was the first *open* meeting of the Dorp Council, a group of elected residents supplemented by advisers from the Administration. The purpose of the meeting was to demonstrate how important decisions were made and to try to involve residents more directly in issues of Dorp concern. During the week, I visited all the facilities where the residents spent their time. But most important, they let me into their homes and into their lives. No resident I wanted to see ever refused my request, and many more sought me out. But the communication was never one-way. They were quite willing to tell me their story, but they also wanted to know mine. They asked how I got through school. How did I become a professor? Was I rich? Did I have influence? Were there special institutions in America that helped people like myself?

All manner of questions. Many could be dubbed "mechanical." But the residents were concerned not only with how I made it physically but how I made it sexually. Not only what devices I used in helping me walk but whether I needed any help in having sexual relations. And for each question they asked of me, I found that I was asking myself a dozen more and surprising myself with the answers.

The end of seven days found me physically exhausted but mentally exhilarated. I was the possessor of over two hundred pages of detailed notes, supplemented by numerous reports and documents. Though what I saw in seven days was only a fragment of life at Het Dorp, several things have nevertheless prompted me to write this book. First of all, there are few accessible accounts of this rather unusual experiment in living. And while I am critical of some of what has happened and is happening, my criticism is of a situation that both residents and administration are locked into by historical, political, and social events, a situation based on the condition of being "handicapped" in a world of "normals." To answer at the outset a question I am often asked, I regard this experiment as a success—not *the* answer for those with severe physical disabilities but *an* answer. Second, in the very creation and development of Het Dorp there are basic lessons to be learned about social life. Those who live and work at Het Dorp are not only a group of people trying to learn the basic skills that we so often take for granted, but in trying to achieve "optimal human happiness" they are after a goal common to all people. Third, the wide range of reactions produced in audiences when I tell of my experience convinces me of its richness regardless of any interpretation I might place on it.

But most of all I am writing because I learned something special. Seven days at Het Dorp, fifteen years of psychological counseling, twenty-five years of professional sociologizing, thirty years of living with a disability, and over forty years of just living, have finally raised to my consciousness what having a handicap in a healthist society is all about. But this is more than an exercise in "telling it like it really is." My story is one of rediscovery—not only about how "it" is, but why it took and is taking so long for the world to see and hear "it."

It is to capture such multiple aims that I have chosen a rather unconventional format for a social scientist. The book is a first-person narrative. Everything is seen through my filter. I begin with two background chapters, which describe my first trip to the Village and provide the building blocks for the chronicle—Het Dorp's founding, its architecture, its residents, its staffing and organization. The next seven chapters are a seven-day slice of their life and of my own. While I have tried to deal in the daily accounts with many issues arising from my resident experience, there are some questions that require more time and space. It is to these matters that the final three chapters are devoted.

The style of a chronology deserves some further explanation. It is more than a traditional set of field notes. What is presented are my edited observations (amplified occassionally by later recall) intermixed with what I felt about what I saw and heard and overlaid with some interpretations. Sometimes the basic source of data is a resident experience, sometimes it is my own. Finally, a word about the speakers in my story. Though a person may recognize his own words, it is hoped that no one else will. I have taken the liberty of altering times and physical descriptions, changing names, age, and gender, and occasionally putting the words of one resident into the mouth's of one, two, or even three others. The names and faces may be fictional but the words and deeds are exactly as they happened.

All in all this book is a series of progress reports: of me a man in transition; of Het Dorp as a social experiment; of the Villager's struggle to be regarded as fully human; of society's difficulty in integrating those it labels "invalid." What I have produced might well be called a socio-autobiography, a personal and social odyssey that chronicles not only my beginning acknowledgment of the impact of my physical differences on my HIS life but also my growing awareness of the ways in which society invalidate's people with a chronic disability.

Het Dorp wishes to encourage both
itself and others never to settle for
half-measures or partial solutions to
human problems.

Arie Klapwijk

Sitting at my desk in early October, I was leafing through the annual research bulletin of the Netherlands Institute of Preventive Medicine. I was in Leiden, it was 1971 and I was beginning my first sabbatical. I had avoided looking at this dry booklet for several weeks now. But as a consultant-in-residence, I knew I should be aware of what my colleagues were up to. In perusing the lengthy list of ongoing projects, my eyes stopped at the name of Dr. Willem Metz. He was reported as being involved in the study of what one of my colleagues called "diminished persons"—the mentally retarded, the physically handicapped, the neurologically damaged. I was interested in similar areas, though I referred to my field of specialization as rehabilitation. When I remembered that he had been a practising physician for most of his life, turning to social research only in his late forties or early fifties I became curious to meet him.

A few weeks later, while eating lunch at the Institute cafeteria, I had that opportunity. He was pointed out to me as the man at a corner table, animatedly discussing some issue with a younger man. Tall, white-haired, with rosy cheeks, he was a sparkling man of sixty. Apologizing for the interruption, I introduced myself. In the next hour camaraderie developed as we realized how much of a mutual history we shared. Trying to give voice to the lives and troubles of patients, we were regarded by many of our Dutch colleagues as overemotional and subjective. This concern earned us the somewhat puzzling label of "phenomenologists."

Though Dr. Metz continually apologized for his English, we had no difficulty in talking about our current interests. One especially held my attention: his work at Het Dorp. Though I knew of a long European tradition of "therapeutic communities," I knew of none that was either "free-standing" or devoted exclusively to the physically disabled. Dr. Metz assured me that indeed Het Dorp was unique, but there was a part of me that just couldn't visualize "a village." My experience with traditional institutional care was too deeply ingrained. Metz laughed knowingly at my bewilderment but had an answer. Since he had done research there, he would be glad to arrange a tour. We looked at our respective calendars and set a tentative date for early January.

My curiosity was piqued and I sought to learn something about the Village beforehand. With a brochure, an annual report, and conversations with friends (everyone seemed to know something about Het Dorp), I got a glimmering of how the Village came to be. In 1959 a physician by the name of Klapwijk was appointed head of the Johanna Stichting Foundation. This was the first Dutch institute for the non-adult physically handicapped. As a center it was eminently successful—yet Klapwijk was bothered by this very fact. He and his staff were "physically rehabilitating" a large number of very severely disabled young children only to see them go off into a world in which they could neither fit nor function. To a large extent he felt this was due to the outside world's unwillingness socially, psychologically, and architecturally to integrate them. He also saw that the available alternative—seclusion in institutions or in their parental homes—was not what he would call "living." In reality these people were being given a kind of a life sentence, or more appropriately a death sentence, the end of life as the rest of us know it. Like many, he felt this was unjust, particularly in a land of plenty, but like relatively few, he decided to do something about it. As he put it, "I wanted a way to find and help severe invalids achieve optimal human development and optimal human happiness." This was a goal that ultimately led to a statement of principle by Klapwijk and his colleagues:

Those of us who are not handicapped and who live in a modern welfare state, take several minimum comforts for granted. All of us create our lives on the following six building stones:
1 The privacy of our own living quarters.
2 The opportunity to work or at least pursue useful occupations.
3 Recreation and relaxation.
4 Participation in cultural life.
5 The opportunity to fulfill religious needs.
6 A democratic right-of-say in our private and community lives.

Translating these principles into a program for everyday living would not be easy. Like other "experiments in living," it was based on disillusionment with the current way of life. To quote the founders, they wanted a place

where life could begin anew, where its physically handicapped inhabitants could live with dignity and independence, *without the sense of futility and hopelessness of being restricted in medical institutions.*

Dr. Klapwijk had the idea, but no takers. He went to government agencies and to public and private foundations. They all said, "Yes, yes. What you say is true. We understand there are many people like that but we don't have the money for that kind of thing." Finally, in a move of both desperation and inspiration, he took his case to the public. In November 1962 he and several show business personalities created what is familiar to American audiences, a twenty-three-hour radio and television marathon. It was a fantastic success. They pricked the conscience of the nation to the tune of 21 million guilders, or 6 million dollars. Few contributions were large, but they averaged about $1.20 for every adult Netherlander!

The phrase "pricking the conscience of the public" is intentional. I was not there and have only the scantiest reports, but let me create a speculative image. The show was, of course, an entertainment. Yet lurking behind the gay facade was a horror show. Out of the corner of my eye I see some famous performer or some smiling "everyman" who either tells about or shows me a crippled child crawling or staggering or dying. And I am asked, "Don't you want to help him walk, make him smile?" Certainly the host conjured up the current state of affairs in long-term institutions for the physically debilitated. The crowding, the emptiness, the stench, all of it must have been there. And the residents' suffering was contrasted with "your good and plenty." For the early 1960s was a time of economic boom in

The emblem of the television funding marathon that opened the hearts of the Dutch people and the doors of Het Dorp. The key could unlock the door to a resident's own home and provide an opportunity for self-reliance unavailable elsewhere. The emblem expresses the purpose and design of the Village. It shows a person finding protection and security beneath a roof held aloft with the person's own hands, a symbol of the shelter and independence that Het Dorp offers to handicapped people.

Western Europe and the Netherlands was no exception. In this Calvinist country, one could not help but feel guilty. But absolution was around the corner. Available to the audience of this telethon was something rarely available to their American counterparts. Americans are usually asked for money to aid in an ongoing process, such as research, that has only a hope attached to it. The Dutch were given the promise of a final answer. "Give us the money and we will build a new world for these people." They gave the money, and Dr. Klapwijk and his colleagues built the "new world." Construction began in 1964, the first Villagers arrived in 1968, and by 1972 Het Drop was in full operation with four hundred residents.

That Dr. Klapwijk and his associates did not really promise a final, "once-and-for-all" answer and were quite aware of the problems to come (as their planning documents show), is sadly irrelevant. They were perceived as promising a utopia; anything less would be regarded as a kind of betrayal.

Who were the beneficiaries of the plan? Not unexpectedly, no accurate figures could be found for the prevalence or incidence of people with physical or mental handicaps in the Netherlands. (Nor were such figures available for the United States.). It was clear to the founders, however, that there were many "out there." Based on their clinical experience and their hopes, they created the following admissions philosophy:

> *Selection Policy*—Het Dorp, where a team selects residents, wishes to ensure the physically handicapped, living, social, and work opportunities in an atmosphere where these elements can best contribute to a large measure of happiness. *Criteria:*
> 1 Het Dorp is open to the handicapped of all creeds.
> 2 Het Dorp is, in principle, intended for the handicapped of all ages. In reality, however, handicapped youth usually are still in stages of rehabilitation until their eighteenth or twentieth year, and the handicapped older than sixty or sixty-five—at least at present—can preferably be placed in homes for the aged.

3 Het Dorp prefers to accept only the handicapped who have achieved maximum rehabilitation before arrival. In this connection, of course, the age of the candidate and the nature of his handicap must be taken into consideration.

4 Het Drop is not open to the mentally handicapped, since its community can in no way help them. With respect to this criterion, first consideration is not the intelligence quotient of the candidate but rather his degree of social competence: whether he can provide a positive contribution to the community and profit himself from the association.

5 Het Drop is not intended for those who are handicapped in the sensory organs only. However, the limited hearing or sight of the physically handicapped is not in general a deciding factor so long as the other criteria for selection are present.

6 Should the handicapped candidate suffer from chronic illness which would require twenty-four-hour medical and technical care, then accommodation in a nursing home is preferable.

7 The seriousness of the handicap is not a deciding factor for admission to Het Dorp, since both general and individual facilities are adaptable and specifically designed for those who desire to achieve the most rewarding life possible.

8 In selecting residents, Het Dorp strives, first of all, to serve the interests of the candidate. Het Dorp is, therefore, always pleased to take these interests to heart— often in an advisory function—even if they would better be served outside the community. It is then to be expected that Het Dorp will consider these other solutions critically with an eye to achieving the greatest possible degree of development for the handicapped person in question.

I read and reread this philosophy trying to think of its implications. Two things struck me. The first concerned demographics. The Villages openness to all comers solicited a heterogeneity of class and religion absent in most Dutch communities, particularly in village's of four hundred people. How well Het Dorp succeeded I don't know. The only material I could find told me only that there were more women than men (Table 1) and that, since women tended to live longer than men, the age spread reflected this (Table 2).

Table 1   Number of Residents in 1971

Sex	Disabled	"Healthy"
Female	225	2
Male	162	6
Total*	387	8

*Included in the total are 37 couples. In 29 cases both partners were disabled and in 8 only one partner was disabled.

Table 2   Number of Residents in 1971 Distributed by Age

Age	Men	Women	Total
Under 20	1	0	1
20–25	24	30	54
25–30	35	22	57
30–35	20	28	48
35–40	13	28	41
40–45	16	28	44
45–50	21	26	47
50–55	15	26	41
55–60	9	18	27
60–65	7	12	19
Over 65	1	7	8
Total	162	225	387

But what really absorbed me were the diagnosed conditions of the residents. The available data confirmed that their medical problems were serious:

*Diagnosis/Number of Residents**

Cerebral palsy 98	Still-Chaufford's Disease 3
Multiple sclerosis 50	Syringomyelia 3
Muscular dystrophy 47	Congenital luxation of the hips 3
Poliomyelitis 28	
Rheumatoid arthritis 27	Idiopathic kyphoscoliose 3
Spina bifida 27	Morquio's Disease 2
Encephalopathea on traumatic or operative base 23	Chondrodystrophy 2
	Hemophilia 1
Ataxia of Friedrich 13	Myositis ossificans 1
Congenital malformations 7	Sclerodermia 1
Osteogenesis imperfecta 6	Coxitis tuberculosa 1
Other somatic diseases 5	Spastic spinal paraplegia 1
Arthrogryposis 4	Epilepsy 1
Bechterew's Disease 3	
Parkinson's Disease 3	"Healthy" 8

The admission criteria hinted that while a resident with a serious illness would be admitted, the illness must somehow be contained. While no one with a rapidly progressive disease was admitted, the implication was that a dramatic change for the worse might force an individual to leave. An official document did little to allay this suspicion:

> There is no age limit upwards, but those inmates who through old age should become mentally or physically helpless or permanently bedridden, will have to be persuaded to be moved to a hospital or other institution. The same applies for residents who develop mental or physical illnesses requiring nursing or medical treatment.

A later document apparently available to the residents sought to mitigate this policy:

*Sixteen residents were not classified.

It can be easily understood that if a person comes to the Village knowing beforehand that as a consequence of his kind of illness he has to leave the Village at an uncertain future moment, this has a heavy psychological bearing on his person, which in his total attitude could prove fatal for his/her social adaptation and so for his/her happiness in the Village. . . .

We are for the moment of the opinion that in these cases the principle of personal free choice must be maintained. This could imply—for the future—that we would have to organize a 24-hour-a-day nursing department, but this is at the moment still being studied. For the time being, we have succeeded in supplying the necessary nursing help in their own living quarters.

My instincts told me that these statements were equivocal and that there was a shadow, however small, over this utopia.

This was all I could learn from the documents about Het Dorp. Then I began to feel the necessity for some inner preparedness. Two weeks later on November 10, I was sitting at my desk with time on my hands and a nagging memory on my mind. This date would have been my fourteenth wedding anniversary. (I had separated from my wife that fall.) With nothing more than the wish to put some part of my life in order, I reached for a yellowing but carefully preserved set of notes. They had been written on May 2 and May 3, 1969, when I was on assignment in New Delhi, India, for the World Health Organization. For two and a half years I had kept them close at hand, promising to put them in coherent form some day. Today was that day and so I began to write.

With Hieronymous Bosch in India

I had expected many unusual things of India but the welcoming remarks were not among them. As I walked from my plane, a government official, a Sikh, resplendant in his turban, rushed forward through the crowd to greet me. After we introduced ourselves and shook hands, he asked in quick succession: "Where in the States are you from? Where was your undergraduate degree from? Your graduate degree? What happened to your leg?" The latter, as any American would know, was hardly a typical opening between strangers. I answered in turn, "Boston, Harvard A.B., Harvard Ph.D.," and then, somewhat hesitatingly, "polio complicated by an auto accident." The question bothered me and I began to wonder about Sikhs. When we reached our car, I was introduced to his colleague, a Tamil, who asked my home, my schooling, and what happened to my leg. The next several hours produced more of the same. Whether it was heads of bureaus or government ministers, the introductory questions varied little. While my response seemed to be taken as but pertinent bits of information to be received and stored, I was curious, even a little put out, at this intrusion into what Americans regard as so private a matter. It had been many years since I was made directly aware that I wore a back support and a long leg brace, used a cane, and walked with a limp. But I decided to ignore it and turn my attention to the business at hand. This was, however, an omen of things to come, of an event a week later which would make me acutely conscious of "what happened to my leg."

On Friday afternoon about 2:00 P.M., I was sitting outside the posh Oberoi Hotel. It was hot and dry, nearly a hundred degrees in the shade, but my excitement overcame my usual dislike of heat. A week of conferences had been interesting but today was to be my first "adventure." After touring several impressive medical facilities, I was anxious to see something more local, and secretly I thought, more real. In response to my request, colleagues had arranged a visit with an Ayurvedic healer, a local folk physician. And so I waited and wondered about the questions I would ask.

A horn sounded and the bus, decorated with the familiar WHO symbol, pulled up. In the rear seats I could see my guides for the day, Doctors T. and M. They waved and I saluted back. Paying more attention to Dr. M., who looked exquisite again in a sari, I pushed myself to a standing position. As I did, I heard a crack. It sounded as if it came from within me, but I felt all together. As I stepped toward the bus, there was an unpleasant squeaking and clicking sound. I climbed in and when I sat, my trouble became obvious. Something was trying to poke its way through the knee of my trousers. The brace, one I had had for 15 years had snapped somewhere just below the knee.

Here I was thousands of miles from home, in a strange land, without friends, and needless to say, without a spare brace—and on my way (of all things) to see an Ayurvedic healer. I had a certain confidence in his ability to deal with a myriad of problems, but a welder he was not! I turned, somewhat uncomfortably, to my hosts. "Ah," I stammered eloquently, "I seem to have a problem," and pointed to my leg. Unfortunately, as an explanation this did not suffice, so with great embarrassment I rolled up my trousers to show the dangling part. "No problem," they said, and gave the driver new directions. By this time I was soaked in sweat—partly from anxiety, and partly because this enclosed car bus felt like an oven.

In a few minutes we arrived at a series of low buildings, paint peeling and baked a dull orange by the sun. With an air of confidence that I lacked, Dr. T. identified the place as the Nehru Rehabilitation Center. As I limped toward the door a hundred yards away, the "clickety-clack" of my brace seemed to announce my coming. Neither the appearance of the building nor my first glimpse of its occupants reassured me. I was confronted by what I can only describe as an Hieronymous Bosch painting in *too*-living-color. While my Indian colleagues explained my problem to those in charge, I tried to absorb—or deny—the scene before my eyes. Within comfortable touching distance was a panorama of physical suffering. An old man in a turban, toothless, blind in one eye, with his foot missing below the ankle, stood quite straight, almost proud; a young man, twentyish, wandered around, speaking to many but with no one returning the attention; countless children limped to and fro; still younger ones, some with shrivelled limbs, some crying, some just staring, were held and occasionally rocked by their mothers. So many had missing extremities that I flashed to "read about" scenes of wartime surgeries, where one after another limbs are amputated, cast aside, and stacked in piles. Hardest to take were those who moved about in what felt like grotesque ways. Kneeling on a cart, a man in his mid-twenties pushed himself forward with his hands—a Porgy but without his grandeur. Another with no legs used his hands to hop from place to place with a slowness that was painful to watch.

But this was no whining mass of humanity as in the Bosch pictures. If anything, there was an air of resignation. And I seemed to be the only one showing signs of discomfort. As my stomach did flip-flops, I wondered what the hell I was doing here. Why did I leave safe Geneva for this? After days of hearing of the problems in the delivery of medical services, was I about to experience it firsthand? This was far beyond the limits of my intended participant-observation.

My distress was momentarily alleviated by a young boy. As he stared at me, I stared back. When I saw that he was wearing a long leg brace just like mine, I wanted to shout for joy. This meant that not only could this center help me, but that also at least some of the younger generation were receiving up-to-date rehabilitative care. I heard Dr. M. call me and then saw Dr. T. approaching. "Everything will be taken care of and we will pick you up in about two hours. All right?" I nodded my head in approval, not really meaning it. Were they really going to leave me here alone? I was embarrassed by the thought. What was it I feared? And so, acting braver than I felt, I shrugged my shoulders. Directed to a bench, I limped over and sat down. From this less vertical position I felt even more overwhelmed, almost suffocated, but I didn't know why. After all the time I had spent in hospitals, I was surprised at my reaction. Suddenly I understood. My hospital time was spent among people who were getting better or were struggling to. The troubles here were chronic and the patients not likely to improve.

Maybe my thoughts showed themselves, for people began to introduce themselves and explain the surroundings. They were trying to be helpful and friendly, but I could not understand a word they spoke and could only smile in return. Then as if he had hit on the source of my discomfort, a young man said something to the man beside me. When my bearded seatmate nodded approval, the young man excitedly jumped up, and dragging his left foot, rushed off through the crowd. In a few minutes he returned. In his outstretched hand was an opened bottle of Coke. My stomach sank and I hesitated. I remembered that just two days earlier my WHO colleagues and I had been wedded to our toilets because of dysentery contracted from the drinking water. Was I going to go through all this again? Noting my despair, he smiled knowingly and took the first drink himself. Turning to the crowd who had gathered around us, he nodded affirmatively his head and handed me the bottle. Embarrassed and I suppose grateful for his kindness, I couldn't resist. I drank and then passed the bottle. Everyone seemed pleased, including me.

There was little time to relish my bravery before a clerk in a long white coat appeared. "Dr. Zola, please come with me and we will take care of you." Out of the corner of my eye I noticed someone carrying a young boy from a cubicle. It was to that place that I was directed. "You'll be more comfortable here. So please take off your brace." He left and I looked around. He had closed the tattered curtain, which provided at best only a psychological sense of privacy. The table on which I was supposed to sit held a pool of urine perhaps left by the child made anxious when he was carried out so quickly to make room for me. I felt embarrassed. But it made little sense to insist that he be brought back to his puddle. So I sat on a rickety chair, took off my trousers, removed my brace, dressed again and then limped out, now moving more slowly and unsteadily, brace in hand, its right side cracked and dangling. I handed it this time to a young woman in white.

Calmer now, I returned to my bench. All I could do was watch the hubbub. People were moving about. Because of their herky-jerky motion, they seemed part of a movie in slow-motion. A wheelchair came speeding through the door and a teenage boy with dark curly hair, muscular above the waist, withered below, gave a piece of paper to the clerk. Then I noticed that many of those going back and forth had pieces of paper. But I had nothing. Nothing to do. Nothing to read. No one to talk to. More confused than scared I smiled at the children, and they smiled back. Amidst the rags and disfigurements, one thing began to stand out—all the medical staff in their stiff, gleaming white coats. All these men and women looked so young, so beautiful, so handsome. Was it just that they were healthy and we were not, or was some selection process going on? Were they chosen, or maybe motivated to work in such a place because of their appearance? I kept thinking of all the times I have sat at the mercy of a dentist and his dental hygienist as they, with sparkling, cavity-free teeth, proceeded to pick at my gums and instruct me about the perils of failing to brush properly.

My reverie was eventually interrupted. "Dr. Zola, it's ready." I rose and there was my brace—repaired and straight. Once again I was directed to the cubicle. I began to dress. A head poked in: "I wonder if you would mind coming out or just standing there with your brace." For a moment I did not grasp the man's meaning. He continued, "It would be nice for them. So that they could see their work." More out of gratitude than understanding, I rose. Embarrassed, I walked forward one step. My trousers were draped over my arm and there I stood—above the waist a jacket, shirt, and tie; below, undershorts, with my brace and me more publicly exposed than usual. With barely a glance, the attendant announced my presence and called for the staff to appear. Still another shock awaited me. There were five men: one missing an arm and a leg, one on crutches, one with a withered arm, and off to the side a big fellow, who carried in his arms a co-worker whose legs dangled as helplessly and lifelessly as my brace had a few hours before. Part of the hubbub was now explained, the people with pieces of paper going back and forth, even the numbers. For the past few hours I had been not only at a rehabilitation center, but at a sheltered workshop.

I thanked everyone, proudly pointed to my brace and even shook my leg as if to indicate its regained strength. They smiled, giggled, and left. I finished dressing and looked around. For the first time I was aware of the striking absence of disabled women. Surely they too must be suffering, but where? Were they in some sense considered not worthy of being given even this semblance of rehabilitation? As women and crippled, were they twice cursed? Still another attractive person presented me with a bill. The price in American terms was cheap enough, under a dollar. Yet what I felt was a bitter taste in my mouth. I could afford what many here could not. How typical was the little boy? How many such places were there? In a country of such scant resources, rehabilitation for anyone might be considered a luxury. Maybe that's why I was such a curiosity when I first came. One doesn't expect crippled people (ugly phrase) to hold high, or at least public, positions.

With such thoughts, I departed. I felt quite guilty and sure that I was fleeing something, but I was not sure what or why. I knew I was glad that I was once more whole. My medical colleagues reaffirmed this with an Americanism, "You look as good as new." I was uncomfortably elated with this cliché. As we walked to the car, they asked almost perfunctorily about the care I had received. When I said, "Fine," they asked no more and went on to talk about the next stop on our itinerary.

Like the opening words of greeting a week ago, my three-hour experience was just another piece of information, just another incident in their busy day, recorded and quickly forgotten. But not for me, not for me.

With a sense of satisfaction, I put down my pen and reread my story. It was dark outside. Most of the staff had gone home. I felt good but it was more than just a sense of closure. Only months later did I realize that writing this document was as much a beginning—the first step in reincorporating my physical handicap into who I was.

Forewarned about Het Dorp and to some extent about myself, I awaited Metz's call confirming my visit. In late December it came and on January 5, 1972, I travelled east across the Netherlands to Arnhem.

And I believe that man will not
merely endure he will prevail.

William Faulkner

The recollections of my first visit to Het Dorp seem strange. It was a silent tour. Though Dr. Metz and I were always together and were accompanied by numerous guides, I remember little dialogue. Maybe that was true. Since my time was limited, each official tried to explain his work as fully and quickly as possible. The tape recorder in my mind clicked away, my fingers noted data, but my eyes and thoughts were often elsewhere.

The morning was beautiful. Travelling across the Netherlands by train was pleasant, but so flat that I had the fantasy that from a tower in Amsterdam, I could see all the way into Germany. During the train trip, I thought surprisingly little about Het Dorp, but as Metz and I approached in his car, I was taken aback by the irony of its location, another tribute perhaps to Dutch tenacity to overcome the elements. While most of the Netherlands is flat, Het Dorp, this small 65-acre appendage to Arnhem, is built in, on, and around a series of hills and ravines. The primary reason for choosing this site was its availability and closeness to the parent institution to Dr. Klapwijk (the Johanna Stichting). Its seeming disadvantage to everyone with a physical disability was deceptive. As Dr. Metz explained, the chief architect of the Village was J. B. Bakema, who created the Lijnbaan, the pedestrian walk in the rebuilt city of Rotterdam. As in that mall, people came first. Here they were merely wheelchair users. Het Dorp was not designed as a place where a medical staff provided extensive care, but as a place where people lived.

And so it seemed. Standing at the highest point in the Village, I saw nothing striking. Het Dorp looked like a self-

contained middle-class housing project. Its three-story buildings were built into the landscape and, like most Dutch households, surrounded with flower gardens. The Village abutted a
busy four-lane highway. Along this outer edge were the administration building, a supermarket, a restaurant, a gasoline
station, a travel agency, a post office, a beauty shop. There was
also a place of worship, a public library, and far out of sight a
sports hall. Everything a village needed. And all these facilities
were open not only to the residents of the Village, but also to the
citizens of Arnhem. This was the tangible contact point and start
for integration of the two worlds—valid and invalid.

Behind me I heard the hum of a passing car but my reverie
was broken by a strange noise, the quiet whirr of an electric
wheelchair. Turning abruptly I saw my first resident. Paying
little attention to me or my colleagues, he drove into the supermarket. Shaking off my desire to follow him, I looked around
again to orient myself. The largest physical structure was a
six-story tower. I asked our administrative guide (he was one of
several to join Metz and me on our tour) what it was. "That's
where many of the staff live." I greeted this with an impassive
face but an inner twitch. I could not escape the symbolism of the
staff looking down upon the residents.

A question about resident housing brought an enthusiastic
reply. The dwellings ranged from a relatively new ten-unit
building for married couples to much larger ones containing
thirty, ninety, or one hundred twenty units. The guide seemed
particularly proud of the newest addition, the housing for couples, and I got a sense of the special place of marriage in the
history of Het Dorp. Then I recalled the picture in a brochure of
the first marriage and wondered for a moment if there had been
a "first child." "Though the building of married quarters was a
late addition, this was only natural," he pointed out, "since 84
percent of the residents are single and *prefer* to live alone." I
wondered if he could really be serious.

When I asked if it was possible to see their rooms, I was
quickly corrected. "Where they live is called their 'home' not
their 'room.' " My request was nevertheless granted and our

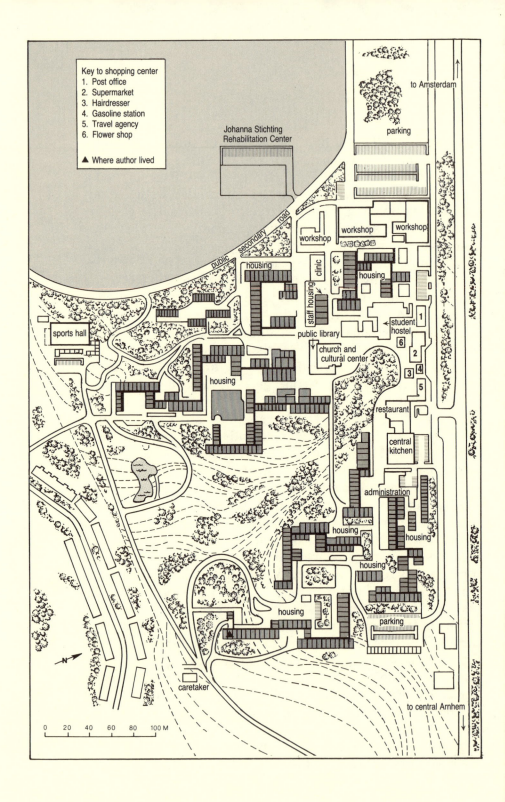

Key to shopping center
1. Post office
2. Supermarket
3. Hairdresser
4. Gasoline station
5. Travel agency
6. Flower shop

▲ Where author lived

Johanna Stichting
Rehabilitation Center

to Amsterdam

parking

public
secondary
road

workshop

workshop

workshop

housing

sports hall

staff housing

clinic

housing

student
hostel

1

6

2

public library

4

3

church and
cultural center

5

housing

restaurant

central
kitchen

administration

housing

housing

housing

housing

housing

parking

housing

N

caretaker

to central Arnhem

0   20   40   60   80   100 M

next stop was a nearby residence. I was immediately struck by the size of the living quarters. The individual rooms were large by Dutch standards, sixteen feet by fourteen feet, and had a number of subtle architectural features. Electric outlets were a little higher, windows a little lower, doorways a little larger—all very important to someone in a wheelchair. The bathroom was enormous by my standards. Sinks were lower, mirrors tilted, and grab bars were bolted to the walls at key points. Each home can also be fitted with electronic and mechanical devices to open and close doors, operate telephones and televisions and reach objects.

The most impressive achievement of the Village was its attention to the more subtle features of daily living. I remembered an early planning document which made the following modest statement:

> Though, of course, formally and officially Het Dorp is a subsidized establishment for the treatment and nursing of physically handicapped persons, for the sake of its inmates, its character will avoid any resemblance, both in its architecture and in its organization, to an institute.

The designers went at this task with enormous sensitivity and imagination. Each room was flexibly arranged. There was no set place for the bed, as there would be in a hospital or nursing home. Of course, each apartment had its own door and lock, but it was the resident who had the key! Missing were the large key rings that too often have dangled from the belts of the staff of institutions. Even more dramatically absent were the white coats. Of course, medical personnel were always available but that is just what they were—available—like a well-endowed university clinic where you could go if you felt sick on a particular day. For more serious problems consultants were on call, and across the street was the Johanna Stichting Rehabilitation Center where Dr. Klapwijk, "the parent" of the Village, worked, nearby but not hovering.

This lack of hovering was characteristic of the one ever-present staff person, the "dogela." The title itself is an acronym: do = dorp (village), ge = gemeente (community), 1 = leider (leader), a = Arnhem. The dogelas were a cadre of women especially created and trained by the Village. They were on duty in three shifts of eight hours and available any time of the day or night when a resident indicated that their assistance was needed. The resident's call determined the dogela's work. Her mandate was not to anticipate needs. The only scheduling that might occur was in response to recurring simultaneous needs such as those related to the starting times for work.

There were other anti-institutional features, too. In ordinary villages, homes are on streets. Here, too, though the streets were closed to cars. Outside every entrance was not an enclosed corridor but an enclosed street. The external walls were all brick, street names and signs were very evident, and the floor was a black asphalt roadway. On each door was a number and a mail slot. The name of each resident complete with street address and phone number was listed in the Arnhem telephone directory. And all these features were reinforced by the furnishings. Here there was no institutional sameness but only the sameness common to Dutch households. Through their own resources when they had them, or through subsidy when they did not, the residents furnished their own homes. Only taste and money determined the color of the draperies and walls, the type of beds and chairs, the quality of the TV's or stereos, the size of the hotplates or refrigerators.

By now there were several of us walking along, Dr. Metz, three administrative staff, and myself. Still somewhat awed by all that I was taking in, I asked my colleagues to tell me something about the general living arrangement and how the residents spent their days. Each filled in some details. Each "street block" had ten apartments. One was occupied by the head dogela. (There were four dogelas in rotating shifts assigned to each unit.) The other nine apartments were occupied by residents and constituted a social unit. According to my guides, each social unit was balanced demographically and diagnosti-

cally in such a way as to resemble the rest of the Village. I took
this to mean that there was some balancing of severity of disabilities. Every three social units had a laundry room, a public
bathroom, and a guest room, a place where friends and family
from far away could spend the night. At the corner of each street
was a kitchen and a common room. The latter was the main
activity center, containing magazines, books, TV, a piano, and a
large long table where all the meals were served. Eating was one
of the day's fixed events. Breakfast was available at 8:00 A.M.
with people coming and going as they wished. By contrast lunch
and dinner were served precisely at 12:30 and 6:00 with everyone expected promptly. At three other fixed times, 10:00 A.M.,
3:00 P.M., and 8:00 P.M., coffee, tea, and cookies provided a
common gathering.

If eating was the most fixed temporal reference point for all
residents, then employment was a close second. It was in some
form of "employment" that most of the residents spent their
daytime hours. The importance of work at Het Dorp was
stressed in all public releases. No surprise really in this Calvinist
country. And yet of all the Dorp features about which I could
learn on this tour, this seemed the least different from other
medical institutions. Of all aspects of the Village, it also seemed
the one most obviously influenced by outside forces. According
to a new Dutch law, only a resident who was capable of doing at
least one-third of normal production was allowed to be at a
sheltered workshop. Since such enterprises were essentially
funded through government subsidy, this effectively put a limit
on the severity of the handicap of any participant in the formal
work program. My sense of unease was only enhanced by the
brief tour of the workplace. Somehow I felt that the working
residents, operating sewing machines, assembling electronic devices, and molding clay, were on exhibit. And so when someone
remarked that with my time so short we might better spend it
looking over the data, I grabbed the opportunity to escape. As
we gathered over coffee, an administrator familiar with the
work program spread several reports in front of us and began to
explain.

Of approximately 400 residents, 5 percent worked outside the Village. Official documents described their work as mostly administrative. (I later met an accountant, an engineer, and a telephone switchboard operator.) All employment was categorized as either "rewarded labor" or "unrewarded labor." The former included about 1 percent who worked independently in small business enterprises. (I later met a man who repaired watches and another who ran an electronics repair service.)

The other major categories of "rewarded labor" referred to jobs in the sheltered workshop or in the internal organization of the Dorp such as telephone operators, receptionists, post office staff, and librarians. The two sections of the sheltered workshop were called "manual" and "mental." The titles, however, referred to the products, not the skills required. Under "manual" were listed the shops producing clothing, toys, and pottery, or engaged in assembling and packing; while under "mental" were sections creating materials for the blind or working on some special administrative project. This is how the residents were accounted for:

Working outside Village	5 percent
Working independently inside Village	1 percent
Working in Village internal organization	7 percent
Working in "normal" sheltered workshop	22 percent
Working in "mental" sheltered workshop	15 percent

Thus, about 50 percent of the residents had some form of gainful employment. This did not mean that the remainder did nothing. On administrative charts they were listed as being involved in "unrewarded labor." This term was part truth, part euphemism. It was an easy inference that this group contained many of the most severely handicapped adults, at very least all those who could not work up to the one-third "normal capacity" required for participation in a sheltered workshop. It probably also contained some people who simply had no desire to do such "productive" work and found better (at least from their point of view) ways to fill their time.

To deal with this 50 percent, two alternatives had been provided: the Creative Center and the Service Center. The former was essentially a hobby shop or arts and crafts shop and provided tools, materials, and instruction. Its products were occasionally marketed in Arnhem. The Service Center was a place where both residents from the Dorp and from Arnhem volunteered their services to help others, whether it was tending dogs and plants, writing letters, or visiting shut-ins. The very nature of the activities of both these centers made it difficult to measure participation. No one punched a time clock, and, anyway time spent physically at these centers was not comparable to time spent at a job if only because it was not necessary to do the required tasks at the center. Perhaps 25 percent of the Village residents were involved to some extent in these two activities.

What about the rest? I suspect here there were three groups: those who led lives in virtual isolation, those who by physical disability were prevented from participating in any organized activity but managed to be socially integrated, and those who were very active in the Village's inner life—active counselors to the residents, organizers of clubs and activities, members of formal and informal Village committees and study groups.

Almost drowning in the welter of statistics, I expressed amazement at the magnitude of this enterprise called Het Dorp. This struck a responsive chord. First my associates told me of the large staff that was required, and then, almost as if a counterpoint was necessary, they all spoke of the important role that residents played in running the Village. The administrative and support staff was indeed quite large, almost as large as the residents' population, over 350. Of these, 200 were dogelas. They were backed up by medical as well as housekeeping staff. There were about fifty administrative positions, including central kitchen help, and another seventy people mostly concerned with technical services. The latter included groups of unusual artisans—those concerned with wheelchair repair and maintenance and those who invented and modified mechanical and electronic devices so that residents could live and work as easily as possible. Their offices were called, aptly enough, the Adaptation Rooms. While all were concerned with making the Village a "better place to live," the staff was generally divided into two parts, one concerned with "general matters" and the other with "well-being." The latter's charter was to be concerned with "the enhancement of socially optimal functioning" and included administration of the Creative and Service Centers and supervision of other resident social activities.

While there were a number of outside groups and boards which advise the Village, day-to-day affairs were run by the Executive Director and his staff. Here there was a self-conscious effort to avoid paternalism. From the very birth of the Dorp, a group of future residents, ranging in number from six to forty, had served on the planning and design committees. Shortly after the Village opened, a form of self-government was introduced. From each three social units of residents, one representative was elected to the Village Council. Subcommittees of the Council were "entrusted with the care of recreation activities, the editing of the internal newsletter, and other activities of interest." According to official publications, "no important decisions are taken without consulting the Council." In addition, "The Council's function was to advise on internal affairs and plan for new community projects." Finally, two members of the Council participated in Executive Board meetings as full members. I must note, however, it never became clear to me what was an "administrative" matter and what was a "resident" one, how the key words "important decisions" were operationalized, or how seriously the advice of the residents was taken.

There was still another way in which the residents were central to the running of the Village. The money raised by the telethon opened the doors of the Dorp, but more was needed for its survival. Until 1970, 90 percent of all income received by a resident, whether directly earned or through some pension or insurance was given to the Village. A new law for payment of housing costs obviated this necessity. Nevertheless, in June 1970 the inhabitants of the Village almost unanimously voted to continue to share their income in the following way. Each resident with an income could keep f1.200 (about $65 in 1970) of it a month. Those receiving more than f1. 200 paid 50 percent to the community fund. This enabled the Village to subsidize the un-met needs of those with little or no income. "Do you know any villages in the world where people live together in this way?" asked the founder, Dr. Klapwijk. I stammered the only answer that came to mind, "No," and with this my several-hour tour ended.

As we drove away Metz asked what I thought, but sensing something special in my silence, he said, "Think about it now, tell me later." At that moment my thoughts were on the Villa-gers. My mind's eye was recreating them. I had not spoken to a single one. Yet all the while that the administrators lectured and I listened, a part of me was absorbing their silent presence. I recalled the table of diagnoses. By medical estimate 40 percent of the residents suffered from a progressive disease. Probably 90 percent used a wheelchair. They suffered from every imaginable disability and disfigurement. They shook, staggered, stam-mered. They lacked arms, legs, vision, hearing. Extremities were twisted, foreshortened, limp. They were paraplegics and quadriplegics. Yet I did not have the sense of revulsion and fear I had experienced at so many other hospitals and institutions. (See, for example, my India experience in Chapter 1.) It was not merely the openness and cleanliness, nor the aromatic lack of urine and medicine. Something intangible was missing—the pall. Stagnation was gone and in its place was movement! Slowly, sometimes agonizingly slowly, the residents moved, but move they did. As wheelchairs rolled by I heard hard rubber against stone or the whirr of an electric engine. Whatever physical ability residents had, they used. Were it only the tilting of a finger, the raising of a palm, the moving of one's head, the controlling of one's breath—with this and the latest electronic ingenuity, the residents *themselves* could get into their wheel-chairs and propel themselves around *their* Village. What an enormous difference this made to the viewer, if not the viewed! They moved and *no one* pushed them, a small but important step to independence and dignity.

What else did I feel? Like many a visitor I was overawed. Het Drop was unlike any long-term care center I had ever seen. But while it looked like a small village, another image kept intruding—that of college dormitories—an image that connoted to me a limbo state between dependence and independence. Perhaps this was the source of my gnawing unease. My sense of doubt lay in that Het Dorp was so self-consciously a total institution, that it sought to provide everything, including happiness. It was rooted in the traditions of long-term medical care institutions and idealistically linked to the utopian communities.

At the end of the day an administrator had turned to me and said, "Professor, I hope you enjoyed this tour. We appreciate the kinds of insights and work that experts such as you and Dr. Metz can contribute. So I hope you will return soon and we will do everything possible to help you." With so many unanswered questions and a growing personal involvement of which I was not fully conscious, this became an offer I could not refuse.

In the weeks and months that followed, I spent much time thinking about the Dorp. Metz and I met several times and discussed my reflections, but when it was time to set a return date, I kept postponing the decision. Gradually I realized it was not so much fear as anticipation. The whole year had been one of new experiences, new pains, new insights. From somewhere I sensed that this visit to the Village would be similarly important, something to cap my sabbatical, something I wanted to save for the end. When I realized this, then I began to plan in earnest. The date that Metz and I agreed on was some time late in May, several weeks before my scheduled departure for the United States.

In March formal correspondence began between me, Dr. Metz, and the administration of Het Dorp. I asked for permission to stay a week, to interview a number of staff, to live as a resident, and to mobilize myself in a wheelchair. I received no direct communication from Het Dorp but several notes and assurances from Dr. Metz that everything was proceeding smoothly. Finally, with his help I composed a letter which firmed up what I understood to be the arrangements.

. . . Dr. Metz has just informed me of your kind invitation
to spend several days at Het Dorp beginning on May 25 and
departing either May 30 or May 31. As you know I have
long been interested in the field of rehabilitation, professionally as well as personally, and so welcome this extraordinary opportunity to experience Het Dorp on a first-hand
basis. I have already visited the village once, read your
circulars and any available articles. My primary aim is
experiential, I want to get a "feel" for what it is like to be a
patient in such a place. Though a week is obviously too
short a time, I have had many similar professional experiences in hospitals and as you may be aware have personally
been hospitalized in long-term institutions for a total of
nearly two years. I hope, of course, to meet with and speak
to as many staff as time permits, but as Dr. Metz has
indicated to you, I primarily want to be with the patients
and thus my request to live in a patient room and to be
confined for the period of my stay to a wheelchair. Since I
am, however, in reality completely physically independent
and healthy, I will not need any special medical or nursing
care.
    Thank you again for your help and consideration. I
look forward to seeing you and your staff in May.
            Very sincerely yours,

            Prof. Irving Kenneth Zola, Ph.D.
            (On leave from Dept. of Sociology, Bran-
            deis University, Waltham, Mass., U.S.A.)
            Consultant, NIPG
cc: Dr. Metz

As before, I received no reply from the administration but
only a confirmation from Dr. Metz. Thursday, May 25, 1972,
was set as the start of my visit and Wednesday, May 31, as the
end.

PART TWO

DURING

Thursday, May 25

In the days preceding the visit I was torn
between finding out more about the Village
and remaining as naive as possible. I stayed
the latter by default since no one at the Institute had ever been
there. Finally, I tried to borrow a camera. It was as if I wanted
some special tool, something to take with me beside my experience and my anxiety.

On my last night in Leiden I made it to bed early, but my
mind was racing. Why did I plan this trip? Was this really how I
wanted to spend the next week? I kept dozing and waking,
rechecking the time and finally succumbed to wakefulness at
5:00 A.M. I wondered if I'd slept at all but I didn't feel tired. I
took a shower and let the water pour over me soothingly. Were
there showers in each room at Het Dorp? Would I be able to use
them? Everything I did had an air of finality. I was looking at
everything as if I'd never come back. My suitcase was already
packed but once again I rechecked my supplies—clothes for the
rain and heat of May, sleeping and shaving equipment, pencils
and pads of paper, and a stockpile of fiction. As always, I was
bringing more than enough to fill my empty spaces.

The clock said only 6:00 A.M. but my anxiety was out of
control. What if the taxi to the station had a flat tire or what if I
couldn't make the ticket taker understand my Dutch? To deal
with such realistic contingencies I left. Within a few minutes I
had arrived at the Leiden Station a full hour before the scheduled departure. No flat tires. No language difficulty.

Shortly after seven I settled comfortably in my seat on the train and began to contemplate what lay ahead. I decided to do what I always tell my students: "Observation always begins with anticipation." So with pencil in hand, I began to record.

This trip really is a mixture of excitement and trepidation. Excitement because the whole idea of going back into the field is appealing. It is good to know that I still have the opportunity to do participant-observation. Also, since I supposedly teach such research methods, it's nice not to have to do it solely from memory. Trepidation because I feel like an anthropologist going into a foreign culture. Do the local authorities fully know why I'm coming? The only direct communications I have are the informal messages of Dr. Metz. How much will my lack of Dutch—I do not really speak it—be a real handicap? Oh, my first unconscious pun. Like an anthropologist, I will have to rely on interpreters and probably select informants. Who will help me? All in all, what *do* I want to get out of this? Why do I think I can get anything out of it in only a week? What's my rationale?

So much for questions. Now what are my answers? First, this is not a study but a brief learning experience, like my earlier work on prisons and juvenile institutions. Despite my formal credentials I intend, as I did then, to present myself as a learner and not someone attempting any formal research or direct evaluation of their organization. I want only to get some feel of what it's like to work or live in Het Dorp. Second, professionally I know something about chronic disease and long-term care. Thus, I may be able to proceed along on certain issues quite fast. Third, in a personal sense, this is a trip I have made before. I do not just have book learning. I mean my previous hospitalizations for polio and a shattered femur. This may help push through the patient's presentation of self, just as the professional experience will let me push through the staff's view of their work. Intrapsychically I am banking on my own sensitivity and experience. I hope these days will reawaken many old feelings, emotions, and even fears. Maybe I can then get a better understanding of some of my present difficulties, or past ones I hesitate to recall, or even future ones I have yet to face.

There are some issues I must face quite early. How will I present myself? As straightforwardly as possible. First, to all comers I will tell my story, naming the reasons why I think I can make it here, emphasizing the learning and downgrading any evaluative component. Second, no matter how much I act like a patient, at best I only can get "A" for trying. All will know that I am only a visitor, in all senses of the word. Third, in places like Het Dorp there is always the "zoo phenomenon"—people feel they're on view as interesting subjects. Can I overcome this? My being in a wheelchair should help. Maybe it won't be so difficult since on my first visit the "zoo phenomenon" was reversed. They were all staring at me as if to say, "Who the hell is this guy with a long leg brace and a cane?" Last, I will really try to live like a patient. I have refused to bring my own car and am traveling here by train to emphasize to myself and to them that no easy or quick escape to a more pleasant reality is available. I will live in patient quarters with patient privileges. At the earliest possible moment, I will obtain a wheelchair and confine myself to it until I finally leave the Village.

Satisfied with this psyching up of myself, I put my notetaking aside. In a sense this trip, even being on the train, has already emphasized some of the reality of being physically handicapped, some of the realities I have so carefully avoided in my life. Not even thinking consciously of adopting the role, I was faced with a change of train and what seemed like mountains of stairs to climb with my damn heavy suitcase. Struggle I did up the stairs, one at a time, hefting the suitcase sometimes in front of me, sometimes besides me. At one point, it was like the old days, when, usually with some embarrassment, I would back down a flight of stairs with my suitcase in front of me. This time when people offered help I gladly accepted.

To pass the time on the train, I looked out the window at the Dutch scenery, spoke casually to several passengers, and occasionally perused E. H. Hall's *The Silent Language*. The time went quickly and within two hours I was in Arnhem.

I stepped off the train but no welcoming face was in sight. The prospect of negotiating the long platform and the staircases was hardly pleasant, but I girded myself. I took barely a step when I spotted Dr. Metz waving, smiling, and walking quickly towards me. He looked great and I told him so. A psychologist to the core, he explained why. "My work is really going quite well and I've even gotten some good reviews."

From our previous conversations I realized this had been a long time in coming. He was particularly enthusiastic about his current writing on pain, based on his observations at a neurosurgical clinic of last resort.* But even this was a mixed blessing, because it took so much out of him. "Each time I begin as so sympathetic to both the patients and the staff, I see how hard it is for all of them. But gradually when I write, we [the staff and he] come further and further apart. When I see how they are medicalizing everything, as you've written, and then tell them, they don't like it."

He wanted to talk even more about his work, "but, after all, you're not here to spend time with me. If you *do* have time from hearing their complaints, maybe you can hear mine." Almost trailing off, he wondered about "his last work." He repeated this several times, and when I pressed him he reminded me that in two years he would be 65. He feared that because of his unpopular views, people would use his age as an excuse not to give him any more paid research opportunities. I silently feared he might be right.

This pessimism inspired his own reservations about what lay ahead at Het Dorp. "I am not sure that they will welcome

---

*William Metz, *Pijn-een teer punt* (Nijkerk, Netherlands: Vitgeverij G. F. Callenbach B. V., 1975).

you with open arms. I spoke to several people there this week and they all seemed a bit vague about arrangements. They were even unsure about what appointments you'll have." He shrugged his shoulders. "In fact we can't even go there now. There's been some special staff meeting called, and it won't be over till after two. I hope you won't mind but I thought we could visit Dr. Langlett at home instead. Do you remember him?"

I did. Of all those I met on my first visit he stood out. He was the general physician of the Village. I remembered him being just a little more solicitous of me, a little more at ease with the residents, a little more friendly with Dr. Metz. "Sure," I answered, "why is he at home?"

"Well, he's got some back trouble and has to give it complete bed rest. He'll be glad to have the company."

My introduction to Het Dorp was already taking on symbolic overtones. My first meetings with the Administration were postponed and my first stop was at a house of "invalids." Of the five people present, only Metz was "unafflicted." There was me, Dr. Langlett flat on his back, his daughter sick in bed, and his wife blinded several years ago in an accident.

After the usual introductions we sat down to coffee. Dr. Langlett remembered that my academic specialty was sociology. So, it turned out, was his son's. Rather shyly, he asked if I would mind discussing possibilities in the United States with his son. I agreed and we set up a tentative appointment.

Talk easily turned to the Dorp and what I hoped to accomplish. I had barely got a few words out when both Dr. Langlett and Dr. Metz corrected me. When I mentioned that Het Dorp was a type of rehabilitation center, they said that the Village engaged in no such activity. "It is a place where people go when no further rehabilitation is possible." When I spoke of the patients of Het Dorp, they said I must call them "inhabitants" or "residents." "It is essential that the people not feel that they are part of a medical center but part of a community." I was surprised though something similar had happened on my first visit.

Together Metz and Langlett recalled the early successes of the Village, the enormous achievement of its very building and organization. But Langlett had a reservation. "With many of the basic physical problems under control, social ones now surface. There is too little attention to psychological problems. You see this most in the living units. Some have their troubles. Many do not function as social groups. There are constantly a mix of people who wish to socialize and those who do not."

This provided me an opening but I put it awkwardly, "I often wonder what it's like to daily confront people with severe illnesses and gross handicaps."

Dr. Langlett agreed, "It does take a certain type of personality to work with them. People who are too cold, too clinical, too technical in their work will neither fit nor be tolerated." Metz concurred.

But that wasn't whom I meant. "Yes, I guess that's true but I was really interested in the residents. What is it like for them to live constantly amid disease, deformity, and death?"

"It's a problem," replied Dr. Langlett. "It's very bad when someone dies. People get very depressed. Some feel that we should move such people out, away, but I don't. They shouldn't have to die all alone, somewhere else. Besides many fear this and so are sometimes reluctant to come to the doctor when they're not well."

I was reminded of an early Het Dorp memorandum which raised the specter of very sick residents having to leave. Langlett was clearly aware of this possibility and was committed to its prevention.

Again I slipped into calling the residents "patients." And again I was corrected. It was hard for me not to. Was I already distancing myself? Would calling them 'patients' make it easier for me to live with them?

Still absorbed in how people live with so much disease, I pressed on, "Do the residents talk much to one another about their physical problems?"

Dr. Langlett nodded, as did Dr. Metz. "That is a problem. Many of the residents are concerned with this." He told how one resident lamented that "some people seem to have nothing else to talk about."

To myself, I wondered how it could be otherwise. A certain narcissism seems almost inevitable with any institutionalization! "Is there any escape from such daily encounters?" It was more a rhetorical question than anything else. Then I recalled their homes and a privacy absent in most institutions. "Does the fact they have their own homes provide some relief?"

"For some," was the reply, "but still others say that they are more lonely here than before."

"God, what an irony," I burst out, "that this whole idea of privacy, each person having his own home, may be so out-of-whack with his experience, that it mutes its very intention." We all shook our heads glumly.

"What are some of the other problems with which the Dorp is dealing?"

"Well, absenteeism in the workshops is one. Increasingly, residents are calling in sick. No one wants to call them malingerers and yet some people feel they are letting the staff down."

"More likely they are letting the administration know something," quipped Metz.

Again I was struck by an irony but I kept it to myself. After all the criticism that Metz and Langlett had given me for calling the villagers "patients," it seemed strange that the residents could use that role when they wanted to and that the Administration would be powerless to cope with it.

"This whole issue of absenteeism is even more complex," continued Langlett. "Several things are going on. There is some distaste with the general atmosphere of the workshops. [He could not be more specific.] Some people simply find that they want more time for leisure activities. It's hard to criticize that. And finally some really are quitting because of sickness."

"I don't understand what that means."

"Well, I guess we did not realize that there would be such a rapid progression with certain diseases. And this has led to some people working less if not quitting entirely."

This bothered me since it contradicted something he had said during my January visit, that people with progressive diseases seemed to be living longer than expected. I reminded him of this and added, "Do you really think it's a physical deterioration which is taking place? Or could it be of a more psychological sort?" I was not sure what I had in mind, perhaps anything from depression to boredom.

Langlett shrugged and Metz smiled knowingly. "Yes, there always seem to be more problems to be faced." It was said not with resignation but with some optimism, Langlett noting that a new vice director of well-being had been appointed, a person whose full time and energy would be devoted to such issues.

In describing the problems with which the Village must deal now and in the future, Langlett distanced himself from neither the staff nor the residents. They were *his* problems, too. Though she had not spoken, by her gestures Mrs. Langlett had also conveyed both involvement and concern. I recalled something Metz had said about Langlett's "devotion." I wondered if I would be welcomed elsewhere as easily as here.

I tried to relax and rehearse my introductions as we drove to the Village. In a few minutes we had parked near the administration building and were entering a waiting room and greeting the secretary. Metz did most of the talking but since she was fluent in English I quickly joined in. Eventually she turned to me and asked, "When would you like to make an appointment?"

"As soon as possible."

She opened her appointment book and knowing full well that I was going to be there a week, set up an appointment on my next-to-last day.

Dr. Metz turned to her with a not-so-benign smile and said, "Aha! The greeting and the departure are one."

She was upset at this violation of professional etiquette. Answering him only with a scowl, she said to me, "We're very glad to see you, Dr. Zola. We are going to give you every opportunity to observe everything that's going on. We have your room all prepared. It's very nice. It's a guest room."

A sense of something awry was reinforced. "That doesn't sound right. What is a guest room?"

"Oh, you'll be very comfortable there."

My doubts grew. I knew that such a room would not be like a resident's. Even though I voiced this concern, she ignored it, saying, "I am sure you will be comfortable there. So why don't you go see it?"

Reluctantly Metz and I agreed, and off we trekked to my assigned quarters. It was as feared, a guest room with all that implied. I had not seen one on my first tour. It was rather like a small motel room, containing only a cot and a night table. It was not the smallness that bothered me but the lack of architectural modifications.

When the secretary asked how I liked my quarters, I explained as gently as possible why the room was inappropriate. It was to no avail. Somewhat exasperated, I brought out the letter I had written outlining my intentions. "I explicitly said there that I wanted to live like a resident."

Sympathetically but clearly in control she nodded, "I'm sorry, Doctor Professor Zola. There are simply no places for you."

An uneasiness crept over me. I was being rapidly pushed into a role in which they could handle me. Rather than be gracious, I decided to fight. In my most authoritative and professorial tones I intoned, "You've been sending me data about Het Dorp and the latest census tells me you have room for 400 people."

"Absolutely right."

"Well, according to the census there are at present only 390 occupants, which means that there are 10 vacancies, which means there must be 10 vacant rooms."

"You're quite right," she replied, unsmilingly. "Yes, you're right, there are 10 rooms but they're empty. There's nothing in any of these rooms because you know that the policy is that each resident sets up the room to be his or her permanent apartment. There's no furniture in any of the rooms, so you'll have to stay in the guest room."

Not giving up so easily, I built my case. "Hmm, let me see if I understand it right. This is a place to house people with a chronic disease or physical handicap, as well as staff, and so you have lots of furniture and equipment.''

"Yes," she answered a bit impatiently.

"Well, I've lived and worked in medical institutions for nearly twenty years and I've never been in one that did not have spare bedroom furniture. You mean they can find no spare bed anywhere in this institution?" I tried to sound as incredulous as possible. She admitted that there might be some around.

"Okay, then. What I would like in this empty room is a bed, a table, and two chairs. You don't have to give me anything else.''

"We'll see," her voice trailed off, "if that can be arranged. We'll do what we can but we won't be able to have it for you right away because you're making up so many things for us to do. After all, we've got your schedule. People are expecting you to live in a certain place and now we will have to change all that.''

I graciously acknowledged the difficulties but continued, "I know that you will do everything that you can for me because the Director said that they were going to try to welcome me in every way." Then looking around I asked, "Where's my wheelchair?''

"What wheelchair?"

"The wheelchair I asked for in my letters.''

"Oh," she said, "you mean *the* wheelchair." With too bright a smile, she asked, "What type of wheelchair do you want?" and proceeded to name several kinds with different types of electrical controls.

This choice was not something I had anticipated but I felt that any delay in responding would work against my ever getting started. So I reasoned quickly with myself. The role that I was resuming was that of a functional paraplegic, someone who was essentially paralyzed from the waist down. That meant that my upper torso should theoretically be in good enough shape to use a manually operated wheelchair. "Oh, a manually operated one will be fine," I uttered with an unjustified confidence.

She seemed surprised at my choice and indicated that it might take several hours but that they would deliver one to me. When I answered that I did not know where I'd be several hours hence, she assured me that they could easily find me. I found her confidence eerie.

It was obvious from all this that not only did Het Dorp officialdom not believe my formal requests, but also that they assumed they knew better than I what I would need. My early queasiness about this all-too-perfect institution returned, particularly my doubts about the problems that come in the wake of someone's continually deciding what is in someone's else's best interests. I did not linger on this thought because the rest of my morning was spent dealing with my rising anger. It was clear that my visit was not going to be made easy. Some other interesting "mistakes" also occurred. In figuring out the cost of my stay, they shortened the time period. (In fact, I had not realized that I would have to pay anything. But the cost was nominal.) Most disturbing, however, was that all but one of my administrative appointments were cancelled. The one person I did see changed his appointment twice, was a half-hour late finally, and then regretted he could not tell me much about the Dorp since he was quite new.

Metz and I did our best "to grin and bear it." While waiting for some further word about my arrangements, I appreciated a final symbolic accompaniment to all these events. While I spent much of the morning cooling my heels in one administrator's outer office, he communicated about me only through the intercom and never deigned to poke his head out and welcome me. This was in marked contrast to the elaborate greetings and departures that punctuated my January tour. Then I was a distinguished American professor and researcher. Now I had become something else.

Metz and I were finally released from the tedium of further rejections by the noon hour and our scheduled luncheon with a group of residents, the ones with whom I apparently would be taking most of my meals. On the way, Metz and I tried to figure out what was going on with the administration. Everything seemed clear when arrangements were being made. We returned to the fact that in a sense they couldn't believe what I wanted to experience.

We arrived just as lunch was being served. As with everything else that day, we were not entirely expected. The residents had heard that I was arriving in the evening. No matter, there was plenty of food, and space was made for us at the table. Introductions began. My Dutch was too inadequate and my anxiety too high for me to remember names. One man, I think he was called Mr. Landsmann, took the lead. At first it appeared that no one knew English for he translated everything, both their questions and their answers. But later I noted that appropriate gestures seemed to precede his translations, so the others must have at least understood English. Although I could not comprehend all the details, my companions seemed interested and so gradually I began to wind down. Several thought it was a good idea for me to experience the Dorp though they didn't understand why I'd want to. So, already well rehearsed, I told why I was there. My story, which included my background and how I hoped to live as a resident, now expanded to what I might do with the new knowledge. As a teacher and adviser to groups concerned with medicine and rehabilitation, I hoped to tell them of alternative ways of dealing with physical handicaps. My lunchmates were surprised to learn that there was no place in America like the Village, and I sensed a certain sarcasm in their disbelief. The conversation gradually turned more personal. They wanted to know the details of my physical status. How did I first become sick? How long had I worn a brace? Who paid for it? How did it work?

There was a part of me that was taken aback by this sudden foray into my physical condition. Never before had I been so quickly and straightforwardly asked such questions by adults. Only young children would uninhibitedly ask why I wore a brace or if I had to wear it *all* the time. Only after many years would even my oldest friends tentatively ask, "You know, Irv, I always

wondered how . . . but if you don't want to tell . . ." There was
the implication that I had something to hide, or that should be
hidden.

Although the questions about me and my condition were
clearly not exhausted, someone, I think it was Mr. Landsman
again, interrupted, "I wonder if I could ask you something
else?" I wondered if he sensed my unease. But in any case I
welcomed the change. "How are things going with the Administration?"

Out of the frying pan and into the fire. I worried about what
to answer. Training cautioned me to play it cool, but I felt
pushed to a more open stance. Right then I had no inclination to
be a neutral observer, so I answered with a wry smile, "You
know, I don't think the Administration really wants me here."
This did not cause as much surprise as I expected and the
residents pressed me for details. Essentially I reported the
morning's events. They relished it, particularly the interchange
between Dr. Metz and the secretary. There was apparently no
great love lost between them and the Administration. It was
difficult, however, to get a handle on their attitude. It was not
linked to any stories of ill-treatment or neglect. It was a kind of
unfocused disgruntlement. Not so much what the Administration had done but what it had not. No great or very specific
dissatisfactions with how they lived but the feeling that it could
be even better. Clearly, Het Dorp was infinitely better than any
other institution they had experienced but somehow this was not
enough.

Everyone agreed that if I wanted to stay at the Village,
then *they* would have to see to it. Together they worked out
several alternate solutions. There were other vacancies, some
fully furnished. A number of residents were temporarily absent—in a hospital, home for a visit, on a vacation. They
seriously discussed who would mind if I used his room and with
obvious delight spoke about smuggling me in. I thought someone referred to my living with a single woman, but with my
inadequate Dutch I let it pass. Their acceptance of me, all quite
bewildering, went beyond this. They planned my schedule. All

quickly agreed that I must attend the Gala on Saturday night.
One named Mrs. van Amerongen said she would get tickets,
another worried how I would get there. Then they talked about
whom I should see and what parts of the Village I should visit.
My delight at all this attention was undercut by a certain feeling
that it was all going too fast. I was not at all sure that I wanted to
sever connections to the Administration and I told them so.
There were some places, after all, that I needed their permission
to visit, like the Workplace. They agreed but insisted that whatever else I did I must not miss the Gala. I laughed and winked in
agreement.

With lunch ending, Landsmann invited me to his room. I
turned to Metz but anticipating me, he said, "Go ahead. There
are some things I have to check into—your home, your wheelchair." I started to rise but half out of my seat I fortunately saw
my faux pas. There was a final prayer and everyone but me had
their head bent and their hands folded. I was totally unprepared. I'd been in the Netherlands all year and that was the first
time that I had witnessed grace. It was a further reminder that I
was indeed in another part of Dutch society. Only when Mr.
Landsmann moved away from the table, did I push myself to a
standing position. Without a word, he rode off in his wheelchair.
As I turned to see which way he was going, a question stopped
me.

"Are you married now?" asked one of the women.

"Why no, I'm divorced," I answered quickly, still looking
after Landsmann.

"Was it related to that?" she gestured, pointing to my leg.

"Of course not," I blurted out and started to walk away.
"It's a much longer and more complicated story . . ." She
seemed momentarily satisfied with my answer but I was upset
with her question.

Walking as fast as I could, I tried to catch up with Landsmann. Hearing me behind him, he laughed over his shoulder,
"What's taking you so long?" So preoccupied was I with keeping up, I failed to notice that I in turn was being followed by a
young woman. When we both arrived at Landsmann's door. I

was embarrassed. She was more at ease than I and introduced herself as "Monika, Pieter's fiancé." She wasn't a resident but was staying at the Dorp with Landsmann.

The next half hour was spent in small talk about my stay in the Netherlands and some differences between that country and the United States. We were interrupted by a phone call telling me that my wheelchair had arrived. Thanking Pieter and Monika for their hospitality, I went to the door. Instead of goodbye, Pieter asked if I would like to go shopping with him at 3:00 P.M. It sounded like a fine idea, and I agreed to return after picking up my wheelchair and saying goodbye to Dr. Metz.

I felt fine. My disappointment over the early-morning rejections had dissipated. They might even have turned out to be a bonus. I had made some new friends. And there waiting for me in the dining hall was Metz with a look of triumph on his face. All we had asked for had come through. He informed me that I would take all my meals with my luncheon group but live somewhere else. It was a bit strange, but who cared. It was settled. The room was not far away, "just a short ride," we both joked. With this Metz gleefully gave me the keys and pointed to the wheelchair. I gave him my cane, knowing this was the last time I would use it for seven days, and sat down with an unaccustomed plop.

The next half hour was weird. Partly it was my getting used to being in a wheelchair after almost a twenty-year absence. But it was much more than that. Subtly, but all too quickly, I was being transformed. As soon as I sat in the wheelchair I was no longer seen as a person who could fend for himself. Although Metz had known me well for nine months, and had never before done anything physical for me without asking, now he took over without permission. Suddenly in his eyes I was no longer able to carry things, reach for objects, or even push myself around. Though I was perfectly capable of doing all these things, I was being wheeled around, and things were being brought to me— all without my asking. Most frightening was my own compliance, my alienation from myself and from the process.

Metz pushed me to my room. It was sparsely furnished but it was mine. We stayed only long enough to leave my suitcase and cane. Like little children we playfully congratulated each other on how things were turning out. As we left the room, he mentioned that he would make some appointments for me and, since he lived but fifteen minutes away, would drop in from time to time to see how I was doing. I appreciated the concern but somehow even the phrase "how I was doing" made me feel child-like or patient-like.

As I rode and Dr. Metz walked through the corridors, residents nodded, mostly to him. When they asked how he was, he made a point of introducing me, but strangely, the introductions seemed a bit superfluous. There was an acknowledgment in their greeting that they already knew something about me.

As we approached the elevator, Metz heard himself being called. Marlene, a long-time resident, was obviously glad to see him, and the conversation in Dutch was animated. I was struck by how good-looking she was and then surprised at my surprise. Did I expect someone in a wheelchair to be ugly? Or was I more surprised to be attracted to such a person? Her long dark hair reminded me of my lover Mara back in the States. Only a few seconds passed before Metz introduced me: "She'll be a good person for you to talk with. She's been here a long time and seen the Village change."

Since his statement was in English I immediately felt at ease. "Yes, I'd like to know how it's different from when you first came."

"Well, the big difference is that there are now more diseased people than handicapped."

"I don't understand."

"I mean there are now more people with multiple sclerosis and muscular dystrophy than those who are paralegics or had polio or some injury. And it's not good."

"Why does this matter?"

Almost as if to close the discussion, she replied, "To be handicapped is to be stabilized, to be diseased is *not.*"

Metz reminded us of my appointment with Pieter Landsmann. I regretted leaving and took her address and phone number, promising to get in touch. She smiled, too noncommittally for my taste, and wheeled away. As the elevator descended I asked Metz for details about her. I learned that she was twenty-nine, had lived at the Village since its inception and had some spinal column defect which limited her mobility, gave considerable pain, and occasionally led to other complications. She could occasionally walk and did so in her own home. I wanted to ask more but we were already at Pieter's door.

Metz deposited me there and waved goodbye. Before I had a chance to digest my new ambivalence about Metz or my meeting with Marlene, I had my first physical problem. As I leaned forward to rap on the door I unbalanced myself and nearly toppled out of the wheelchair. What would happen if I fell? Would my experiment be over? Suppressing this thought, I pondered the problem of knocking on the door. I sat back more firmly in my wheelchair, thinking briefly of the seat belts I usually avoid wearing in my own car. I would have welcomed them now. The problem was simply solved. I approached the door sideways, so that I was parallel to it. I energetically knocked and then quickly backed away. "Here I am," I announced in a somewhat unnaturally happy voice. "Let's go!"

I soon realized my enthusiasm was unwarranted when Pieter pointed out where we were going. The supermarket was a considerable distance from here, on the top of a hill, the highest point in the Village. Off we went, with Pieter leading and I trailing behind. Up one hill, then another. My arms ached and I was winded. Every once in a while he looked back and said, "Are you still there, Professor Zola?" I thought the question was really rhetorical. But I did begin to wish I were somewhere else and wondered why, in the interests of realism, I had rejected an electric wheelchair. Finally we arrived at the supermarket. I had hoped for a brief respite but I was quickly disillusioned. While I did have the chance to notice that this and other shops were indeed frequented by people not living in the Vil-

lage, my little time in the store was spent "coping." As I reached
for a can on a lower shelf, the wheelchair and I tipped forward.
No one rushed to my aid as I steadied myself against one of the
shelves. Again "parallel parking" was the answer. But even this
was not enough. Many of the items I wanted seemed either too
high or too low. I had to ask someone's help, and I hated it! That
many people in the Village had similar experiences was not at all
consoling. To add to my growing sense of humiliation, I had
difficulty carrying in my lap the items I had "so dearly purchased." Needing both hands to propel myself, I laid six apples
on my lap only to see them soon go cascading over the floor. A
middle-aged woman kindly picked them up. I said thank you but
I felt awful. Again I was reminded of all the tricks of the trade I
would need to relearn. Unlike Pieter, I had not come prepared.
He had a mesh shopping bag. I then recalled that other residents
had similar devices attached to their wheelchairs. The final
insult at the store was unintentional but that did not help much.
As I approached the cashier and bravely gave her my money, I
thanked her in Dutch. She smiled and answered me in English!

If the trip to the store was exhausting and the stay in it
embarrassing, the return was frightening. For all the hills we had
so patiently climbed now awaited our descent. To me it resem-
bled a roller coaster ride. But Pieter, setting himself squarely in
his chair, folded his arms in front and let go. Off he went in a
cloud of dust, zooming down the hill, barely steering the wheelchair around one corner and then down another hill. I could not
follow suit but the hills were too steep for a truly slow descent. I
let go for perhaps two yards then braked with my hands, let go
again then braked again. Stop and go all the way. I arrived
dishevelled, my shirt sweaty and sticking to my side, my hands
blackened and sore from trying to control my progress. Pieter,
of course, had arrived several minutes before and looked as if he
had not gone anywhere. He acknowledged my return with a
smile and announced coffee-time. A look at my watch indicated
that the total elapsed time for our journey was a little over thirty
minutes!

The coffee break was pleasant enough, but I was too exhausted to notice much. Everyone was amiable, and I managed to pick up some reference to my shopping trip.

True to her promise, Mrs. van Amerongen wheeled in and proudly waved my ticket to the Gala. About four Monika came in and suggested we go back and arrange my room. Again there was the sense of unease that I experienced with Metz. Though she, too, barely two hours before, had seen me not only walking with a cane but carrying a suitcase, she also "took over" without asking. And again, without being fully aware, I acquiesced. I rationalized that I was so tired and that it was a relief to be pushed to my room. When we were inside, she asked if I needed anything, and without being asked, began to unpack and to point out several features of the room. When two dogelas came in, she introduced me, explained who I was and why I was at the Dorp. They seemed curious but shy, and agreed to help me if I needed them. What was it that I would need? Muffling again my discomfort, I mumbled a thank-you and mentioned something about seeing them during the week. Monika asked if I would go back with her to Pieter's but I begged off. I claimed tiredness, but I also wanted some time to digest all that had happened. When she left, I still found it impossible to unwind, so I did what usually works in such situations, I started to write. I got down barely an outline of the day's events, when it was six and time for supper.

Again an unexpected encounter with the physical environment greeted me. I could not close my door. Every time I grabbed the handle to slam it shut, the door hit my wheelchair before I could get out of the way and sprang back open. It became the enemy, and I tried to sneak up on it, but some part of my wheelchair kept bumping it out of reach. I barely suppressed a scream. Closing my eyes, I remembered the strings hanging on the handles of several doors. Now I knew what they were for. Tying a shoelace to the handle gave me just enough leeway to drag the door with me as I wheeled out. With a satisfied yank I slammed it shut, locked it, and off down the corridor I raced.

I wheeled as fast as I could down several connecting hall-ways to the elevator. I backed in and went to press the button for my floor, and realized there was no floor button to press, no indication of the basement, first or second floors, but only street names. Outside the elevator I was more conscious than before of the arrows pointing to various streets. Perhaps it was because now I was driving, whereas before I was a "passenger." As I wheeled into my dining place it was obvious that I was late. Everyone was there, but they had waited for me. After intro-ductions to some people who had been absent from lunch, grace was said and the meal began. The dinner was good (macaroni with sauce) but not very big, not really enough for two helpings all around, with banana as dessert. Everything went so quickly that it took me awhile to realize that my role had changed. Since they had waited and gone to the trouble of introductions, I expected that much conversation at dinner would be focused on me. It was not. There was lots of kidding with one another and some obvious references to my arrival but essentially I was ignored. More quickly than I had hoped or even than I liked, I had already ceased to be so special. I was in some sense just another person at dinner in Het Dorp.

My disappointment deepened when no one remained after the meal. With a promise to return for the eight o'clock evening coffee, everyone headed back to their homes. With nothing else to do, I did the same. Barely forty-five minutes had elapsed since I first left.

If closing my door had been difficult, so was unlocking it. Again I nearly toppled as I leaned forward with my key. I had to maneuver close, parallel park, set the brakes of my wheelchair, and then unlock the door. I never thought that the mere enter-ing and departure from a room would require so much effort and coordination. All this brought out at least one difference be-tween this and my two previous "confinements." Never before, either with polio or my accident, had I had to cope with such problems alone. There was always someone there to help—a nurse, a patient, a friend. Now I was seeing what it took for a handicapped person to independently cope with even the smallest aspects of the world.

Tiredness and achiness were rapidly overtaking me. Resting more than writing, I worked on my notes for about an hour and then as promised returned for the night coffee.

It all passed pleasntly enough. There was mostly small talk about the quality of the cookies and the coffee and I met the night dogela. It was interesting to see how people would introduce me, to see if they'd leave out any details of my story. They didn't. As I turned to leave, Monika touched my arm. "Will you join Pieter and me tonight? There will be some visitors but they will see Pieter. Please come."

I felt awkward, thinking the invitation was just to be nice, but it felt awkward to refuse.

A few minutes after I wheeled in, the visitors arrived. We were all introduced as Monika played the hostess serving drinks. But in a moment we were separated, Mr. and Mrs. Lund with Pieter, and Monika and I huddled near the TV. As we settled in I realized that what I had first assumed was a kind of hobby, Pieter's vast array of clocks and tools, was in fact a business that he had created. He manufactured and repaired various kinds of electronic clocks and timing systems. While he patiently explained what had gone wrong with the Lunds' timer, Monika and I watched a soccer game. After nearly a year in the Netherlands I had become a fan, so our conversation flowed easily. But out of the corner of my eye I watched Pieter. It was just like this afternoon with Marlene. Then I was surprised I could meet anyone so attractive, now I was surprised to see anyone so independent that he'd set up his own business. Already I was being confronted with my own sterotypes.

After the visitors left, Pieter remained at his bench finishing up his work. Then Monika returned with more drinks and snacks almost as reward.

As I bent over to pull up my socks, my brace became exposed and Pieter picked up where we had left off in the afternoon. Again I was asked about my family and they responded with their own marriage plans. Playfully tickling Monika, Pieter said, "We hope in a year or so to find a place and then we will get married and move out from here." This was the first hint I had had that anyone left but I stilled my surprise. They asked if where I lived in the United States was "adapted." More brusquely than I intended, I answered sharply, "No!" This was the second time that I had been caught off guard by someone's question. I tried to cover myself with a joke, referring to the expenses of such adaptation. They in turn were amazed that in the States I or anyone had to pay so much for medical expenses. Every once in a while they brought the conversation around to something like, "What is it really like to be handicapped in America?" I was glad they didn't push me. Somehow my resistance seemed to be based on something more personal than lack of knowledge. I knew that I'd already been pushed too far for one day, and I wanted some space, so about 10:30 I pleaded exhaustion. It wasn't a lie; I really was done in.

Slowly I wheeled my way home. My arms, my back, my whole body was one big throb. Everything ached, even my mind. As I turned the final corner I saw an elderly couple in wheelchairs. As they stopped to let me pass, we nodded to each other. As I rode by I heard them refer to "the Amerikaner." As much out of courtesy as curiosity I halted. They asked how I was, how I liked the Dorp and if I would join them in their home. I was ambivalent but the flattery of their invitation won out over the tiredness of my body. Wheeling in, I suddenly wondered how we would talk. They clearly didn't know English and my Dutch was virtually nonexistent. Anticipating me, the husband, speaking for both of them, said, "English no good." I smiled back, "Dutch no good."

With the ground rules thus established we embarked on a melange of German, Dutch, very occasional English, plentiful pointings, pictures, and gestures, and a lot of patience. As now seemed to be the pattern, we focused first on my "disease" and "handicap," then they responded with details of their own. They both had multiple sclerosis and what they were particularly interested in was how MS was handled and paid for in the United States. I told what little I knew. Like Pieter and Monika, they were surprised at how little state aid there was and the American philosophy of private voluntary support.

Then with obvious pride and a touch of modesty they spoke about their family. It was more than the usual emphasis on success. The fact of their having a family at all seemed every bit as important as what their children had accomplished. Did they think because they had MS I would consider them incapable of being parents? They asked if I had a family, and though pleased that I had children, they were concerned about my divorce. Gently around the edges they probed. And then they asked the unaskable, was my physical handicap related to the divorce? Less shaken this time, I assured them that to my knowledge it played a relatively insignificant role. With this they seemed to brighten up. This also allowed them to talk more freely about their "happy family."

After sharing a drink or two, they asked what I thought of their home and proceeded to give me a tour. It was well furnished, with modern conveniences as well as many momentoes from a former life. What struck me most, however, was the physical layout. The space obviously was not built for a couple. It consisted of two apartments in which various walls had been knocked down. This was my first indication that the Village might not have anticipated the need for married quarters. And I now recalled, that though my head was full of all sorts of demographic statistics, marital status was not one of them. It was 11:15 and while my hosts seemed able to continue, I was not. I was, once more, drained, so I thanked them for their hospitality and left.

I longed desperately for bed, but so much had happened that I resisted. I sensed that something very special was happening to me and I didn't want to lose it. So, tired as I was, I wrote till shortly before midnight. There was, however, a cost. I gave up any pretense at evening ablutions. Besides, I kidded myself, who would notice? I thought seriously of not using the toilet, but the idea of waking up in the middle of the night with an overfull bladder seemed even more depressing. Still in my wheelchair I dragged a seat nearer the bed so that I could hang my shirt and trousers over it. I was simply too done in to take them off, go back into the wheelchair, and then hang them in the closet. By now I was sufficiently aware of balance problems to recall how to get into bed. I parallel parked my wheelchair next to the bed, locked the brakes, and then pushed myself to a standing position. Using the chair for support I turned slowly till my backside was against the bed and then sat down on it. From that point it was a simple matter to disrobe and strew my brace, back support, and clothes on the nearby chairs.

It was time for sleep. My body said "Yes" but my mind said "No." So much had happened, so many decisions had been made. Would the Administration give me a hard time? Had I really been accepted by the residents as much as it seemed? What tests would I have to pass? The word "tests" intruded. Damn it, I had been tested. Something the elderly couple had said suddenly clicked. Their reference to the Amerikaner had something to do with my wheelchair and the supermarket. It all made sense. That trip was not merely a test of my physical endurance but also of my commitment—did I really mean it when I said I wanted to live as a resident? I remembered something from my first visit in January. No one had to go that way to the store. There was a simple and direct way without having to negotiate a single hill. Since all the buildings are built into the landscape, one can go from plateau to plateau by using elevators. One can enter a building at the bottom floor, take an elevator, get off at the top floor, go down a corridor, drive about thirty yards to another building and repeat the process. Eventually one will be on the level one wants with relatively little difficulty and only the slightest of uphill grades to ascend. Maybe the trip wasn't created by Pieter to see if I'd keep my word, but it certainly had that function. Why else would this elderly couple, so far from my dinner companions, already know about my trip? "I passed! I passed!" I shouted. My muscles told me I should have gone into training before the test, but my head told me that the aches were nothing compared to the satisfaction I now felt. I didn't know exactly what I was but I certainly didn't feel like a stranger.

Sleep still did not come. Partly I was too excited and partly I just could not get comfortable. The bed was hard as a rock.

Just as I dozed off I was interrupted. I may have inadvertently flipped a switch, or perhaps the night dogela, just a bit curious, wanted to check on me. In any case, an attractive young woman was asking me if I wanted anything. There were one or two ideas which crossed my mind but I suppressed them. I laughed and she was embarrassed. I assured her that my laughter was connected with something I'd thought of in a book, and I pointed to one beside my bed. How could I tell her about my sexual fantasy? Besides, though my mind was willing, my body was not. As she left and locked the door behind her, I realized something else. It was clear that she had opened the door I had previously locked, and locked it herself after leaving. I knew that, given the needs of some of the residents, such access was necessary, but still it was a little shattering to my idealized picture of the Village and gave me an uncomfortable feel of play-acting. It flashed through my mind that the Administration was letting us live *as if* we were in a real village. It was all too disturbing to think about so I turned over again and tried to sleep.

Friday, May 26

With sunlight pouring in, my alarm clock did not get a chance to ring. 8:00 A.M. suddenly felt awfully early. I lounged around while hoping the morning warmth would send energy into my still-tired body. This day I knew would be a long one and already I faced my first obstacle—the morning wash-up.

Since saving energy had been part of my make-up for twenty years, today would be no different. Over the years I had developed a system for getting dressed. If the bureau was far away from my bed, I placed my next day's underwear, socks, and occasionally my trousers within easy reach. Since at Het Dorp I was not using my legs at all, the closeness issue was even more important. I started to dress as always, putting everything on from the waist down when something made me hesitate. Some memory told me not to put on my trousers even though this would necessitate an extra trip from the chair to the bed and back again.

The recall was right. Washing up was a mess. Though the sink was low enough, I nevertheless managed to soak myself thoroughly. In retrospect I should not have worn anything. Ordinarily when washing my face, chest, and arms, I would lean over the sink, and any excess water from my splashing would drip into it. My body angle in a wheelchair was different. I could not extend over the sink very far without tipping. Thus, much of the water dripped down my neck onto me. Splashing with water was out, and the use of a damp washcloth, what I had once called a "sponge bath," was in. Again a patient- and child-like feeling swept over me, but I was too busy coping to let it stay. Shaving involved no particular problem of dripping, only one of perspective. Although the mirror was tilted to allow better vision for one below, I could not get a very close view of my face. Only a special mirror at eye level would really have worked.

My next task was one all too often neglected in any account of daily living—the necessity to urinate and defecate. I too might omit this except for my awareness of the continuing problem it presents for any of us with a physical handicap. So despite my own squeamishness I record my handling of "unspeakable practices."

Turning around from the sink I now faced the toilet. As in all residents' rooms, the toilet was nestled in a corner. I wheeled as close to it as I could. First I pushed myself to a standing position and then grabbed the long bar bolted to the wall above the seat. Thus steadied, I turned around, backed toward the toilet a half-step, and loosened my undershorts. With one hand I then unlocked my leg brace and with the other I steadied and lowered myself to the seat. Without doubt this was the easiest "toileting" I had ever experienced. With weak stomach muscles and legs I cannot raise myself to a standing position unless I have either something to pull on like the grab bar or something to push off from like the arms of a chair. On more than one embarrassing occasion I have leaned too heavily on a table or a sink and sent it and me toppling. Now I realized how unnecessary all my previous trouble had been.

But two difficulties did remain. For lack of better term I call the first one "cultural" and the second "psychosocial." As a Western man I had been trained to urinate standing with both feet firmly planted on the ground. Thus, to sit and urinate took some getting used to. This did, however, provide a side benefit. Standing I had always needed one hand free to steady myself. Sitting at least made it a more relaxed activity. My second problem was more "psychosocial." Before leaving the bathroom I tried to think if I had "to go" again. Once more I was reduced to the status of a child as I recalled parental admonitions to the effect, "We are starting on a trip so you better use the toilet now." I did the same thing with my own children. What were the toilet facilities like elsewhere in the Village? Would they be as easy to negotiate as the one in my room? So much for "unspeakable practices."

Back to my bed I went. After changing my waterlogged undershorts, I put on my trousers, undershirt, back support and sports shirt. I tucked a sweater behind me should it prove cold and several pieces of paper in various pockets for note taking.

Locking and closing my door was still a bit tricky but I was getting better at it.

On my way to breakfast I passed through several "streets" and by several dining areas. Residents I didn't know shouted greetings and good mornings. It was 8:30 A.M. but my own dining room was deserted. No one in sight, not even the dogelas. It felt weird. Not because I ate alone, but because I knew that somewhere in the building were dozens of people, but I could not see or hear them. Only the distant sounds of music and the occasional buzzing of an electric wheelchair confirmed this.

After all the "peopling" of yesterday, this sudden solitude was strange. But I busied myself with trying to schedule my cancelled appointments. No one was reachable. Frustrated, I decided that if I could not meet anyone, I might as well go somewhere.

The Workplace seemed a good place to see again. Maybe I could understand my previous discomfort if I had a more relaxed tour. Calling the Workplace was difficult and involved several stammerings in Dutch, but finally I was connected with someone who seemed to have been expecting my call, and an appointment was set up for 10:00 A.M.

It was only 9:15 but I decided to start out. Partly I was anxious to see the main source of village employment and partly I just wanted to take a leisurely ride on this bright sunny day. Outside my building I consulted my map. The workshop was even farther away than yesterday's supermarket. Psychologically, however, I was now prepared for a long trip and had allowed plenty of time. But the map wasn't as helpful as I thought. It didn't tell me whether there were hills or short cuts. In fact, in no document was such basic travel data provided. Either no one thought it important or it was felt that old residents would teach the new. As I wheeled toward the Workplace I experienced a further difficulty in finding my way around. In contrast to the "real world" there were fewer street signs and fewer arrows pointing to various facilities. I wondered if there was an implicit assumption that the life of the Villagers was a confined one. In some subtle way, I felt I was being reminded that outside my quarters was a different world. But maybe the reminder was not for me, a resident, but for me as outsider. Maybe it was felt that residents, by definition, knew the way to anywhere they wanted to go, and it was strangers who should have to ask directions.

All this philosophizing distracted me, and I soon got lost— not once but several times. Once I found myself in a dead-end street. And once seeking an elevator, I found myself at the bottom level of a building faced with a locked door. Suddenly Het Dorp had become a frightening unknown place. I was glad it was daytime and not night. Had other newcomers gotten lost as easily or did they venture forth more slowly? Again and again I consulted my map and kept redirecting myself. Almost exactly at 10:00 A.M. I arrived. It had taken me forty-five minutes to travel a relatively short distance.

I took a moment to catch my breath and to rearrange my ruffled appearance. The Workplace was a single-floor construction and straight ahead was a reception booth. As I neared, I could see that the receptionist was a woman in a wheelchair and thus a resident. I introduced myself and she asked me to wait, while she announced my presence to the appropriate staff person. In a moment a sandy-haired man, dressed in a business suit, emerged from a side door.

He seemed of average height but this was getting increasingly difficult to judge. Everyone was taller from my lower-down position. I recalled my children's awe as they looked up at big people. I was not awed but I did resent having to look up and extend myself to reach his outstretched hand. He invited me into his office with an interesting "Americanism," the offer "to take a seat," a gaffe since I was already seated in my wheelchair.

As he served coffee, he reflected on some of the problems he faced as an administrator in running this "sheltered work setting." He began with the current legislation, which required an individual working in a state-supported sheltered workshop to produce at one-third normal capacity. Many of the residents could not even come close, and he felt there was a limit to how much the staff could fudge production figures. This was complicated "by the decreased willingness of some residents to work." He attributed this decline to two factors. Many of the residents were sicker or their diseases progressed faster than the Administration had anticipated, and many simply wanted or needed more time for other activities.

As one example, he noted that "the women needed more time to dress." This was not as sexist as it sounded. It had certainly taken me a long time to ready myself that morning. Given how society expected women to look, perhaps it did take more time for them than for men. Having a physical handicap or chronic disease might well be more threatening to some concept of femininity than to the masculinity of a man. Someone here had remarked that it was easier for a handicapped man to marry than for a handicapped woman.

While I was dwelling on the reality facing the Villagers, he was dwelling on the reality facing an administrator—how to deal with a decreasing work force. His solution was to alter the general selection policy so as to recruit more "healthy" people. This meant more people whose medical conditions were not progressive, such as those with paraplegia. This was a solution that many residents might also favor. Marlene, for one, had voiced a preference for a "less diseased population." Nevertheless, the whole idea bothered me. It offended my notion of egalitarianism. It also seemed ironic that here of all places I should sense a prejudice against certain types of diseased or handicapped people.

Looking again at the administrator, however, I sensed his empathy. In a gesture of exceptional candor, he confessed his own difficulties and prejudices, "You need so much patience. It's hard. The greatest problem is when they can't speak well. Then, at first, I think they have a problem here, too. [He pointed to his head.] I know they don't. It's very hard. I just want to send them out of my office, get them out of my sight . . . But I am getting more comfortable, I am learning."

He was also aware of residents' feeling of being on exhibit, so as a matter of policy there were no formal tours, though special visitors and professionals could enter the workshops. The subtle issue was that it was his and not the residents' decision, as to who could or could not visit. The residents were at bottom "his charges" in the full sense of the word and had to be protected as well as taught. "We have to teach them things they never knew before, like keeping a schedule. It's just like the outside. We have holidays, vacations, and on Friday everybody is happy because it's the end of the week. We have to force them in some way to come to work but it's good for them. Just like we have to force them to get out of their rooms but it's good for them."

I gagged on this last remark. All the feelings of infantilization I had been experiencing had some base! Suddenly I felt no different from the residents of whom he spoke so patronizingly. Just by virtue of being in a wheelchair, I not only felt more weak and dependent, but people treated me as such. And when they did, I accepted it. Why? It was more than just not wanting to hurt their feelings. Somehow I had lost my right of protest. I had accepted their view of me. My palms were clammy and I was scared. Was the process of institutionalization both so powerful and subtle, that I could be aware of it and yet be unable to resist?

My host was unaware of the cause of my pensiveness and interpreted it as boredom. "Well, enough of all this talking. I know you want to see things with your own eyes." Mapping out all there was to see, he suggested that my visit should be in two parts, guided and unguided. This simply meant that I would tour some facilities alone. So it began. He, too, immediately fell into the pattern of pushing my wheelchair and thus physically directing my attention to where he thought it should be placed.

The guided tour covered all the areas of the Workplace. There were shops for woodworking, ceramics, packing, minor assembly, stage assembly of transformers, and sewing. Everyone was pleasant enough. Each staff supervisor patiently explained what the tasks were, how they were organized, and how well some of the residents did them. When brought to the tables, the workers followed suit and showed me all their work. After touring the main facilities, I was left alone to wheel myself. But the parent-child image pursued me. Not only were the workers presented almost as dutiful children but I was just an older, more trusted sibling. I suddenly had the feeling that after everything had been pointed out to me, I was "allowed" to go it alone. And should I get lost or get into trouble, the parents were around to help me out. In fact, the supervisors were not content to let me just watch and think. If I did nothing for what seemed too long a time, they rushed over to explain something. I wasn't sure whether it was their hovering or my presence but the atmosphere seemed very tense. The workers I spoke to were embarrassed, mostly they claimed by their lack of English. After a few moments of awkward conversation they would look up and inevitably a supervisor would appear.

When finally left alone, I realized how suffocating all this felt. It had started in the woodworking shop. I love carpentry and had stopped to admire the beautifully crafted toys. After asking my guide if I could purchase some, I sat watching a worker go through the final assembly stages. Seeing my interest, he introduced himself, carefully mentioning not only his name but how long he had been married. I noticed that he was the only worker present, so I asked, "Where is everybody?" He said nothing but the supervisor answered. "Yes, it's sad that all these good machines have to go to waste," his hand pointing to several, "but the residents just can't operate them. They're too dangerous." With all the electronic ingenuity that went into creating the Village, I could not believe there was not enough left-over ingenuity to adapt these machines. Besides, the use of the concept of danger was questionable, for a basic human right is the right to take risks. "Danger" deprived the workers of their adulthood and their personhood. It was one more link in the chain reminding them that they were no longer valid. Was this the source of all the embarrassment that the workers and I were experiencing, the "distasteful atmosphere" that Dr. Langlett had mentioned during my visit the day before? The workers participating in their own invalidation and on some level they and I knew and yet felt powerless to stop it.

There was something else, something which stimulated a further sense of depression, a sense of *déja vu*. Images of mental hospitals and institutions for the retarded flooded my mind. The jobs here were too simple, too fragmented, too mindless, too meaningless. Granted that my fellow residents might have limited physical capacity, but why such busy work, why industrial products that were marketable only with a subsidy? Could the workers possibly feel they were doing something worthwhile? Of course, many jobs in the outside world were as repetitive and meaningless but at least those workers may have had a rationalization of the job's being a means to an end. To what end were these tasks oriented? Why was work created from the point of view of the limitations of the workers rather than their potentialities? Again and again I had been told that the residents all had good minds. Why weren't they encouraged to use them? Work is not always exclusively physical. Why, in this of all places, was that myth perpetuated?

As I thought over these things, a staff member began to wheel me to our next stop. More snappishly than he deserved, I said sharply, "I can wheel myself." He was taken aback but smiled and pointed the way to the section devoted to "mental skills." This I remembered was the term used for the braille shops where manuscripts and sound recordings were prepared for the blind. As I entered, my spirits lifted. Maybe the name did have a double meaning. As I looked around the room, my eyes were caught by all the movement. It was ironic, for many of the people seemed even more physically limited than those in the other shops. Here the ingenuity so lacking elsewhere was evident. A woman operated a machine with a finger and over to her right was a man typing with a device attached to a headband.

Though many of the tasks were a sort of typing, what stayed with me was their variety. Each word, each name, each fact was different, and required similar but not identical movements. The contrast with filling the same moulds, attaching the same wires, sewing the same hems, sanding the same blocks was unmistakable. Moreover, the sense of accomplishment was greater. Coming to the end of a page, a chapter, or a book seemed more fulfilling than meeting some quota. While all that I was attributing to this work might be projection, there was a sense of purpose present. Here the conversations were different. When the workers explained what they were doing, they expressed satisfaction with their craft *and* with the ultimate use of their product.

Workers and staff alike were aware that the braille shop was different. Job satisfaction was higher and absenteeism lower, but somehow more general principles could not be deduced. It was as if the overall work ethic made this experience seem an interesting exception rather than a normative possibility.

As I drove back home, I thought about some other aspects of my tour. The resident grapevine was amazing. This was only my second day, yet most workers not only knew who I was but where I lived, where I ate, and what I did yesterday. The Administration also had its antennae out, for while there I received two phone calls. This was especially interesting since I had not told anyone where I was going and had not known myself until that morning. The return trip was quite easy. I was getting better at finding my way and negotiating hills.

Shortly after twelve I arrived at my dining hall. Most of my companions had shown up, some even returning from work. My thoughts were still on the Workplace but I listened to snatches of conversations and even began to remember names. Ms. Shultz was complaining about a difficult-to-reach location in Arnhem. As several nodded in agreement, I wondered what places in Arnhem were *easy* to reach. Someone mentioned the soccer match that evening and wondered whether our TV's could "catch" it. From lack of mobility (the Arnhem trip), there was a shift to excessive mobility (the speedy footballers). Soon we were back to a "lack," as several talked about the new temporary dogela. She was a vacation replacement and was not thought up to par. As Ms. Nijhof put it, "She's very slow. She took twenty to thirty minutes to get me out of bed. The regular one only took seven." Monika caught my eye and invited me to watch the match on TV. I gladly accepted.

Pieter asked about my visit to the Workplace and I shared some of my disgruntlement. But because I sensed this was not the time to "tell all," I changed the subject. "And if that wasn't enough, even the Administration knew where I was. Or at least they made it their business to find me with bad news."

"Oh, what was it?" prompted Pieter, the perfect straight man.

"What else but another cancellation? So much for today's afternoon appointment."

Several people had been half listening for there was some knowing laughter in response.

"So what will you do now?"

"I think I'll go to this Adaptation Room I've heard so much about."

At this Mrs. van Amerongen and the Schmids joined in. Almost everyone added something about how "interesting," "important," and "inventive" a place it was. Reinforced in how I was to spend the afternoon, I returned to serious eating and lunch came to a pleasant close.

Wanting some time for rest and reflection I left for my home. It had been years since I had napped in the afternoon. Usually I have to take off all my braces to get comfortable but this time I slept fully clothed. Was I so relaxed or exhausted? At 2:40 I awoke, feeling great. After a quick trip to the bathroom and a wake-up wash, I was pushing myself to the Adaptation Room. Up one corridor, down another, across to another building, up the elevator, in the side door of another building, and there I was without having had to negotiate a single hill!

Wheeling up to the desk I spied the familiar face of someone I saw on my first visit in January. She was the receptionist, and her smile of recognition comforted me. Knowing far more about me than I knew of her, she asked, "Are you enjoying yourself, Professor Zola?" Before I had a chance to answer, my name echoed behind me. "Ah, Dr. Zola, it's good to see you again."

There was Dr. Klapwijk, the founder of Het Dorp. "I'm glad you took us up on our invitation. Has everything worked out well? The arrangements?"

"Everything's just fine," I smiled.

"Good. Good. Have you had a chance to read the material I gave you last time?"

"Yes, it was very helpful."

"Well, I have to go now but why don't you call my secretary for an appointment?" He waved goodbye to me, the receptionist, and several others nearby. The greetings in return were warm.

Hoping not to lose this opportunity, I asked the receptionist if she would call his secretary. As with every administrative appointment there were dificulties. First, we kept getting disconnected and when we finally got through, the secretary was unavailable. As we waited, a young man in a wheelchair approached, "Professor Zola, I am Mr. Geyer, from the Adaptation Room."

"Oh, I'm sorry to keep you waiting. I'll be just a minute."

"No problem, I have plenty of time."

The receptionist chimed in, "We all have time here."

After another attempt to reach Dr. Klapwijk's secretary, I gave up, and together with Mr. Geyer, I wheeled to the elevator. He was as excited about showing me the Adaptation Room as I was about seeing it. He was certainly more enthusiastic about his job than anyone else I had met. His enthusiasm reminded me of the spirit of the braille shop workers, who were so engaged in "socially useful tasks." When we arrived I saw that there was another reason for his satisfaction. As he quickly pointed out, he was the only resident in this group of "normals." While this gave him a certain sense of achievement, he wanted still more. In his own words, he felt "transitional."

"I am taking a correspondence course in electronics. Maybe I'll go on. Do you think that thirty is too old to go back to school?"

"No," I answered firmly, but it was clear he wanted to talk rather than get advice.

"Well, anyway, soon I plan to get married. And then we'll get a place and leave the Dorp. I really want you to meet her. She's a "normal," you know. We'll be at the Gala."

I didn't know how to respond. His reference to her being a "normal" shocked me. I could see how important it was to him but it bothered me. I disliked the fact that we lived in a society which not only made his being engaged to a "normal" an important achievement but also made it necessary for him to announce it. But I saw that I was really no different, a victim of the same pressures. I had merely set up my life so that I would never have to make such a statement. I had separated myself early from the physically handicapped by refusing to attend a special residential school. Later I had simply never socialized with anyone who had a chronic disease or physical handicap. I too had been seeking to gain a different identity through my associations.

Something else he had said stayed with me. He was the second Villager who spoke of specific plans to leave. Maybe this place was not as much a dead-end as I had been led to believe.

By now we had already wheeled through the shop and were back in the main showroom. My first surprise was at the size of this unit—only six people. Yet this was a place which made the rest of the Village possible. With a sweep of his hand, Mr. Geyer pointed to an amazing array of equipment and gadgetry, from electronic panels to open doors and operate telephones, to cup holders and utensil grippers.

If a resident could control his breathing or lift a finger or nod his head, that ability could be used to extend his range of motions. My awe was coupled, however, with a sinking feeling. What was easy for the rest of the world, was for the residents a major expenditure of time and energy. I felt a little ashamed of my morning complaint about all the energy it took to dress and wash. At the time I gave silent thanks that I did not need the devices spread before me—gadgets to help button a shirt, tie a shoe, or tilt a cup. While I was vey impressed with their work, I was a little wary of my ignorance.

"Won't some of these inventions lend themselves to some mass production and marketing?"

"Yes, but we're so busy here. Our emphasis is on selective adaptation to the problem of the individual resident."

It sounded reasonable, but something about the word "busy" bothered me. So many hospitals and doctors are "too busy" to pay attention to patients' personal problems. I didn't know why this came to mind. Was there something else behind this emphasis on individuation? Partly to find out, I asked, "Well, do you have a booklet or listing of all your products?"

"Not really," he answered a bit embarrassed. "We have been meaning to but we haven't gotten around to it yet."

"Doesn't this lead to a lack of coordination with other facilities?"

He admitted that on more than one occasion, after laboriously creating or adapting a particular machine, they had discovered that they were merely engaged in reinvention.

I was left with the why of it all. Was it merely some form of vested interest? Was there a secret which had to be kept? Like the handicap itself maybe there was something stigmatized about the "needed compensations" and devices which people could not or thought they should not share. While this all seemed a bit far fetched, I wondered if the obstacles to rapid accumulation of knowledge and dissemination had the effect of keeping the handicapped in their place here as well as on the outside. I recalled all the very different bags and other devices that existed for people with colostomies and ileostomies and how they confused rather than helped the patient. Then I remembered my own unsuccessful efforts to learn about new types of braces and realized how dependent I was on my prosthetist for information. For the first time in my life I resented the people whose "patient-customer" I had been for over twenty years.

Mr. Geyer's return marked the end of this tour. I thanked him for all he had shared and agreed to meet him the next day at the Gala.

My return trip took me by the Recreation Room. As I wheeled in I saw a sign announcing its hours as 9:00 A.M.–12:00 noon and 2:00 P.M.–5:00 P.M. It struck me as odd that the hours paralleled those of the Workplace and that the room was not open at night. Did this mean that workers did not or could not use it? Was it only for those who didn't work? As I looked around, I could see it was a rather large room like many another hobby shop with places for weaving, sewing, and painting. The supervisor quickly greeted me, and before I had a chance to ask anything, he assured me that "instruction is available for almost any activity a resident could desire." It sounded good but I wondered. As at the Workplace, who chose the activities? Here also was there some subtle push for the residents to do what was good for them?

All in all it looked relatively uninteresting. I recalled my hospitalization and how uninviting I found such places. Since I love to putter, I was puzzled with my own discomfort. Why did I find this so stultifying? Maybe the reason for coming here seemed more like busy work than play. And I wanted play as a reward. Perhaps I and the residents were too much products of a culture where play comes *after* not *instead* of work. The "hours open" reinforced this image. Maybe there *was* something stigmatizing about the connotations of these activities—activities for the lazy, the lonely, the incapable. I knew I didn't want to be there. Apparently neither did the residents. Only two were present. (I encountered the same situation several other times, during the week.)

As I was about to leave I noticed recent copies of *Paris Match* and several other international magazines. This reminded me of the meeting room where I took my meals. There magazines and books were also much in evidence. But most looked as if they had not been moved since the day they were set out. There was also a TV but I had never seen it on. Now the words of someone about a certain lack of community at the living units took on more meaning. But it was more complex. Many bewailed the neglect of many of the "community facilities," from the Recreation Room to those provided at each residence. It was true that after meals or coffee no one seemed to linger. Maybe it was not all bad. Maybe what was being ignored was the residents' needs—in particular their needs for privacy, to be alone, to create their own private pleasures. While there may indeed be a lack of community here, its roots and solution lay beyond the provision of recreational resources and places to meet and socialize. Maybe, ironically enough, it was not that they interacted too little with each other but rather the opposite. There were three meals a day and two coffees when they saw each other and even more occasions for those who worked *in* the Village. What the residents may have created, to use a Goffman phrase, was some "private space." That this seemed to imply a rejection of what others had created for them was incidental.

Lost in my thoughts I almost forgot a coffee invitation from the Falks. They had been introduced to me as a married couple very much oriented to the outside. Perhaps indicative of this we agreed to meet at the Restaurant, the Dorp facility most actively used by the citizens of Arnhem. As I wheeled in they immediately recognized me (I had only spoken to them over the phone) and waved me over. They were a handsome couple, long-time residents of the Village, both in wheelchairs, both in their forties. I don't know whether it was the setting or them, but except for a brief question about how I was enjoying my stay, all the conversation was about the outside—movies, sports, Dutch culture. It was a break from my intense involvement with the Village. Only at the close did the focus shift back, when Mrs. Falk, smiling, said, "It was so good to speak with you. We have so few good conversations around here."

Since we seemed fairly comfortable with one another, I decided to press them. "I have heard something like that from others. What's the trouble?"

Together, they willingly launched into a description of the limited social world of the residents. "They have so little to talk

about, and what they do talk about is uninteresting." At first
they explained it in terms of their fellow Villagers being so
different, coming as they do from all parts of Holland. I had
heard others vaguely speak of difficulties with "other Villagers," but never so articulately. Mrs. Falk warmed to the topic
and came out with a list:

"Education"—"Most of the people are not very well
educated, they don't read or anything."

"Lack of social skills"—"They lived always before in
institutions or with their parents, they don't do anything!"

"Social isolation"—"Some just sit in their rooms all
day. I can't stand them." Picking up on this, Mr. Falk
elaborated: "They look only at their watches. 8:30 A.M.
breakfast, 10:00 A.M. coffee, 12:30 P.M. lunch; 3:30 P.M.
coffee. It's now time for this, now time for that."

"Jealousy"—She continued, "They're jealous that
we are married. That's a big problem here. They're jealous
that we go out so much, have so many friends. They always
know where we go, when we come in. I don't like it." I
realized that they shared my feeling that someone was
always aware of one's comings and goings.

"Their limited interests"—"They only know about
their handicap. Why, for me, it's only something recent. I
used to walk, run, dance, play sports," she said with obvious pride. "So many were born that way. I was not!"

"Physical impediments"—"And with some," she
added with exasperation, "Well it's just so hard to talk to
the spastics." He nodded vigorously in agreement.

I was immediately struck by some of the uncomfortable
perceptions that the Falks shared, not only with other residents,
but with the outside world. Naively I had expected that people
at Het Dorp would be different. Whenever I have learned that a
particular minority group was itself prejudiced, I have always
been shocked. I had the feeling that "having been through it,
they should know better." I kept wondering what was bought by
the prejudice, perhaps a feeling that "I'm not like them, or, at
least I'm better off than they are." Here where so many, includ-

ing the Falks, had progressive diseases such a distancing could
be even more important than elsewhere. That in a sense was
what Mr. Geyer was doing both in his work and in his choice of a
fiancée. Why was I so angry at this distancing? Was I demanding
something of them but not of myself? Again I recalled my own
unconscious decision not to socialize with or date people with
handicaps. Looking up from my reverie I did not see two "prejudiced" people but two people I very much liked.

It was about five o'clock when we parted, and perhaps,
more prone to childhood associations because of the wheelchair, I thought of my mother. It was only an hour to supper and
she (in my daydream) was admonishing me for "spoiling it" by
eating pastry beforehand. I shook my head to get her out and
wheeled toward home. One resident whom I had never met
before waved and said in broken English something like "Don't
forget the Gala." Everyone, even strangers, wanted to make
sure that I did not miss it. I had to admit their caring felt good.
As I rounded the final corner, I saw a resident parked in front of
my door, the delivery man with the toys I had ordered from the
Workplace. He hefted them in his hand, commenting on how
well made they were and how sure he was that my children
would enjoy them. How could he be sure that the toys were for
my children? Well, they seemed to know everything else about
me, why not this?

My arms and back ached so much that I returned to bed for
my second nap of the day. It was literally for "forty winks" as the
alarm jolted me awake a few minutes later. Off I raced to dinner
and this time I almost made it. The "almost" puzzled me since
this was so against my usual pattern of always being early. But
here I was continually misjudging how long it would take me to
get from one place to another. It was as if I were resisting the fact
that I was in a wheelchair and were refusing to make appropriate
allowances, the kind that I had always made previously. As I
wheeled through the door it was clear that not only had they
waited for me again but a place had been kept open. The sense
of acceptance was a bit overwhelming. I was not used to it's

happening so fast. Something about it bothered me but I didn't know what.

Almost as if to make up for lost time, the meal seemed especially fast. I had always been told how quickly I ate, but these people, despite all sorts of physical limitations, ate quite as rapidly. From beginning to end the three courses, including soup, meat, potatoes, spinach, bread, and dessert, took only about 20–25 minutes.

The Gala the next night occupied all the conversation. There was talk about the new acts, reminiscences about previous shows, and commiserations about all the problems involved in putting it on. This seemed to involve more than the theatrical arrangements. Mrs. van Amerongen was pleased that my ticket was taken care of, but the Schmids and others voiced concern about how I would get to the Gala. Pieter and Monika assured them that it wouldn't be a problem since I could go in their car. All joined in to discuss the details, but I felt embarrassed to discuss my own ambivalence. I wanted very much to go under my own power but they were not sure whether I could make it in my wheelchair. I wanted to interrupt, "Yes, I can!" but I was not really sure. The auditorium was many hills away. If I went with Pieter and Monika in their car, then I would have to give up my wheelchair. Only one would fit into the car and that would have to be Pieter's since everyone knew that I could really get along with a cane. But to me reclaiming my cane seemed a personal betrayal. So mildly, but not too confidently, I said that the auditorium did not seem *that* far away. Adopting the role of solicitous parents, Pieter and Monika nodded wisely, "Hmm, yes. We'll see . . ."

I was grateful when Monika changed the subject quite dramatically. She told of an injury experienced earlier that afternoon. Apparently the bathroom cabinet had fallen on her, its contents bruising her shoulder and chest and the broken mirror glass cutting her heel. Both she and the bathroom were a mess. Though I was very upset, she told about it with such a mixture of hurt and humor that everyone laughed. They kidded her about her strength—it was supposed to have fallen as she touched it—and sympathized about her wounds. As she pouted, pointing to the bandaids, I too had a hard time keeping a straight face.

When the conversation turned to the football game that night, it was the sign that the meal was drawing to a close. One by one people excused themselves, saying, "See you at coffee!" or "Tomorrow!" As I started to leave, Monika caught me.

"Will you come tonight? You know Pieter does not like to watch the game. Besides there will be some more customers tonight."

I was a little embarrassed and said, "I really don't want to be in the way."

"No problem. You know it'll be a good game."

I didn't really need much persuasion. When we reached the room, Pieter was already engrossed in his work. I settled in near the TV while Monika did some straightening, started the coffee, set out the cups, and prepared "munchies" for our game watching. The time passed uneventfully. Shortly after the first score, three customers arrived, a young boy and his parents. Their contact with Pieter was minimal and soon everyone was avidly watching the game with all the appropriate oohs and aahs of sports fans.

During halftime, Monika served coffee and cookies. For the first time I was drawn to her gait. When she had first passed by, I dismissed the occasional limp as due to her accident. But it was more than that. Why was I suddenly so aware of her physical problem and why had I ignored it before? I was usually acutely aware of a person's slightest impediment. Perhaps I had so taken over the handicapped view of the world—the "normals" and us—that once I had categorized her as a "normal," I switched her off and did not notice her. Or perhaps such a minor problem passed unnoticed amongst the greater ones here. My social perception seemed to be determining, for if I knew a person lived here I immediately looked for difficulty in mobility among their problems, and Monika was not a resident but a guest. It was only tonight when she lost her balance in a way that did not look like tripping that I reopened my eyes and saw that she limp-swayed, having the balance problem of those with multiple sclerosis. And indeed that was what she had. In terms of the distinction made by several at the Village, this was a "mixed couple," a "handicapped" with a "disease." Pieter was paraplegic and had probably stabilized within a range, though problems would come as he aged, but Monika had a progressive disease which would only get worse. She was now at her best, but I supposed that both of them wondered how long she would stay at this level. Would he some day be in much better shape than she, with the irony of the reversal of their roles?

As the soccer game resumed, Pieter put the equipment through its final paces. The young boy tried to split his attention between the game and Pieter's mechanical instruction. Pieter won out, and shortly they all left, obviously satisfied with his work. I could not help but notice the fee, which seemed considerable, so when the game ended, I asked Pieter how all this got started.

He described it as a small but growing enterprise. "So far it is just word of mouth. Maybe soon I will have to advertise and if business grows . . ." He glanced at Monika. She smiled in return. Suddenly he reached up, pulled her gently to his lap and kissed her. She was more surprised than embarrassed, poked him gently in the ribs, and raised her eyebrows as if to ask, "Now just what has gotten into you?" Both shyly began talking in Dutch. I couldn't understand but it didn't matter. I felt good, warm and comfortable, and I sensed they felt the same.

Later, wheeling back to my room, I was careful to avoid any new adventures. I needn't have worried, most people were already home. Spreading all my little notes on the table, I wrote for more than an hour, then stopped to reflect. As complete as I tried to be, there were always things I forgot or dismissed as unimportant. And there were other things that only penetrated into my consciousness with repetition. To be honest, I think they didn't get through because I didn't want to hear them.

One example of this started to become clear to me. In my preparations, in my notes, and in my hellos I always referred to myself as a "visitor." Moreover, I apologized for this status, a status which I thought separated me from the residents. But whenever I went into my apologia, they looked at me rather curiously. Sometimes they jokingly corrected me. But I had not let the jokes sink in, let alone recorded them. I felt less concerned with differentiating myself as one who had made it with no difficulty and more uncomfortable at the distance I kept creating between *me* and *them.*

All along, however, the residents had been patiently disabusing me of this distinction. They had been trying to tell me that there are two types of people in the world—"normals" and "handicapped." And there was no doubt in their minds to which group I belonged, no matter how much I might wish it otherwise. While I regarded myself as a visitor to the Village, they regarded me as a visitor to the outside world. The latter world, the world of the normal, was one in which the handicapped were *allowed,* but only temporarily and under certain conditions. Again and again they confronted me with a reality I had often denied: "What was I going to do when I got worse, when I got older?" To them I was on a visitor's pass to the outside world and they wanted to know what would happen when my time was up.

I can't claim that I welcomed their insights into my denial, but I was made to reassess my thinking about myself and about rehabilitation in general. I realized how meager are our attempts to write and do research about adjustment and adaptation. It would be nice if, at some point, growing up ends and maturity begins, or if one could say that successful adjustment and adaptation to a particular difficulty has been achieved. For most problems, or perhaps even most basic life issues, there is no single time for such a resolution to occur. The problems must be faced, evaluated, redefined, and readapted to, again and again and again. And I knew now that this also applied to myself. No matter how much I was admired by others or by myself, there was still much more I had to face. "My Polio" and "My Accident" were not just my past; they were part of my present and my future.

I was not sure what about me was changing but something was. Once in bed I tried a little reading, and a little dreaming, and finally dropped into a deep, restful, uninterrupted sleep.

Saturday, May 27

Despite the long sleep, it still took me longer than usual to gather my clothes and to wash. When I did arrive at breakfast shortly after nine, nobody was around. This time I didn't mind. I welcomed the quiet. I felt so full of experiences that I relished not being "on." The silence was interrupted only by the dogela serving coffee, who chatted about the weather and America.

On the way home, I heard footsteps almost mocking my pace. I couldn't turn around quickly enough to see who it was, before a greeting relieved my incipient paranoia. It was Dr. Metz.

"I'm sorry I could not come yesterday. So many things to do. Are you all right? Who are you seeing today?"

"No one really," I said somewhat apologetically.

"No good, that's very bad. Your time is too short."

"But so much has happened. I don't want too much set up for me. I like it more spontaneous with people inviting me to spend time with them." My tone was stronger than I intended. I really was resisting anyone doing too much for me. This very thought weakened my resolve, so when he argued that some people were especially worth meeting I gave in.

He left briefly to call two "old-timers," one a long-time member of the Dorp Council and the other a resident who had married since her arrival here.

"They both use the Village in very different ways. You should find them interesting. So tell me, how were your first two days?"

"Well, I guess that some of our fears and impressions were true." And then I shared my disquiet about the Workplace.

He reminded me of the similar experiences he had in visiting many "caretaker" institutions. Then he commiserated with me about the ambivalence of the administrators of the places we studied. "They always say they welcome our insights but not when they conflict with their own."

He left shortly after ten and I returned to my notetaking. This I interspersed with reading some documents about the Village, finishing shortly before 12:15 P.M.

This time I made the meal with a minute to spare. But I arrived amidst a disturbing incident. Several men were teasing Mieke, a young blonde woman who couldn't see, about a dark hair on her sweater. Her fending off their questions with "Where is it? Where? Over here?" only deepened my discomfort. But as I looked around the room, no one else including her seemed bothered.

My own arrival, however, shifted the residents' attention to the issue of my transportation to the Gala. Mr. Schmid, as gently as possible, questioned whether I was up to negotiating the distance and the hills.

Turning to Pieter, I said, "Well, I've been practicing. First there was the supermarket and yesterday the Workplace. I think if I leave early enough I'm sure I can make it." My earnest, pleading voice sounded like that of a child.

Pieter and Monika, consistent with my tone, assured the others that they would "look out for me." I didn't realize until it was settled how relieved I felt at not having to give up my identity as a resident.

Looking along the rectangular table, I realized that all the names and faces of my companions were at last in focus. By now I could see that with minor variations we all sat in pretty much the same place each meal. As we ate I tried to recall all I knew and felt about them.

At the head of the table was Mrs. van Amerongen. It was her smile which greeted me at every meal. She spoke English quite well and was probably in her mid- or late-forties. I always imagined she had blue eyes, probably for no better reason than that they semed to be almost shining, set off by tiny smiling wrinkles and round cheeks. Though she used a wheelchair, I was always impressed by her above-the-waist agility and strength. This made me think that she had suffered from some injury that affected her mobility rather than some disease. Her energy seemed boundless. She had established an information exchange before coming to the Dorp and continued it here. Perhaps this was why I thought of her as rising early and going to sleep late. With admiration, Pieter once described her as writing more than twenty letters a day. Though I didn't know on what it was based, she also had a reputation of being a fighter and an organizer.

Next to her on the left usually sat Ms. Schultz. I occasionally saw her at breakfast, rarely at lunch, and always at dinner. She was in her thirties, of slight build with long curly hair. Of the group she appeared to be the most physically fit. She walked with only a slight sway. Her slurring of speech made me think she had cerebral palsy. She was perceived to be very shy. She worked in the "manual" sheltered workshop doing assembly work. There too she seemed isolated, working alone at her bench. When I spoke to her at the shop, she was obviously delighted, and had in fact told the others that I was her friend. And yet I didn't really know her.

Then there was Mieke. We had exchanged very few words, but each time we met, her greeting seemed warmer. Several times I wanted to overcome my own awkwardness with some non-verbal gestures but her blindness got in *my* way. Her hair was short and blond and set off her squarish face like the old Dutch Boy paint ads. She used a cane, but from her biweekly visits to the doctor and the pills she took with each meal, I surmised that she might have some chronic disease. Now as I looked at her eating, my eyes were drawn as they often were to her colorful clothes. Something made her laugh and her square face became round. I wanted to know her better.

Pieter sat sternly in his chair. Sometimes I thought this was a role he took, a sort of straight man to the puckish Monika. He was tall, spare, and pale with a crew cut; like many with paraplegia, he had very broad shoulders but was very thin from the waist down. Despite the fact that he was the one who led the first day's discussion, he seemed a bit of a loner, a sort of Dutch Gary Cooper in style and appearance. The fact that he had his own private business isolated him, yet there was a shy warmth which made me trust him.

If trust was what I felt with Pieter, delight characterized my feelings about Monika. Technically she was only a visitor and yet she was extraordinarily well-known and popular and seemed quite familiar with the comings and goings at the Dorp. Her appearance fit her personality: she was in her late twenties, about 5'4" with straight black hair, a small turn-up nose, bright eyes. With her ready quip, she was a perfect counterpoint to the very serious Pieter. They had been engaged for well over a year with their marriage partly dependent upon the availability of "adapted" living quarters somewhere in the Arnhem area.

Next to her would have sat the missing ninth resident. I heard little about him except that he had had to go somewhere for an operation.

Moving around the table in the other direction, on Mrs. van Amerongen's right were Mr. and Mrs. Schmid. He was telling those next to him about an upcoming trip that he and the missus were contemplating. As usual, Mrs. Schmid did little more than nod slightly. His character was quite in contrast to his appearance. He was short, solid, about fifty, and he looked very standoffish sitting stiffly in his wheelchair. But when he spoke there was often a mischievous twinkle in his eye and a liveliness in his tone. He was one of those, who by his own admission, had built a life completely within the Dorp, serving on various committees. "Work harder here than I did on the outside."

Next to him sat Mrs. Schmid, silently eating. She impressed me as a very nice woman in her late forties. She spoke hesitatingly in English. I guessed that she had multiple sclerosis or muscular dystrophy with growing weakness in her upper body. She could stand, however, probably for only a moment or two.

Then there was me. It's hard to describe how I might have looked to others. I've already described my physical limitations. In my mind's eye I was about 5'7", round, stocky in build, broad through the shoulders and considerably thinner below the waist. My dark hair was a bit longer than that of most of the men at the Village. I've often been told I have nice hazel eyes, a pleasant face, and a very wide grin. I believe it. Never known to be particularly shy, I have been called arrogant, aggressive, extroverted, open and warm, not all at the same time nor by the same people.

Next to me sat Ms. Nijhof, a very gentle woman in her seventies, kindly looking, short, squat, almost round. I know only that her condition, whatever it was, had obviously resulted in a general debilitation. She had the strength or movement in her arms to feed herself, but the food had to be cut beforehand. Once, however, I did see her get out of her wheelchair and walk, albeit very slowly, into her room. She seemed the storyteller, the occasional joker of the group, and I often saw her visited by young children.

On my other side usually sat Mr. Altman. Because of his cold, we had not yet met. He had been described to me as in his thirties, quite bookish in appearance with severe limitation and weakness in all his extremities. I was told that he was quite articulate, the most argumentative and politically interested of all the residents, and had many acquaintances "on the outside." He was a good friend of Pieter's.

The dogelas, though they took their meals with us, seemed to sit in no particular place, perhaps to show no favoritism. On the other hand, the chief dogela was on vacation, and most of those I met were only there temporarily.

It is hard to judge how typical my companions were. They were four men and five women (counting the missing residents but omitting the two visitors, Monika and myself), and they ranged in age from twenties to seventies. I cannot estimate the ratio between "handicapped" and "diseased" though the latter seemed to preponderate. As for degree of physical impairment, this depended on how it was measured. There was no one who needed anything approaching continuous care though several may have needed at least occasional help in dressing and getting out of bed. Noticeably absent was anyone with an obvious physical deformity or overall paralysis. Seven of the nine used a wheelchair all or part of the time.

In how they occupied themselves, they seemed representative of the Village modes. Ms. Schultz and Mr. Altman worked in the sheltered workshops. Mieke was a switchboard operator in Arnhem outside the Village. Pieter had a small independent business. Mr. Schmid and Mrs. van Amerongen were active in the inner workings of the Village. I did not know what Mrs. Schmid and Ms. Nijhof did, but I suspected not very much. Very little had been said of Mr. Heslinga, who was away.

Once Mr. Schmid asked if I thought the people in my group were happy. I was flustered by the question and stammered out that at the very least they seemed to get along well with each other. The meals and coffee breaks were lively, filled with jokes, stories, and the day's events. I did not get a clear sense of the friendship networks. Perhaps they were no different from those in any college community: some very close friends came from the same floor (i.e., street); other friends came from other dorms (i.e., buildings). Whatever the networks were, the residents allowed space for me to enter their lives. I don't know why the Administration assigned me to this particular group, but it certainly has proven a good match.

It was 1:30 P.M. and time to leave for my meeting with Mr. and Mrs. Hendriks. I wheeled through the Village with great anticipation. Their home was in a new building created for married couples. In it were nine apartments for couples, two for singles, and *no* place for dogelas. Thus, all the people there were to varying degrees self-sufficient. Either their handicaps were such that they could manage for themselves, or one of the members of the couple was "normal" and could help the other. When they used dogelas, it was on a special, prearranged task and time basis.

I wondered what the Hendriks looked like. I knew a little about them from Dr. Metz. Both were confined to wheelchairs—he as a result of a traumatic injury, she from a congenital deformity. They had met at a rehab center, known each other for many years, and married when they could arrange suitable living quarters. After marriage, one year was spent with her parents, two years in another part of the Dorp, and three years in here; their "permanent home."

Today I was right on time. Mr. Hendriks greeted me at the door and introduced his wife. She seemed shy and promptly excused herself to make coffee. Seemingly at ease, he welcomed me with, "Well, Dr. Metz mentioned that you'd like to see how a married couple lives. Let me take you on a tour."

The apartment was quite spacious and well-furnished. I entered immediately into a small foyer. On the right was a large bathroom, about six feet square, pretty much the same as the one in my Dorp home. To the left of the foyer was a small storage room. Straight ahead was a largish bedroom, with a door leading to an outside terrace. The beautiful garden and his pride in it were a surprise. It was typically Dutch, and this, I guess because of his handicap, I had not expected. Almost reading my mind, he emphasized, "I landscaped it myself," and proceeded to detail the care and feeding of the various flowers and plants. Returning to the living room, I was impressed by its spaciousness. It contained the standard set of wall cabinets, couch, table, and two chairs, with ample room for two wheelchairs. Separated by a curtain was a kitchen especially designed for use by those in wheelchairs, with everything low and within reach. To the right of the living room was another small room which some people used for guests but which the Hendriks used as a study-workspace—he for reading and she for sewing.

With the tour over, there was an awkward pause. Partly to break the silence, I said, "You certainly have a very nice home. I'm quite impressed with what you've done with it. The location is especially nice. All that room outside to . . ."

He quickly interrupted my praise. "You know my work on

the Council had nothing to do with our getting this place. I got it by drawing lots."

It never occurred to me that he had used any influence to obtain this apartment. It was a reminder that the shortage of such quarters made him uneasy at "having it so good."

At this point his wife brought the coffee. When I asked about the kitchen, she excitedly pointed out all the adapted equipment. But almost as if she had gone too far, she soon fell silent. Mr. Hendriks took over the conversation and spoke of all their "outside" friends and activities. "We go out whenever we can. What we both like to do is travel. Last year we went to South Africa and that was very special. Wasn't it, dear?" She nodded in agreement. "We had a friend there who made all the arrangements. He arranged a place for us to live that was all on one floor and there was always someone to help us, especially Babs, if she needed it." This alluded to the fact that she needed some assistance which he could not provide and perhaps also to the fact that *he* didn't need such help.

During all this time I felt pressured to acknowledge in some positive way their outside activities. I found this especially ironic since the reason I had agreed to met them was their status as Dorp "old-timers." At what I hoped was a suitable break, I shifted the conversation to the "inside." "Dr. Metz told me that you've been quite active in the Village from its very beginning. It's clear that this is quite a fantastic undertaking. What to you are some of the problems yet to be dealt with?"

To Mr. Hendriks, two of the greatest problems were the shortage of facilities for married couples and the loneliness of many of its residents. He offered a solution to neither. He emphasized, as had several others, that a background problem was that the residents were from "all over" the Netherlands. To me this "all over" concept was a euphemism for the perception that many people were of a lower class and had less education and social skills than they. Perhaps this bringing people from "all over," separating them from friends and family, further diminished for some an already shrunken social world. With less stimulation, some then turned more inward on themselves and their bodies and became less communicative and less interesting to others.

He went on, "It's really sad about some of the people here. All they want to talk about is themselves and their problems."

I felt the distance that he was putting between himself and the other residents. And yet this distance had not prevented him from being elected to the Council. Perhaps it even helped. He was a long-time resident, close to the Administration, and he had made it on the outside. That was the world he wanted to talk about. To questions about the world of the sheltered work-shops, he pleaded ignorance. I wondered if he had ever been to them.

When he left hanging a reference to "other unsolved prob-lems," I asked if he were referring to the medical instability of many residents' conditions.

"I'm not sure what you mean."

"I've heard several people mention the fear of what might happen if their disease got worse. I guess they were worried that they might have to leave the Village."

His answer sounded too glib. "For married couples this really isn't a problem. At least one member of each couple is usually stable, so if one gets worse, he can help out. Besides they could merely ask more help from the dogela. It's really no problem." I nodded somewhat unbelievingly, since I knew that most of the Village residents were single!

He changed the subject and focused more on himself. He kept referring to his "lucky breaks," such as an employer who was willing to "take a chance" on him. He had now been working as a draftsman for ten years. But most of all he was grateful to the Dorp for all it allowed him. "Without this place it would be very hard. It means also that we will never have to worry if things do go bad; we will always have a place to go." I could not help but wonder if this was more wish than certainty.

Talking about the Village and what it offered led naturally enough to what was available in the United States. As usual, the conversation started with questions about my own personal

medical care and then moved on to comparisons of the United
States and the Netherlands. Here I shared one observation. "In
almost every village and town in the Netherlands I see handicapped people, either in wheelchairs or using other special
motorized vehicles. I can't honestly recall seeing so many in the
U.S."

"But why is that so strange? Maybe it's because of your
more advanced technology. Surely this not only prevents many
such problems but also cures those that arise!"

His "Pollyannish" attitudes were beginning to get to me,
but I tried to be gentle. "Somehow I doubt if that's the case. I
know of no data telling me there are any fewer handicapped
people or crippling conditions in the U.S. than here. In fact,
given the size of the population, I would expect to see many
more such people in the streets." Asked to explain further, I
speculated that the visibility issue reflected the polarized U.S.
attitude toward the handicapped, one consistent with a "man-
over-nature" perspective. "It's as if there is no force of nature
we in my country cannot control and no difficulty we can't
overcome if we only try hard enough. As in the case of the poor,
underneath it all, there's a feeling that in our land of opportunity, if you do not make it, it's your own fault. Thus, the only
handicapped people one is likely to see or meet in the U.S. are
the ones who have either "passed," or have made it, who are
just like you and me. The others, the ones who are a reminder of
man's failure, are somehow made invisible and kept isolated
from the rest of the world."

It was hard to know how he felt about this. For him it was
something that took place far away, not here, and certainly not
to him. "Here things seem better. The attitudes toward the
handicapped are changing. Why it's even much easier today for
a handicapped man to marry a "normal" woman. And during
the last ten to twenty years, there have been 'normal' men who
would marry handicapped women." Here his wife interrupted
but in Dutch. I sensed that she strongly disagreed that the
situation was getting any better for the handicapped woman. If
it was, she felt it had been only within the past five years.

I recalled that one administrator commenting on the over-balance of women at the Village felt that it reflected the fact that "the disabled man needs the protection of the Village less than the disabled woman, because the man can be more easily cared for with the support of his family." But was this simply a matter of protection? Here, just as in the outside, it was still "a man's world."

The conversation had been informative, but not very comfortable. The Hendriks had answered my questions but volunteered little. I was surprised that they were not better informed about the Village. They lived in the Dorp but were not of it, at least in their own eyes. As we were about to part, Mr. Hendrik suggested that I might like to meet Mr. Veere, someone who "is very different from us." My curiosity was piqued, and I agreed. Within a few minutes, shortly before five, I was off to meet "the notorious rebel, Jacob Veere."

Frankly, it was difficult to picture what a Het Dorp rebel might look like. In fact, more than anywhere else I have ever been, I found myself curious as to people's physical appearance. I wondered if this was due to some unconscious fear that the next person I met might present me with something I had not expected, like a reliving of my India experience. I knocked on Veere's door. There was a call to enter, and as I moved forward, the door swung open. There on the other side of the room was Mr. Veere. It was a case of "like at first sight." He was a stockily built man, early thirties, in a red turtleneck sweater. His large mustache surrounded a full, friendly smile. A glance told me he had little physical mobility. His face by contrast was exceedingly alive. His lips, eyes, even nose seemed to take on the liveliness absent in the rest of his body. Though he did not move, his words reached out, replacing the usual handshake with, "I am Jacob Veere. And you are . . ."

"Irv Zola," I replied, smiling inwardly at my censuring any possible reference to myself as Herr Doctor Professor.

"Come in, Irv, and make yourself comfortable. It's quite a place, isn't it?"

Indeed it was, a tribute to modern technology and what could be done to make life livable. The door which swung open so swiftly was directed by a relay device attached to the arm of his wheelchair. This lever when pressed a specific number of times operated the door, the TV, the telephone, and the radio. He dialed the telephone by clenching a pointer in his teeth. My respect for him deepened as he explained the devices he refused to use, such as an elaborate mechanism for holding a glass. "I don't like it. It's a great nuisance. I have to keep on looking around it to continue talking. It's like a bowl of flowers on a table that comes between people. I don't need anything more to get in my way." He also told of his fight with the doctors over wearing a neck brace. "It interfered with what little movement I have and makes all my clothes look ghastly. They said I could not live without it. But I knew different, and each day I wore it a little less. After several weeks I threw it away. They were amazed, but I knew I could do it."

Jacob, I thought, "Is there anything you could not do? You remind me of myself, or at least that part of myself I'm trying to come to grips with. I want to do as much as I can for myself, resist, even fight for the risks that any activity might entail. Yet I want to be able to give up some things and be comfortable doing so. I don't know if you're succeeding but I can't help but identify with your struggle."

His voice boomed, as with the air of a storyteller he wove tales of his previous life. "Oh what good times! Once in Malaysia . . . in Egypt . . . in Rio . . ." He was apparently working his way around the world when he had an accident which resulted in a broken neck. This left him with only very limited use of his arms, neck, and head, and as far as I could tell, no movement at all elsewhere. He was clearly the most physically disabled resident I had met.

About life in the Village he had much to say. "On the one hand, everything I need is here. It gives me more freedom than any other place. I know, I've been there. I've been in and out of many institutions. There's no comparison. Here I'm much more independent and free. It's even better than my home. I'm too much of a burden for them." Then trailing off, "And for me too." I barely caught the phrase but he was not waiting for me to respond. Despite his praise for the Dorp, he was very distrustful of all the authorities including members of the Village Council. "They're too friendly with the Administration, too willing to keep them informed of all Council and Dorp activities. I think this closeness gets in the way. They are not as strong advocates as they might be. That's part of the reason the Administration does not really understand the problems of the residents. They get yes, yessed all the time and they yes, yes the residents." He told in particular of the great trouble he had in obtaining a meeting place for a youth group of people under thirty-five. "Somehow there was never enough time, or money, or space. It was as if they didn't think we really could do anything worthwhile if we did it ourselves." The sentiment had all too familiar a ring. It was the benign paternalism of the sheltered workshop all over again.

He described his life as a full one, filled with many Dorp committees and a large number of loyal non-Dorp friends. In contrast to the Hendriks he seemed both of the Village and linked to the outside, but it was a link that took considerable effort to maintain. And so recently he had purchased an "Iron-sides"-type vehicle named after the TV program popular for several years both in the Netherlands and the United States, a small van into which a wheelchair could be easily pushed. This eliminated all the problems of lifting and carrying, although someone else had to drive. Showing the same control over me that he exercised over his environment, Veere pointed out that it was almost six and time to eat. We agreed to meet again the next night at 7:30.

My rushing was to no avail, the meal had already started. As I pulled in, Mr. and Mrs. Schmid excused themselves to leave for the Gala. I tried to eat quickly, but I was distracted by two men who were teasing Mieke. They seemed to be taking advantage of her blindness, by touching her and then moving out of her range as she waved them off. One even took her walking stick. I was overwhelmed by the bad taste of it all, but again no one else seemed as upset as I and I wondered why. Was I missing something subtle that was going on? Was she in some way asking for it? Was this another inside joke? Could I get away with teasing Mieke that way? I wondered for a moment if my greatest regret was at being excluded from their playfulness.

The mention of my name brought me back. Monika and Pieter were saying we should start. As we prepared to leave they assured the others that we would make it easily. I wondered if I was as confident. In truth, I felt a little scared. Would I really be able to make all the hills? Or, more embarrassingly, would I slow up people with my pace? It was amazing that this thought came to me here. I was obviously a little slower in mobility no matter where I was. Outside, people had to adjust their pace so that I could keep up with them, and the same would be true here. My own words struck me as "funny," the euphemism that I'm "a little slower." It was still another way of making me appear less different from the rest of the world than I really was.

As we left the dining-room, Monika excused herself to say something to Mieke. Their giggling made me feel left out for the second time in the evening. Mieke waved goodbye to me, "Hope to see you soon." As I returned the wave both Moniks and Pieter laughed.

With Pieter in the lead and Monika keeping pace beside him, we rolled to the farthest exit. The map in my head told me the auditorium was at the bottom of a hill at the far end of the Village. In anticipation I took a deep breath. As we wheeled out our door, others poured out, as if on cue, from their own homes. We formed a parade of walking wounded. Instead of upright precision, our march was an uneven close-to-the-ground movement. People drove themselves, were pushed, or limped along. "Normals" stood out if only by their height. Through it all we were accompanied by a chorus of greetings and what I occasionally interpreted as shouts of encouragement.

Around one building, by another, up a pathway the crowd thickened. Though Monika and Pieter were in sight up ahead, occasionally I feared I'd lose them. Then I heard a familiar voice. Much to my surprise it was Mrs. Hendriks, who wondered if I'd like her to wheel along with me. I welcomed the company. My feelings about her had changed from the moment she had disagreed with her husband's conclusions and mine about the problems of handicapped women.

We didn't speak much but it didn't matter. As we rolled along two memories came to me. The first concerned my grandfather. My family lived with him in a house at the top of a hill in Boston. Occasionally he and I would meet going home, he returning from work and me from school. Sixtyish, with asthma and other chronic ailments, he took the hill very slowly. I would fall in beside him, exchanging few words, for he spoke no English. Maybe my presence made him feel as good as Mrs. Hendriks' made me. The second association was to a younger generation, to my son. For tonight I had taken over the slow-moving characteristics of my old Daf—a car—about which he and I had a running joke. As one vehicle after another would pass us, he would ask if *every* car and cycle was faster than a Daf. So, tonight, everyone seemed to be going faster than me.

At last the hall loomed ahead. Actually the trip had not been so bad—mostly downhill. The way back would be worse, but I postponed worrying about that. The hall itself was originally intended as a sports gymnasium and that made me flashback to men in wheelchairs playing basketball and others who were paralyzed below the waist playing water polo. But I had never heard of anything like that in the Netherlands.

Tonight, however, we were clearly in a theater. The theme was Paris–Café Chantant. The draperies were decorated with French scenes: a statue of Napoleon, a café, a night scene, the Eiffel Tower. Balloons were strung along the walls. Paper streamers descended from the ceiling. Center front was the stage, center left had a small performing area and a bar. To the far left was a space for the orchestra and to the far right was a raised platform for the chorus. The vast expanse of the hall was filled with wheelchairs, moveable beds, and occasional folding chairs. At the back of the hall, clearly distinct from the residents, were about a dozen raised rows of seats for guests and other "normals."

We followed Monika's lead and found a place in the middle of the hall where the sight lines seemed good. As we were maneuvering for position I realized that something was going on. With winks and glances to Pieter, Monika kept telling me to leave "ample space." I thought her instructions were kind of silly until I saw Mieke in a wheelchair being pushed towards us. I was doubly surprised, first at her presence and then because of the wheelchair. Maybe the long distance and hills were too difficult for her to negotiate. Instead of pity I felt a little envy. Hills were no easy task for me when I walked with a cane, and occasionally I'd wished there were some other way for me to climb them.

We arranged ourselves all in a row—Pieter, Monika, Mieke, and me. I couldn't suppress a grin from ear to ear. It was Saturday night and I had a date for the ball with an attractive woman! My one concern was quickly dealt with when Mieke began asking me questions in quite passable English. Together we evolved a pattern. She asked me to describe in detail the scenes around us, and in turn she agreed to translate the performances from Dutch into English. It became a game. She was my ears and I was her eyes.

The show consisted of skits and music. It seemed disorganized, and the sound system did not function well. When the entertainment was good, I was not distracted by the performers' handicaps, but when it was not, I felt uncomfortable. At least two people sang very poorly, one with real breathing difficulty. Was I supposed to marvel at their guts for trying or merely feel sad? I felt some of both.

After a while we were paying as much attention to the audience as to the performers. Monika started it by referring to the dogelas, who mostly mingled in the crowd, as "sex bombs." When I looked at them closely I saw what she meant. Ostensibly to complement the evening, they were dressed in "cutesy" outfits befitting a French waitress or maid: black sweaters, tights, shoes, mini-skirts, tiny aprons, and white caps. Sexuality was also evident in some of the humor, but to me the most provocative performance was that of a non-resident Indonesian woman in a long silk dress, who sang perhaps a dozen love songs all in English, songs like, "Close to You" and "I Don't Know How to Love Him." Was I the only one who felt this emphasis on sex and love odd, if not paradoxical, in this setting? Or were my prejudices showing? There was a gnawing feeling that all this was too stimulating. But I wasn't sure whom I was trying to protect.

My attention was drawn back to our group as Monika started to sing. We four joined hands and kept time to the music. Curiously it was only our upper torsos which moved. It was the only way I ever danced even on the outside, and then only when I was very comfortable, but here it seemed natural and we swayed without embarrassment. We were joined by others and the circle expanded, but Mieke and I stayed close together. With Monika I just clasped hands, but with Mieke our fingers intertwined and when they did, I pressed them gently. The first time I initiated it but the second time she seemed to reach for my hand. Tonight was clearly going to be a time for sexual fantasies! I really could not tell if all this—the hand holding, the being together—meant anything to Mieke, but it did to others. There was much giggling when one of Mieke's friends came by, and I heard my name in their conversation. When she left, I asked Mieke what all the laughter was about. In rather matter-of-fact tones she mentioned that the girl friend kidded her about going back to America with me.

From time to time we were visited by others—Mieke by a few friends, Monika by literally dozens, and myself by people I had met during my various travels. About 9:30 P.M. I saw Marlene approaching. I was happy and uncomfortable at the same time. Ever since Metz had introduced her I had wanted to meet her again. Now when I did, she found me with "someone else." I was caught in an embarrassment of riches. Since she was with friends we didn't have much of a chance to talk. But when she mentioned offhandedly that she'd like to get together, I seized the invitation and made a tentative date for late Monday night.

About an hour later, Mr. Geyer, my guide in the Adaptation Room, came by. He wanted me to meet his fiancée, the young woman whose "normalcy" he had noted when we first met. She was not only "normal" but quite attractive, sweet and pert with short blond hair. He yawned and joked in English, "*All* I am going to do is go home, shower, and sleep." She leaned forward and coquettishly whispered something in Dutch, kissing him lightly. He responded kiddingly, "Nay! Nay! I must sleep." As for the evening, he was upset about the lack of coordination, planning, and rehearsal time. But most of all he felt that it was ending much too early. It was only 11:00 P.M., and he had hoped that people would stay till 1:00 A.M. It was only then that I noticed that people had been leaving in a steady trickle.

Some administrative staff and the dogelas had stayed behind for a brief celebration of the birthday of one and the engagement of another. All joined hands and sang. I recalled seeing them that way earlier in the evening and how odd it seemed, a chain of singing dogelas weaving their way through the immobile audience.

As they sang they surrounded Frank, one of the resident organizers of the Gala. Some sat on his lap, stood on the footrest of his wheelchair, and then several raced with him around the hall. It made me recall my own "playing" with nurses when I was hospitalized and in a wheelchair. I wondered if they realized how stimulating it was for Frank to have so much youth and beauty dancing around him. I had always wanted to go back to my hospital to see if the student nurses were all as beautiful and sexy as I remembered them. But he seemed to be enjoying himself. Would a depression set in later, a near-and-yet-so-far sort of feeling?

It was about 11:30 P.M. and the major departure had begun. As I glided out of the auditorium I again wished for a camera. Many of the wheelchairs were equipped with lights. With beams shining in the dark, they reminded me of the Swiss ski-night torch parade.

The four of us agreed to meet at Mieke's for a party and she and I left together. The fiancé of one of the dogelas took turns pushing each of us. With the trek all uphill the assistance was most welcome. When I pushed myself, it inspired the teasing of my companions. Pieter and Monika said that if I did not reach Mieke's by midnight, they would send out a search party. I fell further and further behind so Monika and Mieke devised a signal. Every few minutes they yelled out, "Ooop, oooop," and I answered with an "Oy!" indicating I was still with them. Along the way we sang and a response echoed from somewhere in the dark. Occasionally people came to their windows and we waved to each other.

As we wended our way home, my thoughts returned to the Gala and all the different clusterings of people. Not only were there obviously tight little circles, but some people were clearly "favorites" of the dogelas and other staff, who made a point of sitting and chatting with them. There were also many isolates, speaking to no one, just looking and waiting. Compared to these people, we four seemed to be like the lonely smile amid a sea of tears in the Charles Addams cartoon.

On the final hill and with the moon lighting my path, I glided alone the final few hundred yards to Mieke's.

My arrival was greeted with joking about my being lost but I was more distracted by the surroundings. Mieke's home was by far the most attractive I'd been in. My own stereotypes were partly to blame. I couldn't imagine her being able to decorate her place so colorfully.

Pointing to the right wall, she explained some future plans. "These are my latest purchases. With all these cabinets so bright and white, I'm going to get some new chairs and a couch–bed to make everything more compatible. When I'm able to afford it, I'll have to get rid of that." She pointed to the refrigerator behind me.) "Don't you think I can get one to match the room better?"

She was right and I was surprised at my surprise.

I could not help but be the observer again, watching her manage as I had watched Jacob Veere. I particularly admired the limits she both set and acknowledged. While she served the food and changed the records, she showed no embarrassment in asking Monika to pour the drinks.

As we settled in with food and wine, the record ended and Mieke asked me to choose a replacement. Again a pleasant surprise: there was one of my favorites, called the "Indian Flute." Holding the record in my hands, I admitted that it inspired me to try once again to learn a musical instrument.

Mieke joked about teaching me and about her own playing. "Last year I was in the Gala playing my ukulele. I would have done it again this year but they weren't interested in my doing spirituals again, so I didn't. But I didn't mind, it was just as much fun watching this year."

"It must have been the company," I teased.

She nodded. "You know next year if things work out, I want to learn to play the flute. It's such a beautiful, delicate instrument."

Her interest not only brought us closer together but reinforced my own musical desire. To be able to play, if only for oneself, always struck me as an immense pleasure. I wondered if that was it, the sense of independence, of doing it to and for myself, which was so appealing.

By chance my hand rested on a record by Santana. On the cover was a surrealistic picture of two naked women, one black, one red. Monika laughed. "Many men," pointing at Pieter, "like the picture better than the music." As with many such off-color remarks, the conversation quickly switched into Dutch. When I asked them to translate, Monika refused, saying, "There are some things that it is just as well you don't understand."

Our drinking continued apace, and four of us finished off about two bottles. I had the distinct impression, however, that Pieter and I did the major portion of the drinking. Mieke and Monika voiced mock concern about my ability to hold my liquor. Pieter assured them that I could, and asked what tricks I could do in my wheelchair to prove it. As Monika called him tipsy, she promptly lost her balance and plopped into a chair. The whole scene was escalating in silliness. When Pieter tipped his wheelchair to balance himself on edge, I laughingly refused his challenge to follow suit.

All in all, it seemed a long time between drunken episodes in a wheelchair—twenty years to be exact. But the memory was so vivid that with their urging I decided to try to describe it.

"When I was sixteen and hospitalized for polio, a favorite orderly was leaving. A party seemed the natural send-off. By now all of us patients were 'on the way out.' None of us was sick, only convalescing. Almost all, male and female alike, had polio, though unlike here we lived in very separate quarters. The night of the party, John, who was a fellow patient, and I were assigned to make the punch. I managed to get two bottles of vodka smuggled in, and with it, we spiked the drink. Ordinarily, this would still have been fairly tepid, but perhaps because of our 'weakened conditions' we were extra-sensitive. Naturally, John and I needed to continually sample our work. Nothing seemed to happen for a while and then it hit us. We went sort of wild and, as in many cartoons, began to chase the nurses up and down the corridors. Luckily there was no one sick around. Back and forth, like a character in a slapstick comedy, I careened off the walls, smashing my wheelchair off the vacant iron lungs, miraculously not falling out. Finally, John and I were cornered. My favorite nurse, Olive, told me to get into bed like a good boy. I refused. She then put her arms around me to lift. I laughingly said, 'Please don't, I haven't been with a woman for nearly a year.' I guess I looked too helpless, for she neglected my warning, and as she reached down, I reached up. Her hands were touching my waist but mine went firmly but gently to her breasts. The next thing I remembered was a knocking on my head. It was morning and I was strapped to my bed. There at the foot with a crutch in her hand stood Olive, tapping me with its tip. 'Little boys should learn to keep their hands to themselves.' At that point, I think I was more embarrassed than she."

After this story, the door was open to being even more autobiographical, though the direction was unexpected. Pieter asked how one became a professor in the United States. I didn't really understand what he wanted to know and told him so. He seemed primarily interested in what "achievements" were necessary, so I explained about teaching and publishing and how old I was when I got my degrees, jobs, and promotions. There were several simultaneous interruptions. Pieter asked about my children and family. Mieke was surprised that I was married, more surprised that I was getting a divorce, and astonished that I had been married fourteen years. Pieter commented that "to have gotten so high a position you must have no hobbies. You must do nothing but work." In response to my divorce, Monika blurted out "Why?" then laughed and covered her mouth. Mieke simply shook her head, "Impossible!"

We all picked up Mieke's comment and began to discuss why I didn't fit their image of a professor. By being only in my thirties, by dressing so informally, by just living in the Dorp, and most important, all the joking and drinking this evening seemed to belie the distance they expected to exist between us. Good-naturedly, but with a touch of sarcasm, Pieter said, "I guess we're not used to people like you as professors. Professors must have a lower status in the United States." Maybe I should have defended the status of American professors, but I was into the sheer comfort in being here and only laughed. Picking up on this, they kidded me about how I would have fit into the Netherlands because of my resemblance to the radical youths in a hippie-type Dutch political movement several years back. I took it as a compliment.

With wine finished, noises were made about leaving. Partly to be cute, partly because I was having a good time, partly because I wanted to see what would happen, and partly because of some sexual fantasies, I made no effort to move. The small talk continued until Pieter said the evening was too long for older folks like him and left. Monika said she would follow immediately but she did not. The conversation from here on took place in a mélange of drunken Dutch and English. First Monika chided me, "Do not stay too late and keep Mieke up."

"Don't worry, I will tell him when to go home, so I can get to bed."

Monika chimed in, "Well, maybe you should make it

soon," and turning to me, "Will you be coming to church with us tomorrow?"

Surprised, I replied in kind, "No, you must be kidding."

Monika, feigning hurt, said, "Well, then you must be with us for morning coffee."

"OK."

"Be sure."

"I promise. Yes, yes."

"Do you know what will happen if you do not show up?"

"What?" I asked innocently.

Her detailed reply was lost on me. With nods of support from Mieke, Monika vowed that both of them would come to my room, open the window, and throw me out, bedclothes and all, followed by a flower pot. Somehow it seemed that I might be undressed, and thus "like Adam you will have to use the leaves of the flowers for a cover."

Recovering briefly, I asked, "If I am Adam, where is my Eve?"

"Eve is upstairs in my room," Monika quipped, "but will not come out in the cold."

There were several exchanges in Dutch between Mieke and Monika, complete with raised eyebrows and winks, that I was surely not supposed to understand. What got through was Monika's concern. Rather impishly, I asked, "Are you more worried about me or Mieke?"

"Why, you, of course. I'm really worried if in your condition you can make it home."

"To make you feel better, I will ring Pieter's doorbell when I leave—two rings for OK and one for needing help."

In feigned indignation, Monika pouted, "What makes you think I sleep with Pieter?"

Frankly, I had never assumed otherwise. She went on to claim that she had a room elsewhere. But somehow I didn't believe her. There was too much kidding in her tone and besides she kept making me promise to ring the bell when I did leave. Since she refused, however, to tell me where her other room was, I maintained adamantly that she stayed at Pieter's.

We were interrupted by a knock at the door. Pieter was back, wondering what had kept Monika.

"Well, I have to make sure everything is all right here."

Pieter nodded his head, I thought in a kind of disbelief, and in a few minutes, after further assurances about the morning coffee, they left.

Now that Mieke and I were alone, there was a certain awkwardness. We talked again about music and how she soon must redecorate the apartment. But the conversation was clearly winding down. With a yawn, she said it was time for sleep and I quickly agreed to leave. In another time and circumstance I might have quipped something about being too tired to go home, but she had given me no indication that she wanted me to stay. I wondered if I should expect the same cues as in other settings. Or was I as a male supposed to be even more active. I laughed at myself. "Just like a man," I thought, I was looking for some reason to explain the lack of encouragement. Sort of like when a woman said no, did she really mean it? But Mieke hadn't even said maybe.

But as we approached the door, she reached down and touched my hand, holding it when I stopped. She told me what a nice evening it had been and how much she enjoyed my company. I kissed her hand though I wanted to kiss much more. I was really flustered. I didn't know what else to do. I didn't know how to reach up to touch someone when they were standing so high above me. I figured that if I did what felt natural to me, like trying to caress her cheek, I would probably topple out of my wheelchair. Suddenly, I realized how much more purposeful and less "accidental" was all the sexual foreplay for people with any of a large number of physical impediments. Gone was the possibility of a "subtle" brushing against one another. So too, at least with Mieke, was the possibility of "catching her eye." I was reminded of an old TV ad about Volvos in which two people strapped in bucket seats try to kiss one another casually. If it was difficult for them how much more so for someone like me in a wheelchair. Even outside a wheelchair it was not *so* different for *me,* though until now I had done my best to deny it. If someone tried to kiss or even touch me unexpectedly, they were as likely to knock me over.

I can't even casually lean over without throwing myself off balance. To hug someone while standing I have to plant my feet solidly or support myself against a wall. Thinking about all this made me shudder. It was the thinking part that bothered me. It took a lot of the supposed spontaneity out of my sex play. But maybe I was being unfair to myself. After all, how much sex play really is *that* spontaneous? But if it was this hard for me, what must it be like for someone with even less physical agility? A whole physical context was missing! How does one learn to give and interpret signals? I was overcome by the sense that here at the Village one may have to risk so much for so little.

We travelled the few steps to the door, and with nothing else to say, said goodbye till tomorrow. It was after 2:30 A.M. Whistling, I wheeled my way home.

My body was tingling. So much of the day seemed to have been suffused with sexuality. I was puzzled. I'd been here so short a time, yet felt more sexually deprived than during nearly a year of living alone in the Netherlands. It was not just this evening. I'd been feeling a sense of sexuality in the air since I arrived. Just much more sex-tinged joking and touching than I'd been used to, and all of it in a place where I'd least expected it. In fact I felt not only deprived, but also more stimulated than in months. Sleepily in bed, I hugged my pillow extra close. It was Mieke, Monika, Marlene, Mara. . . .

Sunday, May 28

I slept right through breakfast. I probably
would have continued through lunch except for the memory of Monika's threat.
Pushing to an upright position, I consoled myself with all the
good sleep I'd get when back in Leiden.

When I wheeled in for the morning coffee, several people
were already there—the Schmids, Ms. Nijhof, and Mrs. van
Amerongen. Together they voiced surprise, "You've made it!
After so little sleep and so much playing . . ." At times like this I
thought there must be a daily newscast of my activities.

The Gala was the chief topic of conversation and there was
general disappointment.

As Mrs. van Amerongen put it, "It wasn't as good as
previous years. There was something missing. Don't you
agree?"

I was flattered at my inclusion in their collective past, but
with little to compare it with I could only shrug my shoulders.

Ms. Nijhof mentioned the mechanical difficulties and some
of the uneven performances. I was glad that she had expressed
that. It relieved my guilt at making the same observation.

But as Mr. Schmid noted, "It's more than that."

Mrs. Schmid added almost in a whisper, "And it ended so
early . . ."

Mrs. van Amerongen summed it up euphemistically.
"There was an unequal participation. Some helped too much."

Everyone nodded in agreement at the unspoken reference
to the administrative staff. To me it was a complaint I'd heard

too many times before, something that happened to the captive audiences at universities, hospitals, prisons, or military bases. What started out as a "people project" was gradually co-opted by the superstructure.

In describing the arrangements for the Gala, my friends could not point to any specific incidents. They needed permission for certain arrangements and gradually from this flowed certain decisions and then more, until finally it was no longer "their show." As in the examples I knew of, it was a two-way street. The Administration not only wanted to help, but also "knew better" about certain things. The patients, students, or Villagers were used to being helped, and used to thinking that those above knew better. And so it went. It didn't matter that a careful analysis might show only limited staff participation. It was the psychological reality that counted.

Monika arrived and proceeded to regale the others with my "late, late-night behavior." Only the details were necessary, for everyone already seemed to know the outlines. Turning to me, she waved her finger, "And after all my concern, you didn't even knock like you promised. I was so worried that I could not sleep."

With a pained innocence, I defended myself, "Why I would have, but I did not know on which door to knock."

Everyone, including Monika, laughed.

At the same time, a somewhat serious thought flashed through my mind. My mother always claimed she could not sleep till I returned from a date. The next morning she would tell me so, and ask without expecting to be answered. "And just what could you be doing till 3:00 A.M.?" The joke masked her real concern. Ever since I had contracted polio, she had worried that some other mishap would befall me. Like Monika, she did worry if I could "make it home in my condition." Her greatest fear was a late-night accident, a fear which was realized four years later. Eventually, her fear became so unbearable for me that I no longer came home after dates. Instead, I usually returned to my college dormitory or apartment, borrowing the family car on Friday night and returning it on Sunday.

Just as Monika was finishing her tale, Mr. Altman arrived. I'd not met him before and he was introduced by Mr. Schmid as their "sick inhabitant." The words pierced me, but everyone else laughed. Seeing my discomfort, Mr. Schmid quickly explained a fact which I had momentarily forgotten, that Mr. Altman had had a cold for several days. His explanation only partly eased my discomfort.

As if the introduction were superfluous for him, Mr. Altman spoke about his father's impression of me. "When he came by yesterday and heard you talk, he told me he could not understand the funny way you spoke. I told him, 'Of course you could not, that was the American Professor!' " Laughing at his father not understanding me, he apologized for his own stumbling English, "I need much more practice." With a grin, he added, "Will you come to my room after coffee and help me learn better?"

With my late-morning appointment, we postponed our meeting till after lunch. I felt very good about this. We barely knew each other but were already on comfortable terms.

The coffee seemed to be lasting longer than usual, perhaps because it was Sunday. It was already 10:30, and so to make my eleven o'clock meeting, I excused myself.

Before leaving, I checked in with the dogela, telling her that I might not be back for lunch. Metz, who had arranged this meeting with the Jansens, hinted that they might ask me to stay. Telling the dogela was more than a mere courtesy. I had heard Mieke do the same thing when she was to miss a meal. It seemed to be an unwritten policy, so I abided by it. The dogela responded in a way that told me I'd done the right thing.

The trip to the Jansens' was a long one but today I felt more invigorated than tired. I was still not the experienced traveller, however, and managed to make two wrong turns. As I approached their door, I saw a couple coming from the opposite direction, a tall man pushing a woman in a wheelchair. "Mr. and Mrs. Jansen?" I asked. They smiled in acknowledgment and invited me in.

I immediately recognized Mrs. Jansen as someone I had seen during my previous visit in January. She was flattered that I remembered her, then was even more surprised when I described what she wore last night at the Gala. The substance of their remarks in Dutch seemed to be that "he notices everything."

To my innocuous opening that "Last night was certainly quite an extravaganza," they both indicated their general displeasure. Mr. Jansen began, "It's the same thing every year, the same people do the same things. The people of the Dorp seem to be doing less and less. They just sit and nod passively. Bah. So after my wife's friend did her piece, we left. Did you really like it?"

As I somewhat defensively said yes, I realized it was really the company—Pieter, Monika, and Mieke—that made it so memorable.

Interestingly, they complimented the master of ceremonies "for his excellent handling of everything. Do you know who he was?"

"Yes, I met him later. He's apparently been here awhile."

"You mean as a resident?" asked Mrs. Jansen incredulously. "I couldn't tell."

I suddenly recalled Goffman's writings about "impression management." Apparently, since the emcee sat behind a draped table and so dominated the proceedings, he was assumed to be like all the other dominant figures at the Village, one of the staff and not physically handicapped.

Since the Jansens seemed very open, I asked how they experienced the Village. Nodding to each other, they agreed they were quite happy and pleased with most things. Karen, Mrs. Jansen, took the lead and reminisced about the founding of the Village and what it was like in the beginning. It was a story I knew well, so only half-listening, I found myself more absorbed with them as people, and the ways they responded to one another. She, probably in her early forties, a very attractive dark-haired woman, delicately made-up and stylishly dressed, was one of the original residents. She had a rare degenerative disease which had led to certain rapid changes during her stay. Apparently in the early days she had been able to walk around the Dorp, and served occasionally as a guide. As her mobility decreased, she was asked to work in the library. Now confined to a wheelchair, she could occasionally stand while leaning on something. She had limited use of her hands, using one to raise the other, and though she could drink and smoke by herself, she lacked manual dexterity. When she dropped a large cookie crumb onto her skirt, her husband deftly rose, picked it up, and placed it within range of her hands. I could not tell how much help she would need in eating. She probably needed the food to be cut, perhaps placed in a special container or plate. He, on the other hand, was referred to as a "normal" by the other residents.

There was something so natural and loving about their interaction that I asked how they met. Maybe I was responding to some non-verbal cue, for with a delighted smile she turned to her husband and said in Dutch, "See, I told you so. I knew he'd ask that."

In some sense prepared for the question, Mr. Jansen took over. "For most of my life I worked in Gouda, about twenty-five years except for a two-year stay in Australia. (That's when I learned English.) I had a very old friend from Gouda who also suffered from a handicap. All his life he lived with his parents, but when his mother died, it became very difficult for his father to manage. So he moved into the Village. About the same time I was transferred to Arnhem, so it was natural that I kept coming here. I guess I saw him about once a week." Looking fondly at Mrs. Jansen, he added, "And one of those times I met Karen." If my arithmetic was correct, it was a very brief courtship. Mr. Jansen continued. "We decided to get married when we could find a place in the Dorp. I was living in a room in Arnhem and that would be no good. So when this place became available, we had to get married right away to get it. So we did in December."

"Was this one of the newly made married quarters that became available?"

"No, they were already filled. We were just lucky. This apartment was occupied by a couple, but the husband died, so she had to move out."

His tone was matter-of-fact but Karen was visibly shaken by the memory. "I don't like it," she said with a shudder, "I don't like living here, where someone else has died."

Her discomfort resonated with me. The fact of a widow having to leave her home because of her husband's death was very disturbing. If the shortage of space was a reality to be faced, it was a damn depressing one, but a possibility that married couples here must deal with.

Looking at Mr. Jansen, I saw how the Village had really made this "late marriage" work. The Village allowed him to maintain his bachelor independence and work life with a minimal obeisance to his wife's physical handicap. I don't mean that he did not love or want to care for her, but rather that because of what Het Dorp offered in terms of help, Karen fit neatly around his life rather than vice versa. He described with pleasure how the Dorp helped out. "I often have to leave early in the morning to be at work by 7:30 or 8:00. When I get up I do not have to worry about her because when she wants to get up at 9:00 she just rings and then they come in and help her. Then she does what she wants, has lunch here, and then to work. I get home at 4:00 and then I can help her." She did not cook and, other than putting out coffee and cookies or perhaps reheating a dish, they made no meals themselves. On the weekends when they were both home, he simply brought the food back from the central kitchen, and they ate alone. Only when her husband was absent did she take lunch with the other residents and then with obvious reluctance.

This use of the Village to make the rest of their life possible was consistent with the way they organized their social activities. They seemed often on the go—to movies, events, and shops and when possible, on his business trips. A typical evening consisted of making the rounds of friends and relatives, returning to their place only to sleep. I wondered if this meant they took no long trips. Had they so segmented their reliance on the

Village that ironically they had become overdependent on it in certain respects? On the other hand, this distancing of the Village, particularly on her part, must be ambivalent. Could it be accidental that of all the jobs open, she got involved in those which required her to present the Village to the outside? First she was a guide and now a librarian, both fairly "up front" positions. But then, maybe this was a way of keeping links to the outside world, a world she knew and missed. Once during a lull, she reminisced about her life before coming to the Village, prefacing the memory with the words, "when I was valid."

Unwittingly, my attention was focussed on her husband Jens, lighting her cigarette. I must have been staring, for she asked, "What are you thinking? You seem to notice everything."

Caught off guard, I needed a moment to collect my thoughts. My answer was compact, "Just all the things I take for granted and the Adaptation Unit's work at creating gadgets to make life easier." I was glad that she latched on to the last half of my comment. My mind was a tangle of contradictions. I identified with both of them. I was uncomfortable with Karen's enforced dependence and with Jens' reponsiveness. I was neither good at receiving unasked-for help nor waiting on someone when they requested it. Both seemed an imposition. My lack of graciousness at being a patient was rivalled by my impatience with the minor sicknesses of others.

As she and I marvelled together at the ingenious creations of the Adaptation Unit, her husband excused himself to get lunch. When he returned, I saw that he'd brought only two plates, and that ended my speculation about staying. At 12:25 I excused myself as we all joked about the rigidity of eating schedules.

The Jansens reminded me a bit of the Hendriks, with their eyes turned towards the outside. A more satisfying image was of suburbanites. The Dorp was their bedroom community where they ate and slept. Work and play were beyond its walls.

In almost record time, I made it to lunch. On Sunday, lunch was the main hot meal of the day—veal, potatoes, string beans, plenty of fresh bread and butter, milk, and for dessert a double treat, fresh strawberries with whipped cream and vanilla flan. While I devoured the meal, the chiding of me continued. Monika commented to the others about my need to recoup the calories lost from "all his last-night adventures." With Mieke present, she teased her, "Why didn't you have him knock at the door? Do you know how worried I was?" Everyone joined in with some variation on "those American Professors."

Over dessert, the Schmids asked if in my many travels I'd visited Scotland. As it was one of my favorite stopovers I warmed to the topic. Back and forth we compared what the guidebook recommended with the real thing. Only at the very end of our conversation did I realize that neither of us had given any consideration to the accessibility of certain sites. With me it was sheer doggedness, or, as I've come to realize, a touch of masochism, but I wasn't sure what the omission meant to them. Were they just being gracious in response to my unfounded enthusiasms "You must see . . . , and be sure to visit . . . .") or did they figure that the specialized travel agency responsible for the trip would work out the awkward details?

To me, any inaccessibility was always a source of frustration and anger. To them it had an added aspect—whatever the inconvenience, it was an adventure, a chance to be outside, away.

As I was about to leave the table, Mieke caught my eye. She seemed hesitant, almost perplexed. "Are you thinking about a future meal?" was my way of breaking the ice.

She looked at me quizzically, and then remembering my passion for Indonesian food, said "Hmm, well it's been about a month, maybe we will have Nasing Goreng on your last night."

Sometimes I was such a clod. I didn't know why I brought up such an inappropriate subject as food. It was clearly not what she had in mind. I realized it was the most innocent thing I could think of. I stammered, "Look, I have to excuse myself for a minute and answer the phone messages that Pieter gave me."

As I wheeled away I realized that she was still behind me. Almost in hushed tones she asked, "Do you have any special plans for this afternoon?"

I wanted to say no but I'd already postponed meeting with

Altman. I was upset both with her for not asking me earlier and myself for already having plans. I looked around for Mr. Altman but he was gone so I asked, "Can I take a raincheck?"

Her not understanding my Americanism made everything more awkward. Finding a time to see her seemed more charged than a mere appointment. We tried several different arrangements to no avail, finally settling on tomorrow night after dinner. With time so short here, even that seemed far away.

As she disappeared down the corridor, it hit me. Tomorrow night was the open Council meeting! I hoped she'd come with me but something told me she wouldn't. I felt lousy, as if I was about to "break a date."

But my schedule didn't allow me time to worry too long about anything. It was 1:45, and time to visit Jos Altman. My knock elicited an immediate response. A tall, blonde young man casually dressed, ushered me in. In the corner, a blonde woman rose to greet me. These were the friends, Bart and Riet, whom Altman had spoken about, the ones with whom he exchanged visits on a regular basis.

After the usual introductions, Jos asked me about the political climate in America. The conversation moved easily from the presidential races to racial tensions. But as usual, we soon turned to national policies about health insurance, and in particular to what the United States did for those with physical handicaps and chronic diseases. He was surprised, as were his two friends, that in a nation as rich as the United States there was no place even resembling the Village. We reflected briefly on how America had such an emphasis on everyone being independent. *De facto* dependence and segregation were of course widespread in the United States, and yet a place like the Village, with its visibly dependent population and *de jure* segregation, was anathema.

To a large extent, this was a repeat of the conversation with the Hendriks in which I speculated about America's "man-over-nature" perspective. Here, however, the conversation was not so one-sided. Together we wondered why it was so much harder to be handicapped in the United States than here. I think they sensed correctly that to be handicapped, if not sick, was regarded there, as both a personal and a social failure. This reminded me of an incident I had once witnessed at a United States hospital, and I shared it: "A patient was dying and the physician could do nothing to reverse it. He was furious, 'God-damn it,' he said to no one in particular, 'it's un-American.' " As we talked, the image became even bleaker, and I added, "You know, it's not merely that people with handicaps have to do their best, they have to do better."

Bart chimed in, "The movies we've seen, particularly the American ones, all seem to say this."

We reeled off examples, beginning with the roles of Harold Russell in *Best years of Our Lives* and Marlon Brando in *The Men.* Both were portrayals calculated to arouse more than sympathy. Russell, with only mechanical devices for hands, and Brando, paralyzed from the waist down, were both war veterans. As such they had become handicapped "in our defense," and thus we owed them something. The onus of their difficulty was at least partly lifted from their shoulders. At the very least we had more tolerance for them. Both of them, naturally, overcame their problem to live full lives.

For a few minutes we could recall only two others, both sense deprivations and both women—the woman accidentally blinded whose story is told in *The Magnificent Obsession,* and *Johnny Belinda,* who could neither hear nor speak. They, too, were ultimately able to live full lives, their rehabilitation coming mostly through the care of male physicians, who also loved them. Riet barely suppressed her anger, "My God, I never thought about it before. I was so wrapped up in the romanticism and the success, I didn't think about what it all implies. How unreal—what resources someone with a handicap needs to make it! It's even sexist—the love of her doctor!"

After a while, I came up with two other films, *The Miracle Worker* and *The Monty Stratton Story.* The first was about Helen Keller, and the second about a man who went on to pitch major league baseball after the loss of a leg.

Jos added another, *With a Song in Her Heart,* the biography of a famous singer who wore a brace. Interestingly, her "disfigurement" was not visible, for her long dresses hid it.

His observation spurred me on, "Now I see the full meaning in the images some of our advertising slogans build upon. Did you ever hear the one, 'Hire the handicapped—he is better!? It refers, of course, to his low absentee rate and higher productivity." I did not mean my question as rhetorical but I was too involved in what I was saying to wait for an answer. "As a total or even representative picture of those with severe handicaps or diseases, the images are so patently absurd that they cannot help but be a disservice to the rest of us."

Bart summed it up, "Now I really know what you mean about the burden of the handicapped. Since all these people made it, it means that every person with a chronic disease or handicap could do the same, and if they didn't, it must certainly be their own fault. They must not have tried hard enough."

Almost to himself, Jos said, "It's not true. I try and try and try . . ."

I barely heard their remarks, for I was caught up in my own inner conversation. My last words were still ringing in my ear— "the rest of us." Had I ever before identified myself so strongly as someone with a handicap or chronic disease? If anything, I had been at the opposite pole. Whenever I spoke about the views and attitudes of "other" Americans towards the handicapped, I was uncomfortably echoing, it not some of my own beliefs, at least some of my own operating behaviors. I too was one who had made it and to some extent passed. When I was sitting behind a desk in my office or standing behind a lectern in an auditorium, no one need notice that I wore a brace and used a cane. All too often I walked around my office and home without my walking stick. And one habit which I had previously attributed to stereotyped absentmindedness of professors, was my tendency to continually misplace it! It was also clear that one of the nicest compliments which people thought they could pay me and which I all too gratefully accepted was that "I never noticed that you had . . ."

But there is a deeper insight than this shock of personal recognition. It only came upon me as I wrote up these notes. Several times during my stay at Het Dorp, I had been asked about my social life. In particular my companions had wanted to know about my handicapped friends and relatives. Consistently I had not only denied that there were any among my circle of friends and relatives, but even among my outer circle of acquaintances. I had to struggle to recall meeting any handicapped or chronically diseased people in *any* social, as opposed to professional or research, situation. My internalization of the American social perception had been virtually complete. Only now did it sink in, that the most significant male figure in my early life, a man who was virtually omnipresent till I was in my late twenties, had a physical handicap. He was my maternal grandfather and he had no hearing for all the years I knew him. He had deafened himself while a young man in Poland to avoid induction into the army, a conscription which, as a Jew, he feared would cause permanent separation from his family. He was no shadow figure to me. Until the age of eight I saw him once or twice a week. When I was between the ages of eight and thirteen, we lived across the street from his home, and I saw him daily. From then until I turned twenty-one, I lived with him and my family in the same apartment in his house. Though he spoke no English and could only lip-read Yiddish and Polish, we talked, and later argued, nearly all the time. He was my only living grandfather, and I was the first and favorite grandchild. He rose from the ghettos of Boston and held at one time three jobs. Always a tailor and never having his own shop, he somehow managed to accumulate property, own a home in the suburbs, supplement his children's income whenever they needed it, send money to relatives in Europe, help others escape the concentration camps, and set still others up in business. In short, he was quite an impressive figure and the one whose approval I sought above all others? Yet until now I had never associated the word handicap with his presence. And it was only now that I realized that, without a word on the subject ever passing between us, he had become the most influential model in my own adaptation.

Meanwhile Jos was talking about how he had come to the Village. Apparently he had been "sick" since childhood and between the ages of sixteen and twenty-three had spent most of his time at the Johanna Stichting Rehabilitation Institute. "After they could do no more for me, I spent two years in a nursing home. It was horrible, very depressing. It's a place where people wait to die. So once on a home visit I said I would not return . . . and I did not. But I could not forever live with my parents. They were getting very old and found it hard to help me. So I wrote to Dr. Klapwijk, who knew me when I was a patient at the Johanna Stichting. He was great. Only about ten days after writing I was scheduled for a physical examination and evaluation. I was said to be eligible and placed on a waiting list. It was a long wait, but when an opening occurred two years later I moved in."

With little prodding he went on, "It's not as easy as it looks living here in the Village. You've got to make a life of your own here, a life in the Village." Stopping for a moment as if to ponder an unasked question, he continued, "It's the only realistic thing. This is where I live. This is where I work. And I like it. I enjoy the work."

"Really?" I asked disbelievingly.

"Yes, I like the social contacts and the freedom the work gives me."

"What freedom?"

"The work isn't all that demanding. It's repetitive, it allows my mind to wander, to think about other things."

I felt a bit chastized. Maybe all work didn't have to be so meaningful. After all, I had done assembly-line work throughout college. The job had been so automatic that I really did enjoy letting my mind wander to other things. Maybe I was being too patronizing in not allowing the residents the same possibility.

On the other hand, he did regret that those who ran the workshops were necessarily concerned more with productivity than with people. It did not matter that the people at this sheltered workshop were treated much more humanely than at most similar settings. "As long as productivity is of some importance, decisions, I guess, will be made which are not always in the best interests of the residents."

The idea of "necessity as a factor in life" led us quickly to our own "hard truths." "You know what my blackest moment was?" Jos said. "When I was told, 'you are as rehabilitated as you can be.' " Looking over his body, he continued, "This meant no use of my legs, limited use of my right hand, little of my left, and a life where I would need continual help to go anywhere or do anything."

We were both silent and I thought back to that time in my own life. How I wanted truth, and how I hated both the facts and the physician who gave them to me. I was angry at him, at the world, at God for doing this to me, and mostly at myself. What had I done to deserve it? Since I had once been "valid," it was not so much the things I would never do, but those I would never do *again*. Which deprivation was worse? Was it the one who had never experienced things who was the real loser? A cliche ran through my mind, "Better to have loved and lost than never to have loved at all." Anything I'd ever read or heard supported this perspective. But maybe this was just literature produced by people who were either "normal" or oriented to that standard. Loss was loss! And one's reaction probably depended most on the context within which it was experienced. Jos and I caught each other's eyes again. The reverie ended and he went on. "It was then I wished I was dead." It was not clear what made him "turn the corner." All he could say was, "I had to."

So do many, I thought, but so many do not.

For him "turning the corner" meant not only building a new life within the Village but continually keeping alive in other ways. He read voluminously and took courses "when possible, though such opportunities are not plentiful in the Village." Almost to himself he said, "One must always learn from mistakes. I always want to try new things. And I know I need people." It was a need he seemed pretty capable of meeting. His father had just been with him for two days and now his close friends were visiting. He pointed to their pictures on the wall, saying, "They are essential to my life." Bart and Riet seemed a little embarrassed but I sensed they felt this more as a compliment than a burden.

"I am happy at Het Dorp. I have all I need to live. I will
never get any more."

To myself, I wondered what would happen if his friends
moved away.

"I now have a secure place to live. Now my parents no
longer have to worry. If I were living with them and one of them
died, what would I do? I can come and go when I want. If I want
to get up at 3:00 A.M., I get up at 3:00 A.M., if to sleep at 8:00, I go
to sleep at 8:00."

This wasn't the first time he had referred to being freer and
more independent at the Village than at other institutions, or
even his own home. And he was not the only one who mentioned it. There was something more than mere institutional
constraints from which Het Dorp freed its residents. When Jos
used the example of sleeping and waking, it clicked with a
memory of my own. I recalled the experience of confinement at
home after my accident. As much as my parents assured me of
their love, I could not help but feel that I was a burden. So
gradually I tried to adjust: to eat, to sleep, to defecate when it
was convenient for them. They never asked for that adjustment,
but I knew that if I made them stay up later, or get out of bed to
fetch something, I would feel not only more like a little child,
but guilty for making demands! This was the freedom available
here, a qualitative freedom from guilt. Of course, there would
be some carryover of guilt for "having to bother someone." But
the dogelas were supposed to be on duty twenty-four hours a
day. Helping us *any* hour of the day was what they were *paid* to
do. Though they might like us and do certain things out of love,
their help was not contingent on love. It was their job. As such
they were there not to parent but to serve!

There were, however, things about the Dorp which dis-
turbed him. With some bitterness he said, "Too few of the
people in the Administration have a real warmth or social
awareness. And others, well, they're here just for the money."

I didn't understand the sudden harshness in his tone, so I
pressed him.

Gradually a surprising picture emerged. His bitterness stemmed more from disappointment in the staff's general understanding than from any specific instances of callousness. In exasperation he said, "With all their experience and willingness they just cannot seem to understand the residents." Sadly he wondered, "Is each person's view of his life and handicap so personal that it cannot be shared? For many hours I have talked with my friends here about how I feel. They understand, but they can never understand."

His friends agreed but added, "But maybe it's also that there are things that a resident *will not* or *cannot* share."

Almost not hearing, he concluded, "Even my parents do not understand."

The scene recalled to me the last lines of George Bernard Shaw's *St. Joan,* when Joan, too, despaired of people's understanding and asked, "How long, Lord, how long?"

For a few moments we all seemed stuck in our own thoughts. It was Jos who broke the mood and in the vein of "Now here's a funny story," began to tell his friends of my escapade at the Gala. I listened with a sense of wonderment, for though he was not there, he reported it like an eyewitness—not only how Pieter, Monika, Mieke and I had closed up the Gala, but the party afterwards, as well as the fact that I did not get home till 3:00 A.M. He even knew in detail about Mieke's disbelief of my "professorship." Warming to his subject, he went on, "If you think that's something . . . ," and told the story of my shopping trip with Pieter. The story was a good one and told better through his eyes than mine. "And there you were still huffing and puffing behind." By now the sadness was behind us and we were all laughing. It was nearly four and it felt like time to leave. I knew that he would want to spend part of the afternoon alone with his friends.

Supper was at six, and like so many Sunday-night school meals, cold cuts provided the main course. This was apparently also the time that people took to visit and eat with friends elsewhere in the Village, so several of the regulars were missing—Mieke, Ms. Nijhof, and the Schmids. There was apparently no restriction on this, save the one of notifying the dogelas. Maybe this had the double function of keeping the dogelas aware of the whereabouts of residents, and putting some "reasonable" limit on visitation. After all, if you had to tell someone when you would not be there, then the implicit assumption was that this was where you ordinarily would or should be.

Someone mentioned an upcoming tour for eight hundred handicapped people. The large number was awesome to all of us. We wondered at the complexity of the arrangements, and I wondered at the possibility of seeing nearly a thousand handicapped people and wheelchairs in one place. The Gala probably brought forth only a third of that number, and it was quite a spectacle.

Tonight was the last time I'd see Monika. In the morning she would leave for home. "You know how important birthday parties are for us in the Netherlands. Well, this one is for my favorite uncle."

I envied her. During my stay in the Netherlands I'd known both the sadness and the happiness the celebrations brought. Within about ten days in January, I'd been invited to my closest friend's, excluded from my daughter's, and had passed over my own. So with a sadness born of many things I toasted her departure and nodded to the "grieving" Pieter.

Monika mocked him, "It will only be two or three days, then you'll be coming." After a brief vacation at her home, they both would be returning to the Village. This prompted my curiosity about visitation.

"Well," said Mrs. van Amerongen, "technically there is a limit on how long a guest can stay, only six consecutive weeks, and there's a yearly total, but," she smiled, "there are ways the rules can be bent."

When Monika and Pieter began speaking in rapid Dutch, I knew they were kidding each other about more than the rules. As best as I could make out, it was about how much time they spent together, and to what this might lead. She, pouting at the allusion, playfully built a wall of jars and bread between herself and Pieter.

It seemed odd to expect to miss someone I had known so short a time, but miss her I would. As if anticipating my thoughts, she rose and came towards me. She wished me happiness and I returned the wish. She added, "I hope you return to Het Dorp some day, but I do not know if we will still be here." Smiling at Pieter, "We hope to be out in our own adapted place next year but it could take longer." She bent down and we hugged.

After a stop at my room to freshen up, I arrived at Jacob Veere's around 7:30. It was like a meeting of old friends and we quickly fell into a relaxed conversation ranging from movies to sports, from politics to music. But when we spoke of a recent music festival in Southern Germany, Jacob expressed some sadness.

"I guess I don't get around as much as I'd like. Since my accident I have travelled quite little. There are lots of reasons— some medical, some not. . . . There are some places I guess I just don't want to return to yet, some places where I had fun when I was "valid." I am afraid of these memories. Maybe they'll be too much for me, maybe being there the way I am now will destroy the pleasure. I don't want that." His medical difficulty offered some realistic problems. His catheterization necessitated having a nurse-companion on long trips and the fact that he would have to be repeatedly lifted was bothersome.

"Besides, those planes are just too damn small. I can never get comfortable."

"Neither can I. I don't think I've ever been able to sleep even on a transatlantic flight. It's all this equipment [my right hand swept down over my body]. Some day maybe I'll be unembarrassed enough to take off all my braces and lay them beside me."

We both laughed at the sight of me limping down the aisle, with a cane in one hand and an "extra leg" in the other, and everyone trying not to stare.

Comparing ourselves to others led to some contrasts between people in the Village. As Jacob put it, "There are so many different kinds of people here. Don't you agree?"

At first I thought he meant social types but something in his voice made me doubt that. "I'm not sure. What kinds?"

"Oh, you know those that don't seem *that* physically handicapped. Just what are they doing here? Are they social rejects?"

I didn't know the answer and I admitted it. "Yes, I do see people here that don't look that bad off, but maybe it isn't true. The only thing that they seem to have in common is that they walk. Maybe." I tried to lighten the tone, "from the perspective of us in a wheelchair, anyone up there looks better off than us down here."

Jacob nodded noncommittally, noted that it was coffee time, and suggested that we might take it with his social unit. As we entered, it became immediately clear that part of the context for his evaluation of the fitness of others must be by comparison with his companions. They were certainly the most visibly disabled group I had met. At least four of them, including Veere, needed help to drink or smoke. As I looked at them, he explained who I was. It was more than an introduction, it was my "story," from why I was at Het Dorp to the nature of my physical difficulty—a commanding performance in all senses.

In retrospect this encounter with his fellow residents seemed but a prelude. About an hour later, when Jacob said he felt thirsty and also wanted a cigarette, I could not help but feel that I had already been coached in what to do. It was not difficult to learn exactly how and for how long to hold the cigarette, or place the glass correctly on the back of his hand, tilt the glass, or wait for him to puff. These were all essentially technical tasks. It was the *when* which became the issue. I simply could not find the right timing for offering him another puff or another sip. He could ask, of course, but obviously this was a bit of a drag. I knew he was aware of this. He may not have felt awkward, but I did. He was giving me a peek into the two-sided nature of social interaction with someone severely handicapped, and it was driving me up the wall. Without a word being exchanged, I had once more been made aware of the minutiae and emotional load that are part of the most simple human interactions. Most important, I appreciated the effort it would take for two people to restore all the niceties to make it again a comfortable "taken-for-granted" interaction.

Almost, I thought, to let me know that this particular lesson was over, Jacob asked if there were other aspects of the Village about which I was curious. Searching for a lighter topic, I asked about the physical design. I loved the fact of the Village being built on hills in contrast with the eternal flatness of the Netherlands but wondered if this architectural layout had created any problems.

Jacob thought for a minute. At one time there had been talk of connecting all the buildings through a series of tunnels but the cost had seemed prohibitive. "Besides, there are some benefits to the current arrangement. It forces people to go outside. The wheelchairs are also designed to make the resident use his maximum ability. Unfortunately, the hills sometimes work against this. There were people who could walk but who simply could not negotiate the hills. Thus, they were forced to use a wheelchair to travel long distances."

When he said this I was reminded of Mieke. While she seemed to use a wheelchair sparingly, I imagined that for others it might prove an easy out. Several times on my first visit I had wished that I'd had some way of getting around other than walking. And with that thought came the fear that once I got in the chair I might not want to get out.

I shared with Jacob another view of wheelchair use. "I do marvel at the skill and fearlessness of some drivers. They just let go! They never seem to care. I would be scared to death. Maybe because they've always been in a wheelchair, they have no idea how frightening it appears." He nodded but didn't seem overly impressed. I recalled my visit to the woodworking shop, with its machines that were "too dangerous" to use. Perhaps this seeming recklessness was one of the few risk-taking activities available to the residents of Het Dorp, one of the few moments when they could escape the protectiveness of others and be responsible for their own lives.

Jacob was still on another wavelength. "I like the physical

openness of the Village. I don't feel so confined. You know that's one of the other reasons I don't like to travel by plane anymore. I would have to be strapped in and not moved for hours. I couldn't stand it. Even now you notice that I'm constantly moving even if it's only to change my position a little."

Not only did I notice that he was doing this, but that I was as well. In fact, not only did I often move my chair around, I also shifted positions, and crisscrossed my legs more frequently than I usually did. Since I was primarily sedentary away from the Village, this activity seemed more than just an effort to make myself physically comfortable. It was another small area over which I had control, a little reminder that I could feel that I was real, as if I were continually pinching myself to see that I was awake.

It was nearly eleven, and I had some things to do before retiring, so I bid Jacob adieu and began the trek home. As I travelled, I realized that this was the first time I had been out alone at night. It was a beautiful feeling, and several times along the way I stopped to relax and take it all in.

Tonight two new tasks faced me, washing my clothes and showering. The former proceeded without major incident. But as I had done the first day while washing myself, I misjudged my leaning ability and managed to drench myself thoroughly while ringing out the wet clothes. I simply could not get them far enough away from me nor could I, in a braked wheelchair, agilely move out of the way of a splash. But since I was already undressed this did nothing but provide me with a kind of presoak.

Showering was more of an adventure. The shower hung in an open corner of the bathroom where the floor was slightly depressed. Under the shower spout was a beach chair with plastic lattices and beneath it was a drain. The spout itself was removable so that the spray could be directed by hand. Next to the chair was an iron bar solidly implanted in the wall. This could be used either for assistance in raising or lowering myself or for support if I wanted to stand rather than sit. The trick, at least for me, was to get everything within easy reach but at the same time out of the water's range. I braked the wheelchair, faced into the corner, pushed myself to a semi-standing position, then leaning forward on the arms of the beach chair, which was set against the wall, reversed direction so that I could lower myself. Once in, I pushed the wheelchair out of water range, but not so far that I could not reach it when through. I wondered if the shower could possibly be worth all this effort. As the warm water soothed my aching body, however, I knew that it was and let myself soak.

In fact, this was the most comfortable shower I could ever recall. The why was surprisingly simple. Bathrooms are simply not designed for any but the extremely fit and stable. While most bathtubs are comfortable enough once inside, the getting in and out is always extremely difficult. There is no easy way for me to let myself down or lift myself out. The rims of most tubs are so slippery that they provide precarious holds at best. And once one is in, it is not easy to turn over. I usually have to wedge my legs against the end lest I slip too deep into the water. Showers are even more of a problem. Most are really tub-shower combinations, which are difficult to climb into and which usually have very slippery, rounded bottoms. There is also the problem of maintaining balance. I, for one, need something to balance myself. I inevitably hold onto a shaky shower curtain or towel rack, and this forces me to wash myself with one hand. In this position, there are also parts of my body I cannot reach. Without something firm to hold onto, I cannot bend over and wash my legs. And trying to stand on one leg, particularly my right one, always invites a tumble. Often I slip and tear the shower curtain and end up cursing myself for my awkwardness. I never fully appreciate the soothing penetration of the water unless I can lean somewhere. It does not take long for my legs to tire if I am not wearing my brace and all the weight feels heavier, so I usually cut a shower shorter than I want to. And for twenty years I have never complained or thought I had the right to. . . .

7

On the Problem of Sharing Power and Love

Monday, May 29

I woke at 8:30. Unrecorded thoughts, untranscribed slips of paper, and unread documents all taunted me. There were people for me to see, but I didn't want to lose all that had already happened. A bird in the hand, I thought, so I remained at my writing table. There would be plenty to do tonight—the first open council meeting of the Village. When I looked up again, ninety minutes had passed, enough time for me to guiltlessly take a coffee break.

But I arrived to an empty room. For this lack of company I could have stayed home. During my second cup, Pieter entered. His usual silence added to the pall. Should I ask him about Monika? Was that why he was so glum? One cue, the dogelas came in and broached the subject. I missed the exact words but what they said was something like, "How sad it must be, all alone with nothing to do. . . ." The tone was teasing, but the concern real.

"Well, at least now I'll have time to rest," quipped Pieter. And we all gladly laughed.

Several times I excused myself to call Dr. Klapwijk. As usual, I was unsuccessful. Today I was even having trouble getting his secretary, so I asked Pieter's help. He suggested trying it from his room. This time I reached the office, but found neither Dr. Klapwijk nor his secretary in. With Pieter's permission I left his number for a call-back. The time passed slowly. There was little talk between Pieter and myself. He worked

busily at his bench, and I looked over his shoulder, glancing
through a magazine. I sensed an emptiness. We both missed
Monika. I waited, wondering if I'd be able to reschedule any of
my other cancelled appointments with administrators. By now,
however, I had become ambivalent. My time was rapidly filling
up, and if all the staff people kept their appointments, I probably would have missed many of my resident contacts. The call
came from Dr. Klapwijk and we set a luncheon date for the next
day.

Pieter looked up from his bench, "What will you be doing
today?"

"Nothing much."

He nodded, still looking at the watch in front of him.

"Lunch?"

"Fine," I answered as I wheeled out the door, laughing at
his monosyllabic question. Somehow this made me feel good
rather than hurt. I sensed the mutual acceptance of two friends.

Outside my room, a large envelope protruded from my
mailbox. With an excitement which surprised me I tore it open.
Out dropped an Institute memorandum, a postcard, and a letter
from Mara. With all my notes spread on the table and a letter in
my hand, I realized an omission in my daily chronicle. Note-
taking was always more than that; it also included a considerable
amount of letter writing. That was rather ironic, since during the
rest of my stay in the Netherlands, I had been a rather lax
correspondent. All this writing was clearly more than the wish to
share my excitement and insights. It reinforced my links to the
outside. It reminded me, perhaps consoled me, that I was still of
that other world and that soon I would be returning there. The
envelope and *all* its contents seemed precious. The other residents had their links to the outside and so did I! Someone out
there still remembered me.

In another hour I left for lunch. As usual, I was greeted
along the way but now I realized that the residents' salutations
were often slightly inappropriate like "Nice day," "Goodbye,"
"How is life?" "Okey doke!" They probably just wanted to say
something in English.

The conversation over lunch began with general talk of travel, then turned to whether I had any difficulty travelling. "Do you need any special arrangements?"

Once more I bridled at the thought of "difficulty" and abruptly replied, "Of course not!" And then I was ashamed of myself. Though no one had to lift me onto planes, the rides were always physically uncomfortable. I never had enough leg room and always asked to be seated so that my braced right leg could be in the aisle. While the seats were soft enough, all my "bodily equipment" prevented me from sleeping no matter how long the trip. And frankly the idea of removing all my braces to make rest possible was too embarrassing.

⌐ Partly to change the subject, I mentioned that travel always allowed plenty of time for "Clavye Jacques," a Dutch card game. What followed was almost a repeat of the conversation two nights ago at Mieke's, where my interest in games and sport had seemed inconsistent with their image of a professor. This led me to tell a story in which I was treated inconsistently with *my* image of a professor.

"While out for dinner at a rather exclusive restaurant in Amsterdam I was informed that there would be about a ninety-minute wait. It was long, but the food and surroundings was worth it. While waiting to register our party, I had been talking with my companion about certain academic matters, so when asked my name, I responded without thinking in the Dutch manner, 'Professor Doctor Zola.' The headwaiter looked up and whispered, 'Perhaps we can serve you a bit sooner.' We were barely back into the lounge when we were beckoned, 'I am sorry, but this is the best we can do.' He then pointed the way to a table which had just been set up for us. The headwaiter was delighted, she was impressed, and I was embarrassed—but only slightly." They seemed really taken with the story, perhaps because of its double meaning. For it was not only as a professor but as a *handicapped* professor that I had commanded such respect.

When I asked if anyone planned to go to America, I was in turn surprised at their lack of interest. Mr. Schmid described it as too vast, too unknown, too far away. Mr. Altman may well have spoken to their other fear, "I don't want to go there. American people are too harsh. They wouldn't help the handicapped. They would say, 'Do it yourself.'"

Some of my own words and interpretations were returning to haunt me. I consoled myself with the thought that while I might have given them some words, the data were theirs. American movies, TV, Vietnam, and tourists, had already done much to convey a harsh, materialistic image. The best I could do was argue that *that America* was not all America, nor all Americans.

As we finished, Jos asked if I'd join him after dinner. I begged off because of the open Council meeting. They all knew about it but no one planned to attend or was even interested in talking about it.

Like the joking yesterday about Mr. Altman's sickness, today there was much kidding about Mrs. Schmid's accident. She had inadvertently accelerated her electric wheelchair and smashed into a wall. Instead of extending sympathy, my friends compared the strength of her wheelchair to the weakness of her wall. The latter was dented, but not the former—and neither was she. The discomfort was again mine, not theirs. It was an inside joke. Like the black who can call a fellow black, "nigger," they could laugh about the sick being sick.

Lunch ended on another travel note. Pieter summed up the problem, "There is a lot of trouble to travel if you have to do it yourself. It's nice when someone else makes all the arrangements." It was a statement of a dilemma which went far beyond travelling. It evoked all my conflicts between wanting to be taken care of and wanting to do everything myself. I wondered why it always felt so "all or nothing," why there was no middle ground.

Back in my room and still lost in my thoughts, I was startled by a knock at the door. I was irked as I always am when something interrupts my absorption. I was also a little surprised, since I couldn't recall anyone, so far, knocking at my home. Wheeling toward the door, I remembered that Dr. Langlett's children were coming to talk about graduate study in America.

At first, we were all a little awkward. I never said it, but I wondered if they felt uncomfortable by my presence in a wheelchair. That was, however, the only Village-related thought that intruded. And yet while the content of the conversation was divorced from the Dorp, the experience of the conversation was not. For the second time during the day I was transported, and willingly, from this world to the familiar world of the United States and academic sociology. It was another contact with the outside, another reaffirmation of my other self and my other world.

They left after nearly two hours and I returned to my notes. It was only as I was preparing to leave for supper, that I reflected on what an atypical day it had been. But was it? In a way I had created a natural experiment of another dimension of Village life—its potential loneliness and emptiness. My other days had been overscheduled. I remembered the words of the receptionist at the Adaptation Room, "We all have time here." Many of the Villagers spent long hours alone in their homes. I was reminded of my own period of confinement with polio and especially after my accident—the long hours in bed, reading, watching TV, all alone in my house. Those were very long days, punctuated by important breaks like an unexpected though always hoped-for letter or phone call. And then the constant noting of the time. How many more minutes before the six o'clock news? How long would it be before someone would come home to fill the emptiness? And how much longer till dinner, when there was a reward for my long silence? Dinner was always the best meal, if only because it was the most peoples. And evening, also peopled, and perhaps topped by an especially good or bad television program. In a way all the time references that punctuated my notes had functions beyond observational preciseness. I've always been preoccupied with time, as if it were limited, as if I had to make each moment count or account for it. But it was more than that, I now realized: time gave me benchmarks, gave me control, and even meaning. My little black appointment book crowded with scribbling was liv-

ing proof that my current life was not empty but filled to over-
flowing.

That I needed such reminders, such ties to the outside, was
a bit unsettling, since, after all, I was only here for a week and
my previous periods of restriction paled in comparison to those
of my companions. Despite the length of my confinements—
nine months and a year—I knew that at some point they would
end. For my friends at the Village, that was a dim possibility at
best; for most, it was not even worth thinking about.

Dinner was at six as usual. For the first time the conversation turned to world events. Soon we were talking about cam-
paign humor, and then American humor in general. Here I was
immediately at home. Television was the medium, and I was the
unexpected expert on "I Love Lucy." It was again as if professors were not expected to know such things. From favorite
episodes of the ever-popular domestic situation comedies, we
slipped easily into the telling of sexy jokes. Most escaped me but
they were pretty much one-liners like; "What was the best
season for Adam?" ("Autumn when all the leaves fall off.")
"What was the best season for Eve?" ("Spring, when she could
buy a new leaf.") I was struck by how un-Dutch the atmosphere
felt. Never had I heard so many sexy jokes nor witnessed so
much touching, as I had in the last few days. It felt unnerving.

As dinner ended, Mieke asked if we were still getting
together. Like all my companions, she had no interest in attend-
ing the council meeting. Since she went to sleep early and I had a
tentative date with Marlene, I was in a quandary. Mieke must
have sensed it and asked if I could join her now. As we entered
her place, she switched on the TV asking what I'd like to watch.
Unthinkingly I suggested a film. More embarrassed for me than
for herself, she explained that movies were almost impossible
for her to follow. I forgot that she most enjoyed programs to
which she could listen, such as musicals and discussions. We
both laughed uncomfortably at my faux pas and chose Top-Pop,
a program of the most popular recordings in the Netherlands.
While she excused herself to get us drinks, I thought of my

grandfather's TV-viewing. Although he could not hear, he claimed great satisfaction from just watching the affect and movement of the performers.

After serving us, Mieke lay down on the couch, explaining that she always rested but did not sleep after supper.

This made me comfortable enough to ask, "You know, I did wonder about you at the Gala. I never saw you in a wheelchair before and I know there's not one here in the room."

Patiently she described the congenital deformities in her leg which caused her to walk stiff-legged. "I can walk long distances all right, but if I have to step down or if the ground is uneven, then I have difficulty keeping my balance."

I knew the problem well. I particularly had trouble with slopes and inclines.

"You know, to go many places I need someone to guide me, or help me, or push me." When she was with friends at the Dorp, she used them more as guides. "I can walk behind them and push their wheelchair and since the chairs are so stable, it also helps my balance."

I do the same thing when I am in a supermarket. There I usually put aside my cane and use the cart for balance as I walk along.

But the city of Arnhem presented little choice. "With all its curbs and unevenness, it's easier to have someone push, but this means I really have to depend on certain people and it's not easy." Life became for her a long series of arrangements. A shopping trip, a visit to the doctor, or a concert could not be very spontaneous. In fact, such events tended to become regularized, and because of a more limited social world, an arrangement once created was not easily replaced.

"This girl used to go with me always to the doctor. She was very nice, and since I had to go to the doctor every two weeks, it was important, but she just had a car accident and now I have to find someone else. There is also a nice man at the office who said he will take me to Nijmegen where my parents live whenever I want. He's very nice. He has eight children and I was over to their house for supper."

At first, I thought this problem of arrangements was foreign to me, but again I realized how well-defended I was against it. When I came to the Netherlands, I made sure that I had available my own personal car. For me this assured the independence, the defense against arrangements, that Mieke so needed. My similarity to her came crashing down whenever I was without a car, for then I, too, became dependent on someone else's schedule. And then I felt anger, frustration, and sometimes even fear that I would always be that way, dependent on someone else.

The doorbell rang. It was her girl friend Babs, whom I had met twice before, once at some office as a receptionist, and the other night at the Gala. She was quite surprised, and almost embarrassed, that I remembered her. We continued listening to Top-Pop and joked about the lyrics. Babs never spoke to me directly but rather through Mieke, who translated. Mieke explained that Babs did not know much English, but hoped to learn more next year through a formal course. I kidded them that she probably spoke it far better than I did Dutch. Like many others, she was probably shy of using poor English in front of "the Professor." On the other hand, they thought my Dutch was not as bad as I made out, for after all I did appreciate the songs. All this made me aware of how much my understanding was based on visual cues. When it was time for the Council meeting, I excused myself, mentioning that I hoped to see them later in the week.

I soon realized how in a few short days my concept of distance had changed. The meeting was in the chapel just beyond the supermarket, a journey that I had once experienced as overwhelming. But the night was clear and the trip up the hills felt surprisingly easy. But it was too quiet. My anticipation was now mixed with a sense of foreboding. Why didn't any of my friends want to go? Why didn't I ask them why they didn't want to go? Was I afraid of what they'd say? Even now, as I entered, I didn't know what to expect. It was supposed to be a public business meeting for the purpose of familiarizing the Villagers with general administrative matters and decision-making. But if it had such a straightforward purpose, why the long delay in its taking place, and why the notable lack of interest?

The chapel was a large open facility, obviously used at times for non-religious functions. Though it was arranged for a meeting, my first association was to a performance. The Council, about twelve members plus several administrators, were all sitting up on a stage along a table facing the assembly. Slightly to the left of the stage were about ten rows of folding chairs, occupied almost entirely by staff. I counted nearly forty. They were primarily young women, and from the few I recognized, I guessed most of them to be dogelas. In the middle and extending all the way to the right, were rows of wheelchairs, some fifty residents in all. They were so closely packed together that an "easy escape" seemed difficult. What an enormous commitment it was to attend any activity! Aside from all the bother it took to get from one place to another, especially if one needed help, once one arrived, there was great pressure to stay. You might be dependent on someone to leave, for example, and in any event your departure can hardly go unnoticed. Even "normals," in a place like a theater, must inevitably step in front of someone and ask to be excused. Here a leave-taking caused a minor traffic jam, more like the trouble it took to move a car parked in a crowded lot. In order to move one, many others had to be rearranged. Recognizing all this, I purposefully sat in the last row and as close to an end as possible.

The format of the program did little to alleviate my sense of foreboding. After some brief opening remarks welcoming the audience and pointing out the historic nature of the occasion, there was an audio-visual presentation, a time study of the work of the dogelas which lasted for approximately seventy-five minutes. I sat in growing amazement at this lengthy report replete with tables, figures, and drawings. On and on the speaker droned. He was not even a regular staff member, but an outsider who had been commissioned to do the study! I tried to get more involved but the material was dull. Gradually, I began to feel insulted at audio-visual representations for such platitudes as how hard it is to change something. This was depicted in a cartoon as irresistible forces crashing into immovable objects. I would not have talked to my five-year-old son in that manner! Did they think the audience was on that level? Surely those who had bothered to come would be among the more intelligent and motivated residents. I looked around at my fellow residents. They sat mute. Why didn't they interrupt? I looked again at my program, and if my meager Dutch was correct, there were explicit instructions which forbade audience interruption during the report. Finally it was over, but instead of an immediate follow-up, a coffee break was announced. I was astonished at this disruption of continuity, for coffee in this setting was a major interruption. It was not brought to us, but everyone had to go into another room. Was this all a bad joke, an opportunity for us "to stretch our legs"? I milled around and noticed a heaviness. Some residents took this as an opportunity to leave and I joined them. Never in my entire stay here had I been so physically and psychologically uncomfortable. I had to leave before I exploded. I felt there was no other choice; I had no right, as a guest, to voice my opinions in so open a setting. Besides, I wanted some time to think through what I had seen.

Sitting alone outside, the immediate physical discomfort left, but the outrage remained. I felt as if I had been "had." At the same time I felt impotent. Since this was such an underlying fear of all the residents, maybe that was why I was so upset. I had so looked forward to this meeting that I now felt deflated. In fairness to the Administration, the meeting was probably not a conscious administrative attempt to distance the residents, and it probably did represent a first step in greater participation.

But whatever else it was, it was a further example of the difficulty of fully appreciating problems from the perspective of the "other." The meeting format, though quite a common one, could not have been less suited to audience involvement. It would not even matter, should I later learn that the members of the Council had been instrumental in setting up the meeting. That would only confirm that they had been co-opted into an administrative perspective.

I was speeding along, not only in my thoughts but in my wheeling. Though my date with Marlene was only tentative, I now desperately hoped she would be there. When I arrived shortly before nine, she was there but surprised to see me. "You're earlier than I expected. Why the sour face?"

I was a little angry at myself. Here I was so looking forward to seeing her and I was distracted by the meeting. Before I realized it I had a drink in my hand, some Mozart was playing, and I was spilling out my anger. But instead of agreeing, she questioned my view. "Maybe you're being too harsh, or too unfair to the Administration. After all, many of the people here are quite limited."

Almost as if she were deaf, I yelled, "No!"

She ignored my shout of protest and went on to give me examples of the residents' limitations. In some detail she told of the Administration's unsuccessful efforts to explain the new governmental subsidies for the handicapped. Obviously upset, she concluded, "Much of it had to be explained as if they were children. And still some did not understand."

I could only nod. All this seemed to set off something deeper in me.

Looking at me for support, she said, "I'm sure you've heard this before, but there are really many people who should not be here—like crazy people!"

"I didn't think they allowed any in."

"Maybe, but they're here. On the way to the Gala I kept hearing a woman say all sorts of things. I asked who she was talking to. 'No one,' she said. That kind of person should not be here! It's not nice! And they're not the only ones. There are those who are very old and have lived only in institutions all their lives. They're a real problem." Then shaking her head quite vigorously. "And there are some people here who are not really *that* physically handicapped but they just have no other place to go."

I didn't interrupt. Partly it was because I was disappointed with her. Damn it, why did she share the prejudices of the outside bigots? Besides, even if some residents were limited, why did the Administration have to be oriented to the lowest common denominator of resident characteristics? Such a program as tonight's could not help but insult the more intelligent.

After all, they're not mentally retarded! The more I thought about it, the angrier I became. The whole thing didn't even seem administratively necessary. The very idea of having so many staff was to individualize the approach. Why was it so easy to translate this into physical tasks but not into emotional or intellectual ones? But there was clearly another side to this story. Maybe for a whole host of reasons too difficult to fathom, we the handicapped encouraged this treatment by our own silence, acceptance, and acquiescence. Maybe, too, the staff realized the distance between themselves and the residents, a gap they could not fill or even fully apprehend, and in frustration, they defined their jobs in terms they themselves could appreciate.

My anger ebbed, and as it did I heard a shift in her tone. Her voice had a catch in it as she began speaking of life in the Village and several people she was particularly close to. I remembered someone and asked, "What about that man I saw you with the other day?"

Maybe my tone indicated more than I had intended. "Just who do you mean? There are many men who are my friends."

By now I was clearly blushing. "Oh, you know, the tall fellow, the one who isn't a resident." I couldn't bring myself to say "the normal."

I half-listened to a description of her "outside beau," how he looked, what they did together, some of his problems. When she complained about him, my interest perked up. Grimacing, she said, "I just wish he wouldn't cling so. When he's here he comes to be with me every minute. Sometimes he even comes by when I tell him I'm off to meet one of my friends. They're even beginning to be upset."

"Why?"

"I guess it was Jana. The other day after Willem had left, she asked why he has to be here so much. She said, 'I might as well not come. I feel like a third person, an extra one!' I don't understand. There's really no reason for her to be jealous."

Recalling my conversation with Mieke just a few hours before, I questioned whether she was being fair. I told her what Mieke said about how hard it was to make arrangements.

"Maybe it's the same thing with friendships. They seem so hard to form here. And once you do and invest so much in them, it's natural that people like Jana fear that they might break up and be lost. After all, Willem is a man. There's always the possibility of marriage."

For a moment I thought I'd gone too far. She suddenly straightened up. The silence was killing me, though it was only a few seconds long. Finally she smiled thoughtfully, and the tension left my body—so much so that I instinctively leaned closer to her as I do whenever someone seems to be hurting. Forgetting that I was not in a seat but in a wheelchair, I started to tip. It was not serious, but it served to further break the tension. Marlene smiled again, saying it was all right. Was it for my almost toppling or my question?

Leaning back in her own wheelchair, she began, "I did love him in the beginning, and still do sometimes now, but I think he will be just a friend. Jana thinks I'm crazy that I sometimes love him and sometimes not. You can feel that about people, can't you? But she should know better. After all, I have no future!" A terribly uncomfortable feeling again swept over me. She needed little encouragement to go on. "I don't feel that way when other of my friends come to visit me, even when they're engaged. I'm not jealous of them. I'm happy for them. I know I have no future. And no future with Willem either. He has too many problems. But I don't know what to do. He needs me. I just can't stop and tell him not to come. Besides he's very nice and we go lots of places and have lots of fun. You know," she said with frightening insight, "he's like many others. He has a handicap which no one can see!" She spoke in some detail of this hidden problem, but I barely listened. I was too involved in her view of herself. "For handicapped men it's easier," she said. "They can find a woman to care for them, but who wants a handicapped woman? Men want a woman who is whole, who can do the housework and cook and everything else."

I wanted to shout, "No!" I even wanted to take her in my arms and tell her no, that she was attractive, that she'd find a man. But I hesitated, and I think, rightly. I seemed more anxious than she. I was the one who was trembling. She did not seem half as upset. Nor did she appear to need any convincing about her worthiness. Who knows, maybe she had a better grip on her social possibilities than I did. I knew that she was at least partly right. As a person with a handicap I had had a similar problem in dating. Interestingly enough, most of my difficulty was neither in the asking nor the date itself, nor even with the woman herself. Almost inevitably, if we saw each other more than once, I would hear about a certain parental concern ranging from earning capacity to life expectancy to "marital responsibility." I occasionally felt that I should carry a medical affidavit with me. While difficult enough to deal with, this was nothing compared to what handicapped women went through. As a male, I could actively seek out companions, but a woman at least in pre-liberation days, was expected to wait to be asked. Marlene and Mrs. Hendriks were right. It took much more for a normal male to seek out and deal with a handicapped female, than the reverse. Here the active-passive dimensions of Western sexual relationships were crucial.

Gradually it clicked that all this analyzing had a further personal referent. At least unconsciously, I, too, shared many of the perspectives of the outside world. My identification was with the "normals." I had no handicapped friends. I had never dated a handicapped woman or even one with a severe illness. The realization embarrassed me. But Marlene got me out of it. "Don't worry. Don't be sad, it's O.K. I don't feel that depressed about it." I was speechless. The roles seemed reversed. She seemed much stronger than I. Whatever sympathy I might have felt was gone. Only admiration, and something approaching love, remained. I wanted to hold her, but the moment, if it was ever there, had passed. I also wanted her to hold me but this seemed beyond thinking, let alone asking.

Maybe to cheer me up, she talked about the future she did have. "You know I may not always live in the Dorp. Some day maybe I'll be able to leave. I've heard about a commune of handicapped people in Nijmegen or Utrecht. I don't know much about it, but everyone seems to help out."

This reminded me of the novel, *Tell Me That You Love Me,
Junie Moon,* about three handicapped people who set up house
together. The experiment, though unsuccessful, did hold out
some hope. I told her about it.

"Yes, I guess it's a dream for me, too. I really would like to
room with another woman, share a life. . . . I wonder if it will
ever happen?"

Without speaking, I reached out and touched her hand. It
rested in mine. Gently, without words, our fingers pressed. It
was time to leave. We held hands in a kind of silent communication as we rolled toward the door. Actually we had to let go
every few steps in order for me to drive my wheelchair. For this I
really needed two hands. Damn it, why was every little thing so
complex? But Marlene didn't let me spoil the moment. I kissed
her hand good night.

On my way home I stopped to look at the sky. It was very
clear and full of stars. What a romantic I was! I was not really
thinking thoughts. I was just so overwhelmed that I felt aglow.

A shout from behind interrupted my reverie. It was Johan,
someone I'd met several times before. He was almost exactly my
age and had once visited America. "How about a nightcap?" he
laughed. "You clearly need something to bring you down."

"Does it really show that much?"

"Indeed, you look like some moon-struck lover."

I confessed that I'd just left Marlene.

"A real beautiful woman," he said. "I envy you her company."

Misinterpreting what he said, I overreacted. "Nothing
really happened." I realized then that I wished no rumors to
circulate about me and Marlene.

"Usually, I thought you Americans liked to brag about
your conquests."

The slight edge to his tone was obvious but it led me on a
different path. "I'm not sure I'm into conquests any more."

This time he seemed to misinterpret me and asked with
some concern, "Oh, is it too difficult for you? Are there things
you can't do?"

I started to reply, almost instinctively, "Of course not,"

but in mid-sentence I changed course. "To tell you the truth, there are some things." I was willing to leave it at this level, but he was not.

"Like what?"

For the first time in my life I not only told someone but put it all together. "Well, there is the absence of a certain spontaneity in my courting," and I shared my discomfort at being unable to act out my romantic notions. "There's simply no sexy, subtle, or even fast way for me to remove my braces and get undressed. And though I've often fantasized about having someone disrobe me I've never been able in real life to do it very easily."

"It also doesn't make for quick getaways."

"Indeed, it doesn't!" and I all too happily related a particularly harrowing escapade. I felt I'd fled into bragging, but if I had, Johan ignored it and with little forewarning dropped the heaviest question. "Can you do it whenever you want?"

I gulped, "Well," and giggled nervously, "I've always worried about that since I had polio."

"Why then?"

"It took an awful long time for me to have an erection, and it was even longer before I could come."

"And now?"

With a heavy sigh, I answered. "There have been times when I could not get erect but I usually related it to not being 'turned on.' With someone who was a regular lover I never seemed to have any trouble." I recalled momentarily that I had, however, been accused by someone of having 'a low libido' but Johan's further remarks prevented me from dwelling on this uncomfortable thought.

"Did that get you into any trouble?"

"What?"

"Not being able to do it."

"Not really, I guess I've been lucky. As long as I've had these," playfully moving my fingers and wagging my tongue, "things seemed to work out O.K."

"Hmmm." Undaunted he went on. "What about certain positions?"

What else could he ask me? Amused both at myself and the

situation, I laughed, "Well, it's been a very long time since I've done anything very experimental."

"Oh?"

"It's certainly not easy to do anything while standing, and I've never done anything active like lifting someone. And doing it in chairs or other cramped spaces has never been easy. . . ."

He nodded, encouraging me to go on.

"I can do the standard one all right, though since I support myself on my arms rather than my legs, my hands aren't free to do anything. I guess now I'm benefiting from women's lib, since a lot more women seemed to enjoy being on top and in many ways that's easiest for me."

With a touch of sarcasm and regret, Johan said, "I wish I had such problems. I wish something was easiest for me."

Now I felt very uncomfortable. I knew he'd really been pushing me and wanted to hear all, but I still felt guilty. "I didn't mean to go on so. No one ever asked me all this before and I guess it has just been building up all these years. You just unplugged me. I'm sorry if all this has upset you." Most of this time I was looking down, not at Johan, but now I raised my eyes and catching his understanding stare, breathed a sign of relief. "I'm sure sex isn't easy for you. In fact, I don't even know what you . . ."

"Yes, you're right. There's not much I can do now. It's even hard to talk about. When I was 'valid' I never even worried about it, but now . . ."

His "now" consisted of no use of his legs and limited use of his arms and hands. He could move them but they seemed to have little strength. I thought he must have a spinal cord injury complicated by something else. While he told me something of his sexual past, it was his present that was before me. "I can't do anything by myself. I can't even masturbate. What can I do?" Then followed a series of rapid-fire questions which I could not answer, perhaps wasn't intended to. "How do you ask someone? If you ask it once, how do you ask again? What about them? What will they think of you? What will they say to others? And if they leave, what then? You will have to start all over again with someone else?"

Two separate thoughts ran through me as he talked. Part of

me wondered what I'd do if I were in his place and part of me wondered what I'd do if I were the one asked. If asked, I'd probably agree to help, though not without some embarrassment. But it seemed different from when I was very young and with some other adolescent boys engaged in mutual masturbation. There it seemed only technical, with no ties, promises, or even involvement. And little guilt except at the possibility of getting caught. But now I was an adult. Aside from the homosexual issue, I worried about what emotion I'd have to convey. That I enjoyed It? That I was not repulsed? And would I always have to leave it to him? Would I ever be expected to ask him if he wanted it? If Johan had been a woman, some of these issues might have seemed less problematic. Then it seemed I could more easily ask questions and let myself enjoy it. The sexist nature of sex, I thought to myself. It also occurred to me that what I did and felt with Johan or any man would also depend on what was being asked, hand-masturbation being infinitely easier and more agreeable than oral-genital contact. And then, as if any more complications were really necessary, I thought of the other side, Bart's interest or wish to touch, feel, love someone other than himself. My God, what that would take of me physically and psychologically!

We were both exhausted and a little embarrassed by our confessions. Johan was silent and I didn't know how to continue. As we both made motions to leave, I could only say, "I think I understand."

"Do you?" he asked.

"I hope so." Our chairs pulled closer and I reached out to shake his hand. It was weak, almost limp, but I held it in mine and squeezed gently. "Thank you, Johan, for listening and trusting me."

He nodded his head but said nothing.

Out the door I wheeled, covering the remaining distance home quickly. This had been my most draining day, though it seemed I'd said that before. Sleep came quickly, and with it, a flood of images, none really clear. I was being touched, caressed, almost rocked, and I in turn reached out with both my arms.

Tuesday, May 30

The morning breakfast was peaceful,
broken only by Pieter's and my half-
hearted laments about the service. With
nothing to do for half an hour, I followed Pieter to his room. His
work day was already planned, and he immediately turned to a
half-finished letter in his typewriter. Knowing I had to reach Dr.
Klapwijk, he put the phone on the bed with a gesture almost
calculated to foster my independence, saying, "You can make
the call yourself." I did, and Dr. Klapwijk, found he could not
make it. As usual, the excuse was reasonable, a combination of
sickness and emergency house repairs. He communicated
through his secretary that he would be willing to deal with "any
problems I had by letter." The secretary then asked if I had any
problems. I laughed no.

What a symbolic start to my day! In a few minutes I had an
appointment with one of the administrators of the Village.
Would he also cancel at the last minute? My adrenalin was
already rising. I was preparing to dislike him, partly because of
the length of time it had taken to get the appointment, and
partly because he was a representative of the benevolent tyr-
anny. With my mind thus clouded, I asked Pieter to wish me
luck and took off the administration building, arriving a few
minutes ahead of schedule. To my immense displeasure, no one
was about. Up and down the corridor I drove, till someone from
an adjacent office saw me.

"Can I help you," he asked, in a manner indicating an
unwelcome intrusion.

"I'm here to see Mr. Gans," I said firmly.

"Oh, that's strange, he is not expected until ten. Do you have an appointment?" His tone displayed a certain skepticism.

"Yes!" I answered rather indignantly.

Taken aback, he excused himself. I assumed he was upset by the demanding attitude of a resident.

A half-hour delay! Damn them all. But before I could stew about my predicament, the staff member returned, full of apologies. "Dr. Zola, indeed you are expected. Mr. Gans will be with you momentarily."

I was only partly appeased. Was it my title which changed his tone? Was it the job of this man to fend off other unwelcome intruders?

But there in front of me was an outstretched hand and a smiling face. "I'm sorry for the confusion. Please, after you." And he consciously let me wheel myself in. He was a tall, thin man, appearing more Scandinavian than Dutch. After the usual offer of cigarettes (refused) and coffee (accepted), he apologized for his poor English. "I hope you will bear with me a few minutes. It always takes me a while to switch from thinking and talking Dutch into another language. To give me a chance to get adjusted, why don't you tell me what you want from me?"

This seemed his way of taking time to size me up, whereas I wanted just the opposite. And so I answered that what I essentially wished was his view of the Dorp, its future and its problems.

"Ah, yes, I will be most happy, but first tell me what you hope to learn about the Village."

During this negotiation, we physically settled in. At first, he was some distance away, standing and looking down at me in my wheelchair. Then, almost as if realizing a certain impropriety in this, he came closer, and in a disarming move, sat down in an upholstered chair next to me with his long legs draped over the side. I no longer thought of him as superior. As I sipped coffee, I felt in good company, and warmed to the topic of the Village.

In telling why I was there, I gave the long version, from my original reasons for coming to the Netherlands Institute of Preventive Medicine to why I thought it possible to learn something about the Village in barely a week. He nodded appreciatively, and when I concluded, stated what he was to repeat several times, "I know it will take some time to absorb, but if and when you write up any of your impressions, I would very much like to see them."

I in turn replied what I was to say several times, "Yes, my notes are voluminous, and if and when I write up something, I would be delighted to share it with *both* you and the residents." To me the commitment to communicate to *all* members of the Dorp community was of prime importance.

With several qualifications about the newness of the Village and the unexpected one that "since you are not here as a scientist, I can be more haphazard and disorganized in my account," he began tracing the history of Het Dorp. He also felt that its initial impact had been too great and that its ideals were in some ways too overwhelming. "The public responded enthusiastically to a previously neglected problem and to its solution. This has made it difficult for us with everyone—the public, the government, and the residents." He mentioned several examples, but perhaps the most telling was a request for vans to enable the residents to visit and work beyond Het Dorp. The government's reply was typical: "Why do you need to transport them anywhere? You were supposed to provide all they needed within the Village!" He went on rather sadly, "So many requests for something new seemed to meet with a similar reaction."

"For the residents, the promise of a solution to all their problems also led to difficulties. They expected Paradise. For some it was, at least in the beginning. It was so far better than anything they had ever heard of or experienced. But later on there was a depression. It was not Paradise, but an experiment. There were not only many problems it did not solve but some it even created or made worse, such as interpersonal relations and sex. Finally, because of this idea of Paradise, there is the issue of guilt. For if it was Paradise, why did some want to leave?"

I didn't understand this train of thought. Did he really mean "leave" or was he wondering about the complaints of the residents? I could see, indeed, that many might feel uncomfortable in criticizing what they have.

He brought up an example of "one quick disillusionment." "Why, there was one resident who thought it was all unbelievable, impossible to ask for anything more. And then three months later he was bitterly complaining about the shower facilities."

The example seemed double-edged. While he emphasized the problem of too idealized goals, he seemed to attribute a certain ungratefulness to the resident.

At my urging, he spoke about the eternal clash of perspectives between the residents and the Administration. "This surely is the most difficult problem, and one I am never sure I know how to handle. Typical was last night's public meeting. It's a pity that you don't understand Dutch for then you would really have seen something." Without asking he assumed that I had not been there. I did not bother to correct him. "The residents are interested in different things. They claim they want to be informed of all the big decisions. But when we do inform them— like last night—they are not really interested. Only a few want to know. They are more interested in why something is at this height," raising his right hand an arbitrary level, "but not that height."

Without realizing it, he may have delineated precisely the issue. The residents, at this stage of their "developing consciousness," were interested in things which directly affected their lives—the height of objects and the repair of wheelchairs. Rather than absurd, this seemed perfectly natural.

On some level he must have known this, for with barely a pause he listed similar issues facing the Dorp. "This we must cope with, before we can really work on anything else—personal medical care and services, substitute legs, food, and shelter. With these solved we can go on to other problems. Do you know what I mean?"

"Could you be more specific?"

"No problem, let's start with medical services. These services are masked. There are no doctors at the Dorp, no white coats. All the facilities are physically out of sight. The dogelas provide for all but the most serious difficulties. This works pretty well but there is still the continuing question of how sick one can be and stay in the Dorp. Also what services are justified and what not. I'm not sure what we should be doing about sex. . . ."

He was not really waiting for a response. I was interested, and that was enough. So he continued with the list. "Substitute legs—they are a real problem. There are continual complaints about the wheelchairs. They keep breaking down even though the repair service is excellent. And when your chair is broken, well, . . ."

The comment bespoke volumes. I remembered what it was like when my brace was being repaired. It was not merely the inconvenience. It was the terrible reminder of my immobility without it, a symbol of my ever-present dependence.

My associations seemed to penetrate his thoughts as he spoke of the residents' overdependence on the wheelchairs. "Because there is a need for the wheelchairs to enable some to climb the hills, it is easy for residents to ride all the time. The same is true for those who could use a regular wheelchair, but do not."

I agreed with him about that reality and confided, "Occasionally, I wish that I had gotten an electric wheelchair."

He laughed knowingly. "And then," he went on with a sigh, "there is the problem of food. What can we do? With so many to feed we need a central kitchen. It's tasty and plentiful but there is a sameness to it."

"This centralization brings up other problems."

"What do you mean?"

"Well, isn't that part of the reason you can take coffee anywhere, anytime without notice, but lunch or dinner is not that spontaneous."

"Yes, but you don't think that's really an issue, do you?"

"Well, it's just something else you have to plan ahead for. I guess I have the impression that people feel they can't change their minds at the last minute, or that they have to call someone to tell them, if not check it out. It's just a feeling I have, nothing big, just another reminder . . ." I caught myself. I really didn't want to share what I thought, that it was a reminder of dependence, not freedom.

He did not pick up my reflection and continued talking. "We really have not yet solved all the problems about living arrangements. While many of the architectural adaptations work, there is great difficulty in assigning quarters. There is a great demand for "couples" quarters but still a great shortage, and since people are assigned to places, there is often dissatisfaction."

"But maybe that's part of the problem."

"What is?"

"All this assigning is such a permanent thing. I am not sure that all that attention should be focused on making the ten-unit apartments their exclusive home. In a sense you are trying too hard. While home is a place to eat and sleep, many activities do take place elsewhere. Even with minimal physical mobility, many inhabitants want to and could visit friends on other streets. This should be more possible than less. And, as on the outside, friends should be able to live closer together. While you may not yet have enough space for friends to live together, where possible you could at least make them neighbors."

"That's an interesting idea, but the people don't want to move, and we certainly don't want to force them."

"Nothing could be further from my mind. I just want to make mobility more possible rather than less." With college housing in mind, I outlined how every year some people could move and be assisted by a central planning authority.

He shook his head at all "the work-coordination that such an enterprise would require." I let him go on and he continued reflecting about the Villagers. "As it see it, the major difference is between the progressive and non-progressive residents. In particular, there are among the progressive a number of problems. The dystrophies, while having severe problems, seem as a group, very nice with good personalities. The MS's, on the other hand, have many personality troubles." This was a contrast that many of the residents themselves made, so I pushed him to elaborate. He continued, "Many think we should take fewer of them but it will take time and if we don't take them where will they go? The young MS's are a real problem. When one of them dies it's very depressing and spreads through the rest of the people." He paused, as if recalling the sadness of such an incident and then spoke of other divisions. "There are those who are born with a trouble and those who get it later, like from an accident. Sometimes I think those born with it are better off, more adjusted, less critical."

It was an issue about which I had often wondered. Someone born with a problem may feel the loss less, but that person may have fewer resources and experiences on which to build. It was his last phrase that gave me a shudder, however. If the residents were "less critical," that seemed like an exclusively administrative benefit.

My pained expression went unnoticed and he concluded with a final distinction. "There are the obvious groups of the severely and the not-so-severely handicapped."

"When is this a problem?"

"Well, it's really difficult in the sheltered workshops. I suppose you know about the current law requiring that, in order to be there, a handicapped worker must perform at one-third normal capacity?"

I had, indeed, heard often about this law, but by now I had begun to wonder whether the law was becoming the scapegoat for all the work-related difficulties.

He ended with a sense of righteous indignation, "Why, if the one-third rule were lived up to, barely fifty of the current one hundred eighty could meet it. And so we have to find some way around it. To help those below capacity we may have to hire more 'valids' to lift the average productivity level."

My distaste was evident. It was not merely the solution, it was what would come in its wake. It meant that Het Dorp would be displacing the severely handicapped for the less handicapped. I wanted him to fight the issue, not skirt it.

Maybe he sensed this, for he changed to a more self-critical tone. "I don't like this solution, not a bit. There has been an overemphasis on productivity in industrial nations. Why, after all, in a world of decreasing work, should these people have to work? Many seem perfectly happy to work at the cultural center on activities for which they receive no pay. Maybe this is the wave of the future." Perhaps feeling that he had gone too far, he expressed some reservations. "But I'm not sure I like the idea of enforced leisure. These people should not be forced to be the experimental guinea pigs for society's problems. They should not be forced to live without work."

Satisfied with his own summing-up, he went on, "And sex, of course, is a problem that is always with us."

"Oh?"

"Yes, I'm sure you're aware it's a great problem. And I'm not sure that anyone has a real answer." He told of a recent trip to Sweden, where he visited a rehabilitation center which mixed "men with women and 'normals' with handicapped." In matter-of-fact tones he described some of their experimental programs. "There was a lot of sex there. Even I think some group sex, but what bothered me most was the exploitation I heard about."

"What kind?"

"Of the handicapped by the 'normals.' The 'normals' were not quite so normal. They seemed to be too involved in the activity." Pausing for a moment to let this sink in, he continued, in a softer tone, "Here in Holland we are not so liberal. We even had trouble with building the Dorp. Many were critical of mixing men and women—you know, most hospitals still keep them segregated—but it seemed mad to build one Dorp for men and another for women. That's not normal."

He seemed very proud of that accomplishment. Thinking for a moment of all the sex-segregated institutions in the United States, I felt he was justified and told him so: "It must have been quite a battle."

"It was but we won." Wearily he added, "But there is so

much more to do. I don't even know where to begin. And I don't know who can help us. Several months ago a resident came to me and said, 'You think we're sexually normal but I'm not sure, I've had no experience. I don't know what I can do and what I can't.' " It was hard to know how widespread such feelings were. Some in the Dorp had once been "valid" and had some sexual experience, but the majority, coming as they did from nearly a lifetime in institutions or the back rooms of their parents' homes, could only be novices. I wondered if this was even more a problem today when we are all bombarded with sexual stimuli. "My God, what can they do!" I blurted out.

To my somewhat rhetorical question, he responded very concretely. "You know there really are some very difficult technical problems. For many, even touching themselves is impossible. For instance, I'm sure you've seen people here with abnormally short arms. Such a man cannot even reach his penis!"

As he cited several other examples, I felt two things. I thought of last night with Johan as we recalled our sexual limitations, but today I let myself feel a little thankful for all I *could* do. I also realized how male-oriented the present conversation was. I should not have been surprised. Almost every article I'd ever read about the sexual functioning of those with physical handicaps or chronic diseases concerned itself with the male— his ability to have an erection, or ejaculate, or the strain that either might produce on his heart and the rest of his system. Here, as in the rest of the sexual world, the woman was a vessel, the object of, not the participant in, sexual activity.

Reflecting on the examples we'd discussed, he concluded, "So this means that some need help in having sexual relations."

"Does this actually happen?"

"I think so, but people don't talk about it. It is very embarrassing, particularly for the dogelas."

I wondered how it could be otherwise. Not only were many of the dogelas young but many of the youngest seemed to be assigned to the evening hours. I recalled a similar situation in the United States. Once while reading the field notes about an obstetrics hospital, I noted how little the student nurses, usually between eighteen and twenty years old, were taught about sexuality. Yet as my research colleague pointed out, it was to these students that the first-time-pregnant mother addressed all her concerns and questions about sexual activity.*

I then asked if there had ever been any male dogelas.

Gans hesitated a moment as if trying to choose his words carefully. "Once there was but he was sort of . . . 'abused.' "

"What does that mean?"

"They used him to do all the heavy work. Besides he had a problem. I don't mean that he was homosexual. That wouldn't matter to me. But he was not very . . . well, he was effeminate." With an air of finality he added, "It just didn't work out."

"All this sounds like quite a dilemma," I said sympathetically. "How are you trying to solve it?"

"As you said, it's not easy. There are a group of residents working on it. We call them Work Group A. They have helped by bringing in several lecturers. It had, however, to be at the most basic level, like for a six-year-old. But nearly 70 percent of the residents came. And there is a study group both at the Johanna Stichting and at the university in Nijmegen."

There was something perhaps unconsciously patronizing in his words. I realized, as the women's movement has pointed out, how little we all know about sex and our bodies until we are forced to look at them.†

Thirty years ago Kinsey noted that most of us at some time or other do all those things that we thought nobody did. More recently Masters and Johnson have shown that "doing what comes naturally" does not come so naturally. We might quite aptly conclude that in our culture we are so alienated from our bodies, and thus mystified by the body's workings, that it might be more appropriate to say that we *all* are at a six-year-old's level of knowledge and understanding.

*Nancy Shaw, *Forced Labor: Maternity Care in the United States* (New York: Pergamon, 1974).

†Boston Women's Health Book Collective, *Our Bodies, Ourselves* rev. ed. (New York: Simon and Schuster, 1976).

His remarks about work in progress seemed to end his reflections on sexuality, so I asked about any changes he had witnessed at the Village. "Yes, some things have changed. In the beginning I was an idealist about integration. I thought there should be full integration with the Arnhem community, but it did not work. There was some mutual use of facilities like the shops, church, and sports hall, but on the whole it felt superficial." The only reason he could cite for this failing was that, "For some, living in integrated facilities is good, for others no."

I had no better explanation than he, though I wondered whether he was searching for the fault in the wrong place. Why was it necessarily a failing of the residents? Maybe it was the outside society that shunned the integration.

As he waxed philosophical, I sensed that the interview was drawing to a close. "The problems of the physically handicapped can only increase. Medical science is continually helping many with diseases live longer and helping many survive who previously would have died." He described rehabilitation as primarily a post-World War II phenomenon, one which was only now beginning to take off. Thus, despite his great admiration for the vision of Dr. Klapwijk, he noted, "the time was ripe for a Het Dorp—perhaps not as soon nor as well-endowed—but it had to come."

As we thanked each other for the visit, Gans praised me for my "courage in coming here." As so many others had already done, he spoke of the importance of experiencing things from the other side. And yet I could not help but feel that all his praise was a sort of lip-service. He was aware that what you see and experience from a wheelchair is different from your perspective from a more vertical position; he even noted the lack of this realization in certain architectural mistakes. He also regretted that he had not taken the time or effort to try the experiment. Why didn't he? Did it really take so much "courage"? Maybe that was the correct word. For them, the "normals," to take to a wheelchair would be to enter an uncomfortable world which they could easily avoid. As several of my fellow residents had said, they could not understand why anyone would want to, unless they had to. Such a trip might also prove depressing. It might reveal to the individual too much about himself. It could open up not only fears but frustrations, not only personal inadequacies but personal contributions he was making to the very problem he was trying to solve. I was certainly experiencing all of these things.

As I wheeled out, I looked again at this representative of the Administration. I was now more admiring of him, and as I'd become with Marlene, more aware of his dilemmas. Several staff members like him felt that they were in the middle, pulled in two directions, mediating not only between the larger society and Het Dorp, but also between the inhabitants and the rest of the staff. As he described it, "There are about four hundred residents here and four hundred employees. Thus, there are two equal groups. When there are certain decisions to be made and someone mentions asking the residents, other staff say, 'Why? That's our responsibility.' We have to work so hard to get them to see the other side. In the future there will be greater participation of the residents. While others are opposed to it, I think it is a good and inevitable thing."

Within his remarks, however, I heard the words, "but not yet," echoing. There was an irony here, for he perceived himself as very sympathetic to the residents' needs. To the residents, however, he was one of those who kept saying no.

It was only eleven. Ninety minutes had passed but it seemed much longer. With an hour before lunch I decided to pay the bills for room, board, and my children's toys. As I read one of the receipts, a secretary cheerfully asked about my stay and my experience at the Gala. Did she too know about my night's adventures? I signed the last one, picked up some booklets, thanked her for her help, and wheeled out.

As I turned the corner towards the reception desk, I was reminded of my first visit here four months ago. I looked around. There was no doubt in whose territory I was. This building was an alien place. The very first time I was here I had slipped on their highly polished floors. As I caught myself with Dr. Metz's assistance, I had thought, how unthinking for a place which caters to the physically handicapped. As I left the building this time, I thought of all the architectural and geographic barriers which continually remind the physically disabled of their unwelcomed, unwanted, or at least unexpected presence in the "normal" world.

Things were taking on a certain "last-ness." This was the last time I would visit the administration building, and now I was headed to my last lunch. At first it proceeded like any other meal. The talk was of people eating too much, and particularly the high cholesterol content of certain diets. The sarcasm in it was like some earlier chiding I had heard about smoking. Then Mrs. Schmid had criticized Mr. Altman for smoking too much. "I have all these troubles," he responded, "so why should I worry about what cigarettes will do?" Now several urged me to eat oranges: "They are important vitamins for you to have." Almost on cue, I yawned, and Mr. Schmid called out, "See!"

Quite abruptly, Pieter broke through the small talk. "So what do you think about the Dorp? Is it a good place? A success? Are people happy?"

I felt unsure of myself. "Well, there are some things that surprised me. For one, I did not expect to meet people who *use* the Dorp for all its physical help but work outside and orient themselves to the outside."

Mr. Schmid wondered if I had met "some who live completely within the Village. They organize clubs and committees. They even work harder than ordinary workers but get no pay."

"Yes. I have. I think I'm sitting next to one."

He smiled just a trifle embarrassed.

Mr. Altman added another category, "There are those who live almost entirely through or for one another. Their life is in making the lives of others more bearable."

This elicited several nods, and Mrs. Schmid chimed in, "I sometimes think that the Aministration does not even know they exist. They never acknowledge it."

When others vehemently agreed, I felt compelled to say something. "I don't think the Administration is really all that unaware. Unfortunately, they make reports to other administrators and they report not only what they think is meaningful but what they can count, like hours worked and units produced. It's difficult to measure, let alone convey, good deeds done and units of happiness spread." I was surprised at my own defense of the Administration and realized how I had been influenced by the conversations with Marlene and with Mr. Gans.

There was silence for a moment, at best a grudging acknowledgment of the legitimate existence of an administrative perspective, but it was as if I had only blunted their discomfort. Picking up on my opening comment, they began to speak of those "who but slept at the Dorp." One after another they were described. The ambivalence toward them really came out. They were only grudgingly admired. I couldn't understand the details, but the envy was straightforward. Such people in many ways lived a better life. "So many friends, so many activities, they never seem to have time."

"For us?" I thought to myself. There seemed to be a feeling that they were in some way taking advantage of the Village. Perhaps the social distance that the Hendriks or the Falks felt between themselves and the full-time residents was not well concealed.

Jos Altman summed it up concisely and dramatically, "They take so much and give so little."

Interrupting, Pieter brought us back to his question. "Well, do you think most people in the Village are happy?"

More relaxed now, I was able to respond, "To tell the truth, I don't really know. I get a sense that most are happier about being here than many other places they might be, but happy? . . ."

"O.K.," said Jos, "what about us? You know us better. Are we happy?" It was as if they wanted me to pass judgment on them, and that was the last thing I wanted to do. So I partially confessed my dilemma, saying, "That doesn't really make it easier. You certainly seem to have fun together, joking and kidding at mealtimes. But I honestly don't know if individually you are happy."

Mrs. van Amerongen asked, "Have you noticed any other ways that people have adjusted?"

I was really feeling pressed, both to be prematurely analytic and to be as honest as I could. "If you mean other unexpected ways, I feel that there are some that I've missed. There are many people I did not see. Even if I stayed here much longer there would be people I would be very unlikely to know, particularly someone with little education, or little ability to speak English, or little experience with strangers. I'm sure there are many unhappy, and perhaps even happy, people who keep much to themselves and to their homes."

Mrs. van Amerongen nodded, "I think there's one like that among us, Ms. Nijhof. She never seems to be around. She never comes to festivals."

"Yes, yes," contributed Jos, "she's usually the first one to leave after meals." Others agreed with this appraisal.

"It's funny you should mention her." Again I found myself mending fences. I wondered if because I was leaving, I wanted to smooth out things. "I've noticed the absences you've mentioned. But look at her when she *is* here. She always joins in, even in her shy way. She's really not that isolated. She has visitors—like the other night. And did you ever notice that she makes a special point of coming all the way back here almost every day to share lunch with you? She could just as easily stay at the Workplace and eat by herself." I felt like a bit of a scold until I saw several of them exchange glances, the kind that convey, "I never thought of that before."

As the others began to leave, Mrs. van Amerongen touched my sleeve and asked if I could stay awhile. Curious about my reactions to Mr. Gans, she asked about the morning session. It was not long before we got to issues of power. She summed it up, "Yes, he has his problems, I know that, and as you said several times, it's really difficult to see it from the resident's point of view. Let me tell you how I see the Village being run." Shaking her head in a way that indicated she knew exactly what she wanted to say, she went on, "The best way of putting it, is that the residents have little say in how decisions are made. Yes, the Administration listens to everything we say, but again and again there never seems to be enough money or enough space or enough time. I think they just won't let go of the purse strings, and really, any power." She backed this up with several examples.

When I asked about the role of the Council, she sighed, "It's weak. Nice people, not strong people, are elected. The strong people, the rebels, are given committee and workshop assignments to siphon off their energy."

This implied greater direct control over the residents than I believed the Administration had, so I pressed her.

As she saw it, when there was an election, the Administration was either able to convey, or the Villagers were already aware of, which candidates were looked upon favorably, and this made a big difference in the outcome.

"On the other hand, I am not sure what difference it would make, since the Administration does not allow the Council much power. They seem to think the Council's main purpose is 'to inform the Villagers.' "

"But that's exactly the problem, we are only informed of the decisions that have already been made! 'Here's what we've decided. Now, don't you agree?" Bah! That's not what we want. We want to be part of the actual decision."

"So why do the residents stand for it? Why do they go along?"

"Oh," almost despairingly, "It's so difficult to organize the residents for any kind of political action."

But why? Why? we asked each other. In an effort to answer our own question, we spoke of situations where we had been made to feel impotent. Gradually a picture emerged which seemed so provocative that I asked if she'd mind my taking notes. Scribbling and crossing out, we went at it until we had five groupings of people and factors which obviated the rise of meaningful "patient power."

1 As a result of a background in sheltered living situations, many residents are quite timid, and have had little experience in making decisions or having any control over their lives.

2 Many are truly grateful and feel the situation at Het

Dorp to be so much better than any they experienced before that any present "lacks" must simply be lived with.

3 Some have been convinced that everything that *can* be done for them *is* being done. They stand in awe and respect of medicine and its allied workers.

4 Some are content not to rock the boat because the major lacks of the inner Village life do not affect them. They are oriented to the outside and since the Village makes this possible, they're not interested in jeopardizing it.

5 Some, if not all, fear the possibility of the Administration's retaliation. They are aware that there are certain conditions under which they could be transferred out. They all know that they "could take a turn for the worse," and if they did, they would not want to have alienated anyone who might have a say in what happened to them.

Reading over the list, I knew we had tapped into something that applied beyond the limits of Het Dorp. Many of these reasons were reasons why patients in general found it, not only too difficult to complain, but to organize on their own behalf.

Looking at each other, Mrs. van Amerongen and I were pleased. We both had a better handle on some issues central to the Village. More important, we wanted to use this thinking to strengthen the Village, not destroy it. This place had so much unrealized potential. Perhaps to buttress my confidence, I needed some comparisons, so I asked, "Do you know of any other places like this? To my knowledge there are none in the United States."

"I do know of one. I even visited it. It's in Sweden." Without my asking she proceeded to give me her impressions. "It's better equipped, adapted, more luxurious and spacious, but it's socially backward. You don't see anyone in the streets. The people don't do anything. They sleep in the morning, look out the window in the afternoon, and drink at night. There is, however, one lesson to be learned from the Swedish center.

They have a long period before the person is allowed to move in, a time when they can get to know all the appliances and tasks."

This highlighted the lack of such a break-in period at Het Dorp. In a place so concerned with independence, I would have thought everything possible would have been done to prevent people from slipping into old ways. New people needed lots of support as they literally "fumbled" their way through their opening months, finding out what they could and could not do. Then again, maybe the informal system of socialization was stronger than I or Mrs. van Amerongen realized.

From problems of entree, she turned to the consequences of the view of the Village as a place from which people never leave. "There are other problems of the Village because of how it is looked on, as a final solution. They assume the people here do not need or want certain things, like education or sex."

At the mention of sex, I told her of the dilemmas Mr. Gans had mentioned.

She wrinkled her nose and shook her head in disbelief. "I don't know—like that workshop he spoke about—I can't believe they really want it. Every time some of us press for money to really get it going, they always claim there are higher priorities. And those lectures he spoke of, why they were almost all on reproduction and not really about sex."

As she spoke, I thought of the Pandora's box Mr. Gans had to deal with. "I don't envy him. Maybe on some, albeit unconscious, level, he realizes that if they seriously start talking about sex they may see how totally unprepared they are to deal with all that might be needed. They're still dealing with the issue of marriage and housing. That's at least a technically simpler problem. But sexuality . . ." I shared my own ambivalence about what it entails to help someone else with sex.

She sympathized but wouldn't let go. "I agree it won't be easy. We've got to start some place and some time. Life isn't over for us. For some it's just beginning!" Both her voice and her hand shook with emphasis. And in a more reflective and almost more depressing tone, she continued, "There are so many things that I and others want to learn about. It's as if they think there is no need to teach us anything more. Don't they know there are many ways in which we want to improve?"

No answer was called for and I nodded my head in agreement. As I did, I recalled the times in my own introduction to the Village when I was corrected again and again for referring to it as a rehabilitation center. "No rehabilitation takes place here." From this dead-end perspective flowed all too many negative implications.

Mrs. van Amerongen ended our conversation with a sigh, "The best life is one where there is some integration of the Dorp with the outside."

I agreed with her, but felt the need to elaborate. "Yes, but it's not necessarily just an integration in physical sense. For survival the Village and its residents must always be tied to the outside, share its happiness and sadness, its shortcomings as well as its possibilities. But it must be done in some way that does not always confront them with their 'invalidity,' . . ." When I realized that I was giving a speech, I stopped myself. "Sorry for being so long-winded. I guess you tapped into something I was thinking about." The vague rumblings I had felt when Gans spoke of "integration" had finally surfaced.

"You did the same for me. Thank you for listening to a foolish woman talk," she said.

"I wish all my conversations were full of such foolish talk."

She smiled. I wished I weren't in a wheelchair. What I wanted to do was hug her. Maybe she knew this, for there was something special in her goodbye.

I sat by myself for some time. When I next looked at my watch it was nearly three o'clock. My time here was drawing to a close. Who was the student? Who the teacher? Who the respondent? Who the researcher? The lines were certainly blurred. Maybe they always were, but we social scientists have a trained incapacity to see that. I once more scanned the room. There was much to do. I wanted to capture all that had happened, but today it could wait. In a few hours we were having Nasi Goreng, my favorite Indonesian dish, to "celebrate" my departure. I wanted to return the compliment, so I had to do some shopping on my own. The only logical place was the supermarket, so off I trekked.

Although I knew the shortcuts, under a full head of steam I chose the hills, taking them easily, guiding myself, saving my strength for the steeper parts. Once there, I felt like an old-timer. I window-shopped. The travel posters caught my eye. For me they were no longer a fantasy; within two weeks I would be flying KLM to the States.

In the market I knew where things were, and asked un-embarrassedly for help when I needed it. Savoring the selection before me, I purchased the largest bottle of wine available, a magnum. With it in my web bag and that snuggled behind me in the seat and tied to the edge of my chair, I took off. The downhill trip went fairly fast, perhaps not with quite the grace and speed of Pieter, but getting there. Occasionally I let go and glided, confident that I could bring myself to a gradual halt if necessary. It was a tremendously satisfying excursion—hard to believe that barely a week ago the same trip left me physically and psycho-logically dissipated. By the time I returned home it was just after four, and there was plenty of time to collect my thoughts before dinner.

When I arrived for dinner, everyone was there. There was a tension in the air. Maybe it was all in me, but I broke it with the raising of the wine bottle. The Nasi Goreng was brought out and we ate and drank with gusto. Everyone made sure that I had second helpings. Mieke teased me about not drinking too much. Jos started a series of toasts to me, and America, and I returned the compliment. But a sadness lay over us. The usual joking and storytelling were absent.

We continued to toast one another. I thanked them for allowing me to share their meals and their lives. They, in turn, hoped I would return some day. But we really did not want to part, so one after another we made arrangements to meet again. Some made sure I'd drop by later, or would be there for the evening coffee or tomorrow's breakfast. I willingly agreed to all the requests as well as to a more formal leave-taking after coffee with my two closest friends, Jos and Pieter. True to their prediction, I no longer felt like a visitor. The Village was not quite "my home" but close. Much, sometimes I thought too much, had happened to me here.

At eight I was back again. To my surprise, so was everyone else. Not only my friends but a friend of Mieke's and both dogelas. Jos opened, "Well, I guess you'll be glad to be back home with all your friends?" There was something in his tone which conveyed a different question, "Won't you be glad to leave us?"

It was to the unasked question that I responded. "It's not all that easy to leave." I wanted to say that I would not forget but I did not know how. I took the safer intellectual route, "I know I feel very different now about myself and about this place than when I first came. I hope to write something about my experience. When I do, you can be sure that you will see it."

There was some kidding about their being in print and the pall of sadness lifted. The connection was lost on me, but from being in print, we shifted to stories we had read and then to our old style of sexy jokes and innuendoes.

When the last bit of wine had been finished, Pieter grounded us again. With mock solemnity he intoned, "We would be so honored, Professor Zola, if you would autograph this bottle." I was embarrassed, but with a flourish I wrote my name in full, Irving Kenneth Zola, and dated it. Mrs. Schmid, who I hadn't noticed was beside me, shyly asked if she could have the bottle. Placing it carefully in her lap she wheeled her chair to the side of the room and then pushed herself to a standing position. It was the first time I had seen her stand. Shakily she stretched and placed the bottle atop the highest cabinet. As we all watched, Ms. Nijhof said, "Now it will always look down and remind us." No one, including myself, could add anything, so with the remark we departed, substituting only "goodbyes" for the usual "good nights."

Mieke did not leave immediately, so I quickly wheeled over to catch her. I didn't know what to say but she spared me the opening. "I wish you happiness, and a safe trip and return. I also want to thank you for the pleasure of your company."

That seemed an awkward phrase but real. The usual bana-
lities stuck in my throat. I could not say that I would write or
return soon. The only thing that seemed right was an even older
cliché, but clichés exist because they express some truth. So I
said it, "I will always remember you and the Village. Thank you
for the pleasure of your company." Our hands touched. It was
neither a greeting, nor a parting, just a final bit of warmth. She
left and I turned toward Pieter and Jos, who were waiting for
me.

Jos's room was a welcome relief. He went right to his small
refrigerator, bringing out cold beer and cheese, and we settled
in for an evening of serious drinking and conversation. Jos was
anxious to organize the residents. I supported the idea, but he
wanted more than that. "You must help us. You must help us
see what to do. Maybe stay here longer or do something. I ask
this, for I am amazed. You see things in three days that I only see
after three years. How do you, a foreigner, see what I miss?
How, that is the question."

It really wasn't a question, it was a compliment. The real
question was what we could do for the Village. With no ready
answers I could only share some of my thoughts about living
arrangements becoming even more similar to those on the outside. Like me, they sensed it might be too soon to make concrete
proposals. The conversation became more personal, but it was
just another way of dealing with the same question. Pieter
asked, "O.K., how would you live here? Could you?"

Jos asked, "What would you do if you got worse?"

I sensed that Jos was not saying "if" but "when." "I guess I
would try and make it as long as I could on the outside. If I
couldn't, then I would probably fight to the bitter end any effort
to make me dependent." Jacob Veere's, casting off of his neck
brace flashed through my mind. "I would keep oriented to the
outside world as long as possible. I do not think I could work in
the sheltered workshop, at least as presently set up. I would
more likely work in the inner organization. And though I would
gradually make a life for myself here I would probably never
give up on the outside."

Pieter asked, "What does that mean?"

"I don't think I would ever try to forget completely what it was like, or regard it as all past. I don't mean as nostalgia, but as part of me. Like the other night with you, Mieke, and Monika, I might tell stories about when I played football or something like that, not with any conscious sense of regret, but because what I recalled was just interesting or funny or illustrated some point. I guess all this would depend on the kind and degree of physical impairment I suffered, but that's how I feel about it now."

Both Pieter and Jos seemed to understand, but I wondered if they did. I was not trying to criticize the Village or the way they had dealt with their physical problems. "Do you understand how much of this is all my way of handling problems? I don't mean that I would rather be somewhere else. For some things, I know for sure that I would rather be here in the Netherlands. To give birth or to grow old and certainly to be handicapped, I would want to be here rather than in the U.S."

They look puzzled and Jos spoke for both of them when he wondered why I would want to experience such important events in an alien land.

My only answer was that "if I really had the opportunity or desire to experience these things, I guess I would no longer feel a foreigner." My own words surprised me. Would I really leave the U.S. to come here? Maybe I would. No place besides the Netherlands had ever felt as much like home to me. In some ways it was my home. I had started a new life here, a second beginning.

But for Jos and Pieter, whatever their disgruntlements with its materialism, the United States still held out possibilities. They pressed me with questions about new medical techniques and procedures. "Isn't it right that they have a new procedure for . . . ?" asked Jos. "Aren't there new kinds of wheelchairs being developed in . . . ?" I felt uninformed. They knew far more about new rehabilitation procedures than I.

Within the questions, however, was a more depressing message. Referring to their frustration with new advances, first Jos and then Pieter reported that awful moment when after some operation, the surgeon said, "I'm sorry, nothing more can be done." They were both resigned to this and at the same time not. Their reading of medical literature was more than "hope springing eternal," it was another way of making nothing in their lives a dead-end.

From faraway places, Pieter, the realist, brought us back to the Village. Responding to something we had spoken of nearly a half-hour before, he said, "I'm a little less involved. Perhaps I am less sensitive to the problems because I live alone, by myself." While that was part of it, he also soon planned to marry Monika and leave the Dorp.

Jos must have made the same association and then thought, "When Pieter leaves, it will be a pity for me. I will lose a friend." Where friends were so hard to come by, such a loss was a serious one. Both Mieke and Marlene had said the same thing.

The issue of loss must have led to other associations, for Jos spoke of the "missing resident." "He kept falling, and was in constant pain, so finally they decided to operate. He will never be able to walk again. He will be like us." This seemed more a sad factual commentary than anything else. Jos obviously liked him and went on to say that despite his speech impediment, "He has good brains."

This was not the first time that I had heard such a remark. In fact, I'd heard it so often that I thought it must be a reminder to both the speaker and the listener. To all it said, "Don't judge by our surface appearances or limitations. We are all much more, much more."

From this point the mood lightened and we talked of sports, TV, and travel. At 10:30 our real, final departure time had come. We spoke of trying to maintain contact and Pieter asked for my address. Jos said, "Now we'll have someone to visit there!" Pieter agreed. But to myself I wondered about having a place that was physically accessible, with ramps. Would it be just for them? Would I need such a place some day? Maybe sooner than I'd like to think.

"I'm a terrible correspondent, but I think I will write about the Village or people with handicaps. When I do, I will share it with you. And whenever I return to Europe I will try to return here." They smiled but I wondered if they thought I would ever come back. I would, I promised myself.

Again in an attempt to postpone the inevitable, we agreed to meet for breakfast. Apparently Jos was not an early riser so Pieter kidded him about getting up in the morning. "It will change your whole schedule and what you'll see in the world." We all laughed.

The whole evening had been a delight. I was sorry to see it end. As I wheeled toward the door, I noticed that they had dressed up for the occasion. After dinner, both of them had shaved and Pieter now wore a clean shirt and tie. With things like this, I gradually became aware that I, and my stay, meant more to them than perhaps I wanted to realize.

So for the final time I drove home. I went slowly, savoring this last night trip. I met no one and was greeted along the way only by empty wheelchairs and the low whirring of their electric batteries being recharged. The image stayed with me. Throughout my final note-taking and my deep though restless sleep, I too felt that I was being recharged. And I had the sense that it would "take" and be long-lasting.

9

Gone but Not Forgotten

Wednesday, May 31

I awoke quite early, about 7:00 A.M. The calendar beside the clock caught my eye. In the United States it was Memorial Day, a time to remember loved ones lost in war. That my day of departure was officially set aside for remembering seemed a good omen. Maybe I will always recall my friends on this day.

But more mundane matters like packing faced me. I really hate this eternal moving, leaving what I'm used to, going on to something unexpected. It's not the newness of place which upsets me, but the process of getting there. I seem plagued by questions related to my physical condition. Will I be cramped on the plane? Will I have many stairs to climb and long corridors to walk? Will I have allowed myself enough time? Will I need help? Can I get it if I need it? Packing was somehow a prelude to all these difficulties. Reaching for clothes, balancing them on my lap, folding them neatly into my travelling bags, each was a problem. The table was just a little too high for me to peer easily into my suitcase. The shelves were just a little too low and deep for me to reach. And there, way in the back, was a pair of socks, taunting me. For a moment I thought of leaving them there as a reminder of my visit, the socks for my immobile feet. Letting anger get the better of me, I overreached and my wheelchair tipped precariously. The gesture was wholly unnecessary. It was as if I were trying to prove something to myself as I moved back into the world of the normal. On the outside I would have known that the socks were unreachable and used something to get them. But during this transition, even with no one around, I had to do it "fully myself." The words themselves stuck. For the first time I was getting uncomfortable with some of the behaviors I tied to being a "full" or "whole" human being. Leaning back in my chair, I let this sink in and as I did I saw a coat hanger, the perfect tool for my purpose, and with it retrieved my errant socks. I held the rolled-up pair in my hand, a painful reminder of a new self toward which I was striving. Placing the socks almost preciously in my suitcase, I looked around for other "last matters." On my table was the lamp I had borrowed from Pieter. Placing it on my lap, I left for breakfast.

Balancing the lamp was not so risky a task as it once had been. It and I arrived safely and on time. In fact, no one else was there. To my rear I heard the spin of wheels. It was Pieter and right behind was Jos. Pieter mockingly greeted him, "I'm glad you could make it so early." Jos grumbled in reply and we all laughed.

The sun shone brightly through the window and we talked about the nice weather for leaving. Jos again threatened "to descend upon me in America."

Then Pieter as always shifted to serious matters. "Will you remember how to walk?"

I laughed, albeit uncomfortably, "Yes, I'll probably remember though I guess I'll be rather stiff. It will take me a while to get used to it."

They smiled about an experience they would never have "to endure."

"It's a pity you had such a short time." Pieter's words were well-chosen. It was a "pity" I could not stay longer, but part of me wanted to remain and part wanted to leave. And the latter was linked to a latent fear. The figure in fiction whom I most disliked passed through my mind—Hans Castorp of Thomas Mann's *The Magic Mountain*. Like him, I came as a visitor to a medical refuge. As with him, the line between myself and the others blurred and almost disappeared. The Village became more and more comfortable, and the outside world more cold and inhospitable. But also like Hans, I felt this was not my home, at least not yet, and it was time to go.

Pieter interrupted my reverie with a message from
Monika, who sent her best wishes for a safe trip home. I thanked
him and returned to the now ancient theme of keeping in touch.
Pieter asked if I had written anything that might be of help to
them. I remembered my paper on mutual aid groups and agreed
to send it along when it was published. As we were leaving,
Pieter asked me to stop by his room on the way out of the
building.

After saying goodbye to Jos, I turned to the dogelas with
whom I had a final bit of business. As I matter-of-factly explained what they should do with my wheelchair after I'd gone, a
sense of bewilderment appeared in their voices. In awkard
phrasing they seemed to be asking, "Why should we take *your*
wheelchair? How will you manage?" For them my resident
identity had succeeded too well. Though they knew I was a
professor and a visitor, they also thought of me as a resident and
handicapped. How could I "leave behind my wheelchair" and
"walk away" from the Dorp?

I drove quickly back to my room to meet Metz, who was
prompt as usual. I wanted just a moment to look around. I told
him it was to make sure that I had not forgotten anything, but
really it was to say goodbye to my surroundings. This room had
become more than just a place to rest and sleep. It, like the
Netherlands, had become another home, a place briefly experienced but which would be long remembered.*

When we left, Metz once again resumed pushing me. My
suitcase lay firmly on my lap, as did my cane. I gripped it very
tightly, this link to my old self. I had neither held nor even
looked at it for a week. It felt solid and comforting in my hands.
On the way down the corridors, people waved. They seemed to
know I was leaving and shouted! "Farewell, Good trip!"

As we rolled down the street, I told Metz of my promise to
knock at Pieter's. He must have been expecting me, for my tap

---

*Reading this remark some time later, I recalled that Margaret Mead in her autobiogra-
phy, *Blackberry Winter* (New York: Pocket Books, 1975), describes how she came to
think of many places where she had experienced comfort and growth as "home,"
regardless of the length of stay.

was greeted by an instant opening of the door. We moved forward till our wheelchairs almost touched. Looking straight at me he said, "I hope we will meet again," and after a pause, "I want to thank you for all the pleasure you've brought to us these past few days. I don't know if I say right in English but God bless you," and he extended his hand. I grabbed it but I couldn't say anything but a mumbled "Thank you."

"May I go with you to the door?"

I smiled yes and asked Metz to let go of my wheelchair. We drove silently to the outside entrance, one behind the other, as we had so many times before. He then said a final goodbye.

The door opened automatically as it always did. Metz rejoined me and pushed me outside to within about five yards of his Volkswagen, which he'd driven onto the pathway. He held the wheelchair as I pushed myself to a standing position. My leg brace locked into place and I was fully upright. I was indeed stiff and awkward, but it was good to be on my feet again. He smilingly handed me my cane, and I was once more "complete." I shook my left leg to get the kinks out and then bent over slightly to straighten out my right pants leg. The lining always got caught when I stood but, of course, this had not been a problem these last seven days. I also checked my pockets, something I always did when about to leave home. Assuring myself that all was in "good working order," I slowly, almost testing myself, took my first step toward the car. As I walked these five yards, I had the feeling that I was not alone. The building was behind but as I, turned to back into the front seat I was once more face-to-face with my friends. Pieter had come out a side door to watch me depart and at all the windows of my social unit sat the others, a small phalanx of wheelchairs and movable beds. They were all smiling and gesturing wildly. In my mind's eye they were not so much waving goodbye as cheering me on as one would a messenger. Their arms were raised so high that they seemed to be reaching, but with a clenched fist. I was making it. I was fulfilling their hopes. I was returning to the outside, but miracle of miracles, I was returning in a better state than before. I had been in a wheelchair and *now* I walked out under my own power! Would others leave in a *better* state? "Better" need not just mean physically more able. Maybe that was part of the message from the residents—Het Dorp, a place not merely of "is" but "could be," not merely of limits but potentialities. I smiled, waved, and clenched my fist in return.

The short ride to Metz's house was passed in silence. I didn't realize I'd want to be so alone when I'd accepted this invitation to a farewell coffee. Thus, it was with considerable ambivalence that I sat down with the Metzs and the Langletts, and I guess it showed when they gently pressed me for my impression of the Dorp. Although we covered a wide range of topics, everything I said I'd uttered and recorded before. It was as if by not pushing myself to new insights, I could in an almost magical way make the experience last longer.

The conversation continued uneventfully until I tried to convey the meaning of "freedom" at Het Dorp. I recounted my original puzzlement over resident remarks about how much freer they felt here than even in their own home. "It took me a while to understand this. And what helped the most was when I was able to get back into my own life and recall my own feeling of having to always call on my mother and father. I guess that no matter how much one is loved by the helper there is still the inevitable feeling in our society of imposition and guilt." Obviously identifying with my experience, the recently blinded Mrs. Langlett turned lovingly to her husband and silently confirmed my words.

Interestingly, we ended almost where we had begun a week earlier. Then they had sharply disabused me of the notion of the Dorp as a place for rehabilitation. I now argued that their insistence on this notion did a disservice to the residents. "The Village is many things to many people and its very flexibility is perhaps its greatest strength. For a far larger number than anyone is aware, a great deal of physical, adaptational, social psychological, and vocational learning does take place. There are many residents that I don't know really well. But what impressed me is that so many seem to have grown and learned so much *after* they came, *after* their rehabilitation was supposedly over."

I heard myself almost shouting, but my friends were still with me, though they looked puzzled.

"Maybe I'm not saying it clearly, but I mean more than that they are adapting well here. That seems too passive a term. I mean something more. They are learning social and even physical skills that they never had before."

This seemed to strike a responsive chord, and both Dr. Metz and Dr. Langlett added examples of people who had learned new skills.

As we spoke, I saw the irony in all this. For while the Dorp made it all possible, it did so despite the operating assumption that the Village was the end of the road. I now realized that this was true only in the limited sense that many residents would spend the rest of their active lives here. With its possibilities for living and working arrangements, and a social life, the Village opened up awareness previously closed. It was clear, for example, that those who created the Village never expected that the residents would be able, let alone want, to marry. For some few, the Village was but a way-station, where they put together these new skills, tested themselves and their capabilities, and then departed. What was possible for all was growth and development. In fact, one of the problems of the Village was the increased independence of a significant number of residents. Some, after trying their wings and getting a taste of what life could bring, wanted it *now,* not when someone else told them they were ready. The image of an oppressed minority was not so bizarre. That the administrators keeping them down did not realize it, that much of what was done for the Villagers was done for their own benefit, that their problem was one of sickness not misdeed—all these considerations did not make the end result any less oppressive. For others, many of whom once were "valid," their arguments and criticisms were not just reactions against dependence. They were not fighting for independence. They were fighting for their lives. As long as they struggled, they were alive. In a sense that was what the Dorp was all about, an eternal struggle to be alive and vital. Surely it was not a battle that all were winning. Yet the fact that the battle was even being waged is a tribute to those who founded, staff, and live in the Village.

The warmth I felt toward these people was even greater than a week previous. Then they welcomed me as a stranger, now they bade me farewell as a friend.

As planned, Metz drove me to the station. Again, for two such verbal people, we were notably silent. As we walked down the platform, I looked up at this very special person. I said, "Thank you for your help and your encouragement. Without it I never would have come." But to myself I wondered how to thank him for his example, his courage, his caring. He extended his hand and I grasped it, holding it longer, trying to say with a touch what I failed to say in words. The train noisily intruded. With a heft of my suitcase, a backward glance, and a wave, I left a part of my life. No, not true, I said to myself, a part of my life had just begun. No, that sounded too dramatic. Reclaimed, recaptured, hopefully reintegrated—these words fit better.

Settled in my seat I felt restless. I tried unsuccessfully to nap or relax. Nothing worked. Partly I was overtired. I didn't sleep well the previous night. Images of events and people had kept intruding, so at times during that night I had turned on the light to make notes. As I sat here in my seat, it was as if I were letting myself fully acknowledge what I had been experiencing. With this came the strong wish to talk about the Village.

Partly I wanted to just tell what had happened and partly I needed an audience to help me sort out the uniquely personal from the socially relevant. I sought some limited aspect of my experience on which I could safely dwell. In setting out a pad of paper on my lap, I experienced a feeling of *déjà vu*. I began this trip by writing down my expectations. Now as I returned, I began the long process of figuring out what I'd learned.

These thoughts about comings and goings seemed as good a place as any to start. In any field work situation, there are problems of entree and acceptance. Within my first hours six days before, I had felt "bad vibes" coming from the Administration. As I recorded in my notes, this precipitated a crisis, one I resolved by rejecting a position of neutrality and seeking an alliance with the residents. Whatever I might have lost by this move seemed outweighed by the opening it provided. I still thought of myself an outsider in the sense that I was a foreigner and a professor, but to the Villagers, the overriding identification was my status as a curiously different handicapped person. On the other hand, my very "differentness" also proved to be an asset. My being an American and a successful one in terms of status (being a professor) and family (having been married with two children) made me as much a fund of information to them as they were to me. Thus, the difficulty of starting conversations or even probing sensitive areas (by my standards, sensitive; not necessarily by theirs) was largely mitigated. Many of our meetings began with their questioning me about my handicap and how I managed. To ask them in turn about theirs was not only fair but natural. In fact, I had never felt so comfortable in an interviewing situation. It was as if, for the first time, I was truly able to pay back respondents for what they had shared with me. In so equal but atypical a research situation, I began to understand recent writings of some social scientists who claimed that any research situation had the potential of exploitation because one party gets a great deal but returns very little.

My acceptance by the residents was also expedited by my refusing a guest room and insisting on a wheelchair. These acts made the differences in our physical difficulty something that would not be continually confronted and also proved that I meant what I said about "living as a resident." Saying was, of course, not the same as doing. And so the test of the first day, my shopping excursion with Pieter. A further test turned out to be my using a hand-operated rather than an electric wheelchair. Not only was this appropriate to my "resumed condition," but it also further committed me physically as well as psychologically to "living it like it was." Though I had not fully realized it at the time, it probably also showed to the Villagers that I would not take the easy way out. In fact, as I wrote this, it became clear to me that during my stay, I had never consciously taken the easy way. Put more strongly, I had never "cheated." This was important to me for several reasons. To have cheated when no one was around would not only have seemed unfair and dishonest, but it would have cut me off from some very important behavioral and psychological data. I was only alone when in my room and to have been my old self there would have deprived me of a fuller appreciation of the physical (the details of daily hygiene) and emotional (the feelings of loneliness) aspects of living in the Village.

In this sense, I had gone farther than many investigators who in their private, out-of-the-field space try to create a bit of their old home.

I was also proving something to myself, though I am not yet sure what. Perhaps the journey into Het Dorp was the only way to get back in touch with a part of myself that I had long rejected—my physical disability. What I had done at the Village was to live out in a totally unexpected way one of my favorite denial mechanisms. For most of the past twenty years I have, at least once a day, "mislaid" my cane, usually in another room or behind a chair. I have then had to search all about for my lost "appendage." As a professor, I integrated this into the "absent-mindedness" supposedly characteristic of my occupation. At the Dorp, I really put aside the cane and had to do without it. But instead of feeding my denial, the loss served to reinforce, if not validate, my dependence on the cane.

Whatever else this experience had been, it was one of the most exhausting and intense experiences of my life. I was always "on." Every minute was an opportunity to observe and learn something. If it was not appropriate to talk with someone, then it was appropriate to examine my own behavior and reactions. I felt I retained my "true self" more than I ordinarily would in a research situation. While I was no more active or passive than usual, all my senses felt "finely tuned." But the visit did take a tremendous amount out of me psychologically. As anticipated, it unearthed old anxieties and generated new ones. But my anticipation had been only theoretical. I had no idea how deeply I would feel things.

I was also totally unprepared for the bodily strain. The trips around the Village took their toll. My arms and back continually ached. I had been unaware of how difficult and complex were tasks that in my previous life had been so simple. My bouts with illness and my hospitalizations had not been as directly relevant as I had expected. In those situations, there was almost always someone on hand, a nurse, an aide, a friend, a relative, to help me. At Het Dorp I was expected to do much more on my own. It was in many ways a much less sheltered environment. As a result, a lot more energy, both physical and psychological, had to be expended on mundane tasks such as washing clothes, opening doors, and moving from one place to another.

For all these reasons it was a real pleasure to follow an old field work dictum, namely to spend almost as much time recording as observing. The period of recording became an occasion for reflection and interpretation of the day's events. The act of transcription also had a cathartic value, giving me release from the intensity of the experience, allowing me to work through some of the issues and also establish some protective distance from them.

As I wrote these notes, I realize that everything I had recorded, every word, every conversation, was in English. Many of the residents not only spoke English but were especially desirous of any opportunity to practice it. Where conversations did take place with someone who knew little English, usually there was someone around who was willing to translate. Finally, on those occasions when no English was available, our commitment to communicate overrode its absence. We managed either through some other language (usually French or German) or gesture to tell each other "our stories." Dutch, of course, was used all around me, so my comprehension and vocabulary increased enormously. Had I stayed a month I might well have been speaking Dutch, though with abominable pronounciation. On the other hand, my lack of Dutch produced two interesting results. Since everyone assumed I knew none, many conversations, particularly over the dinner table, took place *as if* I were not there, thus leading to a more relaxed atmosphere. My previous nine months in the Netherlands had, however, not proved a total waste language-wise, and it was soon apparent that I understood far more than either they or I had anticipated. On the occasions when Dutch was used purposely to prevent my understanding, I could usually figure out the gist. The language lack also led me to pay particular attention to nonverbal behavior—not only gestures and affect, but the ways in which people used their bodies and their wheelchairs as extensions of their bodies. On the whole, it was relatively easy to communicate, and this might be partly due to something else that was going on, a special common language. An analogy would be the ease I have always had, because of the similarity in technical vocabularies, in reading foreign sociological journals as opposed to foreign newspapers or novels. With the Villagers and me there was a tremendous overlap in vocabularies—from the technical language of our equipment to the emotional language of our handicapped experience.

What troubled me most was the amount of time I spent at the Village. It was barely a week. I felt the relative, but not the absolute, deprivation. The separation from friends and loved ones was only temporary, and most important, I knew it. The lack of time may have also led me to be too impatient, not merely to expect too much of the Administration and the residents, but perhaps to miss the subtleties and nuances of their situations. Moreover, there were obviously people I did not see. I had no knowing contact with anyone who was severely depressed, completely disillusioned with the Village, or a social isolate, though I did meet people spread along the continua of depression, disillusionment, and isolation. Partly this lack was a matter of time, but partly it went deeper. It is not inconceivable that many such people would either not be selected for residence or would be among those who left quickly. It might also be a fair guess that the most isolated residents would probably be the ones with whom, because of language, culture, or personal disposition, I would have the most difficulty communicating, no matter how long I stayed in the Village.

The group I most regretted not seeing more of was the staff. With the dogelas this was wholly a matter of time. The kind of person it takes to work in such settings is a subject worthy of separate attention. Whatever selection policy was used seemed to work well. I heard residents occasionally complain about efficiency but never about callousness. The biggest problem may be one common to many such settings, namely an air of hopelessness and despair that occasionally affects the staff so deeply that they either leave or become necessarily more distant and uninvolved. This may have been partly solved by the Village hiring policy. With only my impressions to go on, I thought the dogelas were of predominantly two types. One group was of middle-aged women, past childbearing age, perhaps even widowed or divorced, who seemed strong, yet gentle and motherly, good people to have for a neighbor and friend. For them, the job was long-term and familial. The second group was characterized by its youth. Many of the dogelas I met were either engaged to be married or soon hoped to be. They were attractive, friendly, and exuberant women, giving off a spirit that often seemed contagious. To those few I spoke with, working at the Village was temporary. No matter that the job lasted several years, the perception guaranteed psychological escape. These two types of dogelas may also have embodied several key elements of the Dorp. The older women with their strength and motherliness symbolized the importance of shelter, comfort, safety, whereas the younger women stimulated the potential for growth, development, even sexuality.

To know the rest of the administrative staff, however, would have taken more than a longer stay. To get fully into their perspective would have required working in their world. To do it justice my participant-observation would have to have been done from a staff position.

This last statement hopefully suggests something that pervaded all my observations—the shattering of a certain smugness I never thought I had about the ease of trying to communicate

the way it looks from "the other side." Again and again I
recorded my tripping over prejudice I never thought I had. I can
best convey my new appreciation by contrasting two experiences—Het Dorp and the one that started me on the field-work
road many years earlier.

In the spring of 1959 I was hired as a staff member of the
anthropological research team studying the redevelopment of
the West End of Boston.* Through a series of fortuitous circumstances too detailed to be recorded here, I found myself
converted from the position of interviewer to that of "undercover" field observer. In this role I spent nearly four months,
passing as a former resident, never revealing fully who I was,
and eventually leaving the scene, as did many real residents,
when the last of our hangouts was destroyed. It was an adventure in many senses of the word, but what has stayed with me
over the years is not the escapades I engaged in (good for
cocktail-party conversation), but the identification I felt with
those I studied. For instance, one day in a bar, the owner, angry
at several of us for being too loud, picked up a wet rag and flung
it at no one in particular. It hit me square in the face. As it lay
draped across my head, I picked up a glass of beer to toss back.
As I raised my hand, she looked at me defiantly and said, "*You!
You're just like all the *rest!*" With a sense of pride, more to do
with the issue of belonging than imitation, I said a silent thank
you, smiled, and put down the glass.

The West End was an extraordinary experience in part
because it drew upon so many facets of my life that had been
submerged as I climbed the academic ladder. In 1959 I was a
third-year graduate student in the Harvard Department of Social Relations with a Harvard B.A. behind me and a Ph.D.
looming ahead. At the time it seemed quite an accomplishment

*My own research was subsequently published as "Observations of Gambling in a
Lower-Class Setting," *Social Problems* 10, no. 4 (April 1963): 353–361. Other publica-
tions emanating from the larger project included Herbert Gans, *The Urban Villagers*
(New York: Free Press, 1962); several papers included in Leonard Duhl, ed., *The Urban
Condition* (New York: School and Society Books, 1969); and Mark Fried, *The World of
the Urban Working Class* (Cambridge: Harvard University Press, 1973).

for a Dorchester boy, perhaps not so much for my immediate circle of friends (of twenty-five boyhood chums, almost all had gone to Boston Latin School and thence to Harvard or other Ivy League colleges), but certainly from the point of view of the Zola family group. My father was the youngest of eight boys and two girls who lived to adulthood, and at the time I was only the third Zola to get any college education at all.

My involvement in the West End project caused no end of dismay in my immediate family. While my mother was distressed by this "sinking" into the lower classes she was trying so desperately to escape, my father was absolutely delighted. For the first time since I was a little boy, he could not only share an activity with me but also transmit specific skills. It was with great pride that he took me to a local pool room, introduced me as his Harvard-professor son, and then told how he was instructing me in the fine art of billiards and eight-ball. In addition, he re-schooled me in barroom slang and behavior and the ins and outs of gambling. All this made my mother so upset that she never wanted to hear about my work and for the first time in her life stopped asking, "How are you doing in school?" For that matter, the long hours, the night work, and the occasional return home in a slightly inebriated condition did not always sit well with my wife, who at that time was also pursuing a graduate degree.

My West End work also crystallized other issues. Though trained in survey and statistical methods, I had always had a gnawing doubt about their limitations. As a graduate student I was a close admirer of C. Wright Mills and of the psychoanalytic insights scattered interestingly enough by my anthropological (William Caudill, Clyde Kluckhohn) and sociological mentors (William McCord, Ted Mills, Talcott Parsons, Phil Slater). The West End gave substance to this doubt, as I for the first time felt a texture and depth in what I was studying. It also gave me a taste, albeit a guilty one, of what it meant to use every facet of my being in my work. Not only was I able to use my senses, what *I* saw, felt, and heard, but I also could draw on parts of me that traditional participant-observation did not ordinarily mention, like my background. Being working-class, being Jewish, having grown up in Dorchester and Mattapan, having worked at manual labor for several years in a factory, and having had polio were not merely interesting things to talk about with my fellow West Enders but were directly drawn upon in my work. This was so mind-blowing, so contrary to the trained objectivity of the then-current social science, that I could only relish this feeling of totality very privately, feeling guilty that I was betraying my training by using such extraneous and personal factors to enhance my grasp of the research situation.

There was, however, another dimension to this experience, which started then but in some ways could only simmer for a decade. For there was a real surprise in what I *learned*. I don't mean merely the excitement of *learning* something new, but rather the shock of discovering something that I thought, by the very virtue of who I was, I should have known. After all, I was not really investigating an alien culture. What fascinated me was why, in some ways, it had become that. Starting then, and culminating in Het Dorp, was the disturbing fact that my socialization (courtesy of two loving Jewish parents), my education, and all the energy devoted to "overcoming" my polio and my accident had indeed made me distant and separate from part of myself. (It wasn't until I got to college that I even thought of myself as working class. Only then did I discover that I alone of my closest friends had a father who was a blue-collar worker.) Knowing what I do about psychology, I'm not completely sorry that this process took place. I'm not sure that I could be where I am (largely happy in my work and life) if I had not been able to regard certain elements of my life as alien to me, to be overcome, to be put behind me. But it did have a cost, one I'm only now beginning to appreciate and understand.

My Het Dorp experience in many ways paralleled, heightened, and reawakened the West End issues. Once more I saw how incomplete had been previous sociological accounts, in this case of people with chronic illnesses and physical handicaps. (In a sense, the more statistical were such accounts, as in the studies of sexual ability and capacity, the more unrepresentative they were of the experience.) Once more my faith in experiential methods was confirmed. Once more I was able to draw upon aspects of my personal and social background, though *every* aspect of my being seemed relevant to the task of understanding the nature of being "invalid." And all of it was done knowingly and without guilt. This time *I* was no undercover observer with all the attendant ethical issues on my conscience. This time the biggest secrets were those hidden from myself.

While the details of my blind spots may be unique, I am not sure that the process of distancing and its results are not of general concern. In particular I have serious doubts about how much social and emotional separation from those we study *is* necessary. Much, now I suspect too much, has been written about the problems of "going native" or "becoming overidentified" with the people or phenomenon one is investigating. At one historical moment, this was probably a very important issue, for there may have been a tendency to glorify, more than understand, nonliterate groups, exotic cultures, quaint customs. But today awareness rather than noninvolvement seems our best defense against such overstepping.* Many social scientists are in fact beginning to note how difficult, if not impossible, it was and is to be value-neutral or to divorce oneself completely from one's values or one's personal and social history. The new admonition then is to at least acknowledge and state explicitly what these values are.

I would go further. We can make use of these "realities" to continually ask how one is like or different from what one is observing. It's no longer enough to be aware that as a researcher

---

*In rereading this comment, I see an analogy to my work about doctor-patient encounters. There, too, much has been made about the social and emotional distance "necessary" for physicians and therapists to treat their patients. As in the above example, this separation may once have been quite functional. With no anesthesia and with death a common outcome of serious illness and hospitalization, few would have been able to continue their work without such "steeling." Though the realities that produced this distancing have long since passed, the educative process that brought it about still remains. We now hear about cold, unfeeling doctors and therapists who are so removed from the patients they wish to help that they cannot understand and thus help them deal with their pain, their suffering, their chronic loss, and their eventual dying.

one is part of the research situation and thus altering it. As part of the research situation, the researcher himself or herself is worth studying. To fully account for the texture of everyday life, it is not sufficient to relegate to a methodological appendix or later memoirs, "What this experience meant to the investigators."* Rather we must look at that experience and see the anxieties, fears, delights, and repulsions as part of the very situation we are trying to understand. Thus, while social and emotional distancing once provided us with important objectivity and noninvolvement, it has now come to overemphasize the dissimilarities of human experience. Perhaps through the kind of self-examinations I have suggested, we can bridge the gap of understanding and restore some of the universality of the human condition.

In many ways I was neither the same person nor the same field-worker I had once been. Perhaps now I was only more conscious of something that had always been there. I was certainly not the value-free observer. Part of this I had fully incorporated into my research style, not only sharing experiences with the residents of Het Dorp but also ideas for change. I had felt truly on someone's side, the side of the Village against the world. How this had affected what I had seen and understood I wasn't sure, but it would affect what I would do about it and what I would write. On the whole, I felt great, different from when I started the trip barely a week before. In a sense the week had been my entire year in microcosm, a time of assessment of where I'd been and where I would want to go. And with it all, there was the hope that during the week I had "touched" some people. I hoped they were better for it. More than I could count had touched me.

A final reminder of my visit awaited me when I reached my destination. Up and down stairs I climbed, dragging, lifting, hauling my now even heavier suitcase. But now I did it unembarrassedly. This was me. There was no need to apologize. And this time instead of waiting humbly for an offer of help, since I no longer had to prove I could do it myself, I asked.

*Elenore S. Bowen, *Return to Laughter* (New York: Harper & Row, 1954) and Margaret Mead, *Blackberry Winter,* are examples of this genre.

PART THREE

AFTER

10

If Listening Is Hard, Telling Is Worse

Thoughts on the Improbable and Problematic
World of the Physically Handicapped and the
Chronically Ill

Not everything that is faced can be
changed, but nothing can be
changed until it is faced.

James Baldwin

"Why doesn't anyone understand what it's
like?" is a lament not only of the Villagers
but of many who try to convey to others the
nature of being physically handicapped or chronically ill. It is a
story difficult to hear as well as to tell, a difficulty rooted deep in
Western culture. Slater put it well.

> Our ideas about institutionalizing the aged, psychotic, re-
> tarded and infirm are based on a pattern of thought that we
> might call The Toilet Assumption—the notion that un-
> wanted matter, unwanted difficulties, unwanted complex-
> ities and obstacles will disappear if they are removed from
> our immediate field of vision. . . . Our approach to social
> problems is to decrease their visibility: out of sight, out of
> mind . . . The result of our social efforts has been to
> remove the underlying problems of our society farther and
> farther from daily experience and daily consciousness, and
> hence to decrease in the mass of the population, the knowl-
> edge, skill, resources, and motivation necessary to deal
> with them.*

It is, however, increasingly less acceptable to exile prob-
lem-bearers in faraway colonies, asylums, and sanitaria. A recent compromise has been to locate them in places which if not
geographically distant are socially distant, places with unfree
access like ghettos, special housing projects, nursing homes,

*Philip E. Slater, *The Pursuit of Loneliness: American Culture at the Breaking Point*
(Boston: Beacon press, 1970) p. 15.

and hospitals. This, too, is imperfect. So a final strategy makes these people socially indistinct. They are stereotyped.

I never fully appreciated the resultant distancing and isolation until it happened to me. I have previously described myself as using a cane, wearing a long leg brace and a back support, walking stiff-legged with a pronounced limp. All in all, I think of myself as fairly unusual in appearance and thus easily recognizable. And yet for years I have had the experience of being mistaken for someone else. Usually I was in a new place and a stranger would greet me as Tom, Dick, or Harry. After I explained that I was not he, they would usually apologize, saying, "You look just like him." Inevitably I would meet this Tom, Dick, or Harry and he would be several inches shorter or taller, forty pounds heavier or lighter, a double amputee on crutches or a paraplegic in a wheelchair. I was annoyed and even puzzled how anyone could mistake him for the "unique me." But I let it alone—until it happened again at the Village. Within a day virtually every resident knew who I was or what I looked like even without being introduced. Quite the opposite was true for the staff. As I drove through the grounds in my wheelchair. I evoked no sign of recognition. In any other Dutch context, my general appearance—long hair, sideburns, and casual garb—pegged me as a foreigner and an American. But here these characteristics went unnoticed and were irrlevant to my identity. Being in a wheelchair overshadowed all other features and I was assumed to be a regular resident. I was once even incorporated into a guided tour and heard myself described as "a typical Villager probably on his way to work." These experiences concretized a truth conveyed by the residents during my first few days—how the outside world chose to think of me. It did not matter whether I was a paraplegic, a spastic, someone with muscular dystrophy or multiple sclerosis. I was handicapped and "invalid" first and foremost, so much so that in the eyes of the able-bodied I and all the others looked alike!

But more is going on here than goes on in the stereotyping of a stigmatized ethnic group, for example. The social invisibility of the physically handicapped develops more insidiously.

Young children care little about skin color or about semitic or oriental features. Only as they grow older are they eventually taught to attend to these. Quite the opposite is true with regard to physical handicap. When small children meet a person using a wheelchair or wearing a brace, they are curious and pour forth questions like, "Why are you wearing this? What is it? Do you take it off at night? How high up does it go? Can I touch it?" If, however, there are any adults or parents within hearing, they immediately become fidgety and admonish the child, "It's not nice to ask such things" or "It's not nice to stare at people who are . . ." The feature in question—the limp, the cane, the wheelchair, the brace—is quite visible and of great interest to the child, but he or she is taught to ignore it. They are not, of course, taught that it is an inconsequential characteristic, but with affect, if not words, that it is an uncomfortable and all-encompassing one. They are taught to respond globally and not particularistically, to recognize a handicapped person when they see one but to ignore the specific characteristics of the handicap. Is it any wonder that a near universal complaint is, "Why can't people see me as someone who *has* a handicap rather than someone who *is* handicapped?" Young children first perceive it that way but are quickly socialized out of it.

But why all this effort? Why this distancing of the chronically ill and handicapped? Why are we so threatening that we must be made socially invisible?

The United States is a nation built on the premise that there is no mountain that cannot be leveled, no river that cannot be tamed, no force of nature that cannot be harnessed. It should be no great surprise that we similarly claim that there is no disease that cannot be cured. Thus the series of wars against heart disease, cancer stroke, birth defects. They are wars which promise Nirvana over the next hill, a society without disease. It is, however, as Dubos has claimed, but a mirage.

Organized species such as ants have established a satisfactory equilibrium with their environment and suffer no great waves of disease or changes in their social structure. But man is essentially dynamic, his way of life is constantly in flux from century to century. He experiments with synthetic products and changes his diet; he builds cities that breed rats and infection; he builds automobiles and factories which pollute the air; and he constructs radioactive bombs. As life becomes more comfortable and technology more complicated, new factors introduce new dangers. The ingredients for Utopia are agents for new disease.*

People no longer simply die; rather, doctors lose the battle to save them. With society raging against the anthropomorphic "killer-diseases," should it come as a surprise that some of the anger at the diseases spills onto their bearers? In this context, the physically handicapped become objects, permanent reminders of a lost and losing struggle, symbols of a past and continuing failure.

How can the rejection of the chronically disabled be justified if we are examples simply of society's failure? The rejection appears more justified when our difficulties are seen as reflections of our own failure and failings.

In a previous era the occurrence of sickness was often seen as God's will. Not far beneath the surface of this belief was the idea that this "will" was influenced by one's own behavior and failings. Despite contemporary emphasis on illness as an impersonal process conveyed and exacerbated by impersonal forces like bacteria, a similar below-the-surface belief persists. When most people are asked what causes diabetes, heart disease, or upper respiratory infections, the investigators may be comforted by the scientific terminology if not the accuracy of their answers. Yet if this question is followed with the probe, "Why did you get X now?" or "Of all the people in your community who were exposed to Y, why did you get it?" then the rational scientific veneer is pierced and the concern with personal re-

*René Dubos, *The Mirage of Health* (New York: Doubleday-Anchor, 1961) jacket flap.

sponsibility emerges quite strikingly. The issue, "Why me?" becomes of great moment and is expressed in quite moral terms of what one did wrong.

When the "able-bodied" confront the "disabled," they often think with a shudder, "I am glad it's not me." But the relief is often followed by guilt for thinking such a thought, a guilt they'd just as soon not deal with either. The threat to be dispelled is the inevitability of one's own failure. The discomfort that many feel in the presence of the aged, the suffering, and the dying is the reality that it *could* just as well be them. And in high technology America, this means dying *not* of natural causes and old age but of some chronic disease.

All this, then, is the burden that we the chronically ill in general and we the physically handicapped in particular carry. In every interaction, our baggage includes not only our own physical infirmity but the sense of infirmity we evoke in others and their consequent incapacity to deal with us.

There is a complementary question to the one which opened this chapter. It goes, "Why can't *I* make anyone understand what it's like to be handicapped?" To me, the different emphasis implies that the person may be at a loss "to tell it like it is." Part of the problem may lie in the vantage point of the speakers. Erving Goffman once noted that minority-group spokespeople may occupy their positions precisely because they are successful adapters and, thus, in many ways closer to the "normals."* yet to that extent, they are ironically less representative of the group they are supposed to represent. This phenomenon was repeated at the Village. Those elected to the Dorp Council seemed least like the rest of the residents, not so much in the degree of physical handicap but in their vocational and social adjustment. They were more likely to be married and have their friends, social life, and work oriented to the outside world. As such, they were more like the Administration and less aware of some of the day-to-day problems of their fellow resi-

---

*Erving Goffman, *Stigma: Notes on the Management of Spoiled Identity* (Englewood Cliffs, N.J.: Prentice-Hall, 1963), pp. 105–125.

dents, a fact which several ruefully acknowledged. One even mentioned that he had never visited the place in the Village which upset me the most, the manual sheltered workshop.

The message is written even larger beyond the boundaries of the Village. Myself and many other "successful mainstream adapters" have not numbered among our close friends and acquaintances *any* handicapped people—an alienation from our disability which has been raised almost to the level of unconscious principle. Moreover, almost every written account about a "successful" handicapped as well as every "success" that I have met (including myself) usually regards as a key element the self-conception, "I never think of myself as handicapped." Yet the degree to which this is true may have made it virtually impossible to tell anyone what it is like to be disabled in a world of "normals." In a real sense we don't know. If we do not choose to speak for the handicapped, the public may nevertheless regard us as examples of what can be achieved, even though what they learn from us is decidedly limited.

Franklin Delano Roosevelt is a case in point. To "normals" as well as handicapped he is the ultimate of successful adaptation. After being afflicted with polio and left a virtual paraplegic, he went on to become President of the United States. What better evidence of success? Yet the newer biographies reveal a man not so pleasant as an individual, not so happy with his lot, and possessed of certain drives and needs that for another person less famous might have been labelled clinically pathological. Moreover, whatever his political achievements, his social success was more limited. The public knew that he had suffered polio, was confined to a wheelchair, and used crutches rarely, but he was careful never to "confront" the public. He never allowed himself to be photographed in a wheelchair or on crutches. He photogenically passed. With the omnipresence of TV, George Wallace was not so fortunate. In every public appearance, George Wallace and his wheelchair appeared together—pushed, shoved and carried with all the negative connotations of such interdependence.

Few of us can control, manipulate, and overcome our

environment the way FDR did. So too with the other folk heroes of disease. They are not the little people, not the millions but the few who are so successful that they also "passed"—the polio victim who later broke track records, the one-legged pitcher who made it to the major leagues, the pianist who was blind, the singer who had a colostomy. They were all so good that no one knew or had to be aware of their handicap, and therein lay part of their glory.

But increasingly I have come to realize how distorted and unrepresentative such success stories really are. The wish to believe them is great, and we all—able-bodied and disabled— continually seduce ourselves in this fashion. The media is particularly helpful in this seduction. The 1976 Olympics found me, an avid sports fan, glued to my TV set. I was pleasantly surprised by a documentary which related to me quite personally. I think it was called, "Six Who Overcame," and told how six athletes had overcome some problem (five were directly physical) and gone on to win Olympic gold medals. One story really grabbed me. It was about Wilma Rudolph, a woman who had polio as a child. Through pictures and words her struggle was recreated— love, caring, exercise, and endless hard work until she started to walk slowly with crutches and then abandoning them, began to run. And there in the final frames she was sprinting down the track straining every muscle. With tears streaming down my face, I shouted, "Go on Wilma! Do it! Do it!" And when she did, I too collapsed, exhausted and exhilarated. Scarcely ninety minutes later I was furious, for a basic message of the film, had sunk in. In each case the person overcame. But overcame what? Wilma's polio was not my polio! All the love, caring, exercise, and hard work could *never* have allowed me to compete in a running race, let alone win one. My point is that in almost all the success stories that get to the public there is a dual message. The first one is very important—that just because we have polio, cancer, or multiple sclerosis, or have limited use of our eyes, ears, mouth, or limbs, our lives are *not* over. We can still learn, be happy, be lovers, spouses, parents, and even achieve great deeds. It is the second message which I have recently come to abhor. It states that if a Franklin Delano Roosevelt and a Wilma Rudolph could *overcome* their handicaps so could and should all the disabled. And if we fail, it is our problem, our personality defect, our weakness.*

Now this great achievement syndrome blinds not only the general public but also the achievers. We are paid the greatest of compliments when someone tells us,."You know, I never think of you as handicapped." We are asked, "How did you make it against such great odds?" And we answer the question. And yet in both the being and the answering we further distance ourselves from the problems of having a handicap. In a sense they become both emotionally and cognitively inaccessible. I am not using these words lightly. I do, indeed, mean emotionally and cognitively inaccessible. Let me illustrate with a personal example. I do a great deal of long-distance travelling and, like other travellers, I often find my flight located on the runway furthest from the entrance. Taking this into account, I ordinarily allow myself an extra 20–30 minutes to get there. For most of my life I regarded this as a minor inconvenience. If you had asked me whether I experienced any undue tiredness or avoidable soreness, I would have firmly and honestly answered no. But in 1977 my attitude changed. Piqued at continuing to inconvenience myself, I began to regularly use a wheelchair for all such excursions. I thought that the only surprise I'd encounter would be the dubious glances of other passengers, when after reaching my destination, I would rise unassisted and walk briskly away. In fact I was occasionally regarded as if I had in some way

*I do not wish, however, to leave the reader with the impression that the media's, particularly television's, only impact on the public's view of the handicapped is in the distorted picture of success. The general problem is perhaps more depressing. In the most systematic and incisive analysis I have yet seen, Bonnie D. Leonard claims that on prime-time shows not only are the handicapped numerically underrepresented but whether the dimension be demographic, economic, social, personal, or interactional, the handicapped are depicted as almost irredeemably inferior to or dependent on the able-bodied. They are retrieved from this status only by a miracle, such as the unflagging persistence of a skilled physician or the undaunted love of a good person. Leonard characterizes their position as "less than human" and "beyond servility."
(Bonnie D. Leonard, "Impaired View: Television's Portrayal of Handicapped People" (Ph.D. diss., Boston University, 1978).

"cheated." Much more disconcerting, however, was that I now arrived significantly more energetic, more comfortable, more free from cramps and leg sores than in my previous decades of travelling. The conclusion I drew was inevitable. I had *always* been tired, uncomfortable, cramped and sore after a long journey. But since I had no standard of comparison, these feelings were incorporated into the cognitive reality of what travelling for me was. I did not experience the tiredness and discomfort. They were cognitively inaccessible. What I am contending is shockingly simple. The very process of successful adaptation not only involves divesting ourselves of any identification with being handicapped, but also denying the uncomfortable features of that life. Not to, might have made our success impossible! But this process has a cost. One may accept and forget too much. Frankly, Het Dorp made me remember much more than I might have wished.

I remember, however, but fragments of a story, for there is no special world of the handicapped, and herein lies another major problem in telling the story. There are several reasons for this lack. While most minority groups grow up in some special subculture and thus develop certain norms and expectations, the physically handicapped are not similarly prepared. Born for the most part into normal families, we are socialized into that world. The world of sickness is one we enter only later, poorly prepared and with all the prejudices of the normal. The very vocabulary we use to describe ourselves is borrowed from that society. We are de-formed, dis-eased, dis-abled, dis-ordered, ab-normal and, most telling of all, called an in-valid. And almost all share deep within ourselves the hope for a miracle to reverse the process, a new drug or operation which will return us to a life of validity.

What then of the institutions where we spend our time, the long-term hospitals, sanitoria, convalescent and nursing homes? These are aptly labelled "total institutions," but "total" refers to their control over our lives not to the potential fullness they offer us. The subcultures formed within such places are largely defensive and designed to make life viable *within* the institution. Often this viability is achieved at such a cost that it cannot be transferred to the external world. Nevertheless, the problems that we ex-patients have in living outside are blamed on us, not on our lack of preparation.

For most of their history, organizations of disabled people were not much more successful in their efforts to produce a viable subculture.* Their memberships have been small in comparison to the potential population, and they have been regarded more as social groups rather than serious places to gain technical knowledge or emotional support. And though there are some self-help groups which are becoming increasingly more visible, militant, and independent of medical influence, the movement is still in its infancy.† Long ago Talcott Parsons articulated the basic dilemma facing such groups.

> The sick role is . . . a mechanism which . . . channels deviance so that the two most dangerous potentialities, namely group formation and successful establishment of the claim legitimacy, are avoided. The sick are tied up, not with other deviants to form a "subculture" of the sick but each with a group of nonsick, his personal circle, and, above all, physicians. The sick thus become a statistical status and are deprived of the possibility of forming a solidary collectivity. Furthermore, to be sick is by definition to be in an undesirable state, so that it simply does not "make sense" to assert a claim that the way to deal with the frustrating aspects of the social system is "for everyone to get sick."‡

A mundane but dramatic way of characterizing this phenomenon can be seen by looking at the rallying cries of current liberation movements. As the "melting pot" theory of America

*See the special issue of the *Archives of Physical Medicine and Rehabilitation* 60, no. 10 (October 1979): 433–486.

†Rita Varella, *Self-Help Groups in Rehabilitation* (Washington, D.C.: American Coalition of Citizens with Disabilities, 1979).

‡Talcott Parsons, *The Social System* (Glencoe, Ill.: Free Press, 1951), p. 477.

was finally buried, people could once again say, even though they were three generations removed from the immigrants that they were proud to be Greek, Italian, Hungarian, or Polish. With the rise of black power, a derogatory label became a rallying cry, "Black is beautiful!" And when female liberation saw their strength in numbers, they shouted, "Sisterhood is powerful!" But what about the chronically ill and disabled? Can we yell, "Long live cancer!" "Up with multiple sclerosis!" "I'm glad I had polio!" Clearly a basis of a common positive identity is not readily available.

For all these reasons, the world the physically handicapped and chronically ill inhabit is many different worlds, not one. It is difficult enough to integrate one's experience into one's own world, let alone communicate it to others. There is a certain inevitable restraint in this communication for what comes out seems like a litany of complaints. And no one, at least in our society, likes a complainer! But it is a reality, my reality, and as such I record it.

Chairs without arms to push myself up from; unpadded seats which all too quickly produce sores; showers and toilets without handrails to maintain my balance; surfaces too slippery to walk on; staircases without bannisters to help me hoist myself; buildings without ramps, making ascent exhausting if not dangerous; every curbstone a precipice; car, plane, and theatre seats too cramped for my braced leg; and trousers too narrow for my leg brace to pass through. With such trivia is my life plagued. Even though I am relatively well off, mobility is a daily challenge. When I'm walking with companions, they must always be on my right, else they will inadvertently kick my cane and throw me off balance. Socialized into the role of the courteous American male, I was at one time particularly piqued that it meant my female friend, not I, must walk on the outside. My moment-to-moment concerns are even more mundane. I must be extraordinarily watchful about where I place both my cane and my leg. If not, my cane tip will slide on a water or oil slick, or I will stub my toe on an uneven piece of sidewalk, and I will lose my balance and fall. In short, I should walk as if looking for pennies. But I resist impositions which impede social interaction. If I am constantly looking down to where my foot or cane must be placed, then I cannot look directly at the person with whom I am conversing. And so I run the risk and pay the price, which means I trip, stumble, and fall all too often.

Any public travel raises more serious issues. Without a car for much of my time in the Netherlands, I became aware of just what an important sense of independence an auto provided. But it also did more—it freed me from much contact with an inhospitable environment. Travelling by foot, I re-experienced the angry glances as I too slowly mounted the narrow staircase from a train station, impeded the rush to seats on a bus or theatre, or slowed up a guided tour because I could not walk fast enough to keep up with the crowd. At the Village, I realized one of the benefits of letting a specialized agency do all the planning. They would ask the questions and deal with the contingencies that the lone traveller found difficult to confront or did not even anticipate. They would know beforehand what places were physically inaccessible. For example, I would have been spared the embarrassing as well as frightening experience of one castle tour. Having reached the top by a one-way elevator, I found myself forced to descend in the only prescribed way, by a curving staircase with no railing with the apex of each triangular step too narrow for my inflexible braced leg and cane. There was simply no room on a step for both my legs. Using both sides of the wall as bracing, I hopped down one at a time. When my strength ebbed I regressed, and returning to the days of my polio youth, I descended the stairs on my rump.

The problems of long-distance travel go even deeper. Every departure from home base is fraught with difficulty—from how long one can go without toilet facilities to how long one must sit in a cramped position, from the lack of a special diet to the lack of a special bed, from the absence of familiar and reliable surroundings to the absence of familiar and reliable help. Each problem slams home our dependency, our sense of "living on a leash." The leash may be a long one but it nevertheless exists. This was especially hard for me to realize, because I had quite successfully repressed my "leashes." For long-trips, I would almost always pack my spare leg brace and back support, but never for short trips. And then one day the impossible happened. On a trip to New Delhi, India, my brace snapped. And there I was with a piece of steel protruding from my trousers, unable to put my full weight on my right leg, thousands of miles from home and I thought from help. Never had I felt so absolutely helpless. Worse, I felt foolish, embarrassed, even guilty, as if I had had some role in my brace's snapping. I felt a sense of total panic never before or since experienced. I suddenly thought that I would never be able to move again but would forever remain where I was with my leg dangling.

But I am "blessed" with a certain amount of income and position. Even in New Delhi, India, I could "command," and that *is* the appropriate word, resources to deal with my problem. What happens to all those without sufficient money or power to alter their environment, without resources to have railings built or clothes custom-made or sufficient influence to have meetings take place in more physically accessible locations? I suspect that they ultimately give up. Unable to change or manipulate the world, they simply cut out that part of their life which requires such encounters, which contributes to a real, as well as social, invisibility and isolation.

What happens when none of these unpleasant events occurs? What happens when it all goes off without a hitch? With whom can I share the satisfaction that I did not trip, that my brace did not break, that I did not have difficulty with toilet facilities, that I made it by myself? When hospitalized with polio, I was tearful when I first defecated without the aid of a laxative. Even more exciting, after months of impotence, was my first erection. My first walking steps I could share, but not excessively, with my parents and friends. My bowel movements were at least acknowledged by the medical and nursing staff. But my sexual issues were kept achingly to myself. Even among my fellow residents, socialized as they were into the world of the normal, there was only limited sharing. There was an implicit limit on how much "the others" wanted to hear about your successes and failings. One ran the risk of being thought "too preoccupied" or even "hypochondriacal." Gradually the lesson was learned that no one including myself really wanted to hear the mundane details of being sick or handicapped, not the triumphs or the hardships.

I am sure the specific details and hardships of having a handicap or chronic disease vary from person to person. But not the core problem. The story is inevitably difficult to hear and difficult to tell. The teller finds it especially hard to acknowledge the central difficulty. Even to think of the world in such a realistic, paranoid way might make it too depressing a reality to tolerate. The only defense, the only way to live, is to deny the reality. But then it becomes socially invisible to *all*. We are sadly left in the situation Slater has described. Both those with physical handicaps and those without—*all*—are deprived of the knowledge, skills, resources, and motivation necessary to promote change.

11

**Four Steps on the
Road to Invalidity**

The Denial of Sexuality, Anger,
Vulnerability, and Potentiality

We are nothing less than simply
human.

Harry Stack Sullivan

"Do you think we're really happy?"
This was the most disturbing question my
Dorp friends ever asked me, and my replies
reflected this discomfort. I either dismissed it cavalierly, "Of
course you are! Why almost every time I see you, you seem
happy to be with one another," or I reacted defensively, "Well,
that's very hard to judge. Happiness is such an individual matter." Clearly such interchanges satisfied no one, and recognizing
the awkwardness, we let it drop. And dormant it lay until two
years later as my fortieth birthday approached.

The entry to a new decade seemed to call for reflection, and
I began asking myself whether in fact *I* was happy. While the
ultimate answer was generally yes, I was struck by my thought
processes. I would always start with a rephrasing, "Why
shouldn't I be happy?" and then immediately follow up with,
"After all, I have . . ." It was hard to keep from laughing at
myself. There was something about my own words that seemed
"canned," and one week before my birthday, I saw why. Spread
before me were books written by women which I had collected
for a course on sex roles. As I sat there leafing again through
Memoirs of an Ex-Prom Queen, * analogies between my own
situation and that of the "oppressed housewife" sprung up from
the pages. For several weeks it had been as if I were hearing a

*A. K. Shulman, *Memoirs of an Ex-Prom Queen* (New York: Bantam, 1973).

thousand female voices questioning their lot in life. Like me they never seemed to get to the heart of the issue. Before they could even understand what *they* were experiencing, their search was squelched by the incredulous voice of their "over-burdened" husband. The words were the same in fiction and in real life. My own father had used them. "What? You're not happy? How is that possible? After all, I've worked so hard to furnish this apartment, buy you these appliances, provide these clothes, feed all of you, . . ." Often unspoken were the words, "How ungrateful can you be?" For me the issue was not simply whether I was happy but an even more basic one; I was unable to let myself even think about the question without becoming defensive. And I needed no outside person to remind me of how grateful I should be. I had already internalized a patronizing attitude toward myself. Like the women because of their femaleness and their poverty, I too had no right to expect more than I had, question what I received, or dare to wonder if what I received was what I really wanted. Whenever someone told me I deserved what I got, it felt less like an acknowledgment of my hard work and more like a compensation for "my condition." Whoever I was, whatever I had, there was always a sense that I should be grateful to someone for allowing it to happen, for like women, I, a handicapped person, was perceived as dependent on someone else's largesse for my happiness, or on someone else to *let* me achieve it for myself.

It was during these daily debates, that I began to re-experience the questioning of the Villagers. Gradually I saw the resemblances between their issue and mine. They, too, were beginning to question not only whether they were happy but what happiness was. In a certain sense, both the Villagers and I were at similar life stages. We had attained just about all the material benefits we had ever hoped for. Life now was far better than it had been at other institutions or even our homes, and was probably an improvement over the early stages of our disability. Almost every Villager agreed that the six rights that the founders had specified (see Chapter 1)—the right to privacy, work, recreation, religion, culture, and self-governance—were at least being worked on seriously.* Yet these "six building-blocks of happiness" were just that, building-blocks, a foundation which awaited an edifice. Ironically, the satisfaction of these basic needs for the Villagers and for me did not so much make us thankful for what we'd been given but provided us the time and opportunity to be aware of what we had lost—emotional needs that seemed to have been taken away, or never granted.

In fact, an uncomfortable assessment of my last twenty years was that they represented a continuing effort to reclaim what I had lost—the right to act sexy, get angry, be vulnerable, and have possibilities. And while these do not seem the kinds of things that one person can give to another, they are needs whose satisfaction the rest of society has helped impede and deny.†

On Being Sexy   Sexuality is one of the first things to go when one becomes ill, and its return, often noted in standard jokes, supposedly indicates recovery. Much is made of sickness being a period of social withdrawal, when one feels less attractive and less interested in sex. And when one becomes permanently disabled, attractiveness and the ability and interest to engage in sex are often regarded as similarly impaired. More and more I realize that this is true only as long as sex is associated exclusively with youth and physical attractiveness. Our society does not like to picture people who are weak, sick, and even dying, having needs for sexual intimacy. It is regarded as unseemly. Such people are thought to have better things to do with their time than holding or being held. Yet my personal experience

---

*Some, of course, felt that they were not being worked on "seriously enough."

†A prefatory comment seems necessary. While both this and the preceding chapter are analytic reflections on my Dorp experience, the data-base and thus the writing in each are very different. Chapter 10 grows out of concrete observations and is expository. The current chapter is based less on acts of commission (what I saw happening) and more on omission (what I felt was missing.) As such it feels both more personal and revealing, and subjective in the sense of drawing more heavily on myself for the data. In style then this chapter has an unfolding quality which hopefully conveys the process by which I came to my conclusions without blurring the conclusions themselves.

and professional observation has taught me to distrust this notion. The desire I believe is always there, but it is shunted aside, suppressed by fear. We do not express or even show our wishes, because we have learned that in our condition of disablement or disfigurement, no one could (or should) find us sexually attractive.

I need to make a brief aside here about what "should" be. Several years ago I was consulting with a sexuality- and disability-counseling program, and the staff was discussing a project of sexual experimentation in Sweden. It involved able-bodied counselors being sexually involved with severely disabled people. It was ultimately discontinued, *not* because of the experimentation, *nor* because of any lack of success, *but* because it was found that many of the counselors were enjoying themselves. They actually began to find these very physically disabled people attractive, and *that* was regarded as shocking if not sick.

To a certain extent these views were shared by the founders of the Village. Sexual counseling was not a part of the services for residents nor were any housing provisions made for married couples. But proximity led to possibility and the Villagers married in increasing numbers, and eventually separate and larger living quarters for couples were created. But this absence of forethought on the possibility of love and marriage for the handicapped was a sign of a more basic omission, the denial of our sexuality altogether.

Before coming to the Village, I thought of sexual matters for the chronically disabled in pretty much medical or technical terms of capability and capacity. In this I was reinforced not only by what I had read of the professional literature but also by my own experience. Like most boys growing up in the inner city, I learned about sex in the male-dominated culture of the streets. Sex was an activity that was almost all "technique." In my early years there were "techniques" of seduction such as what "lines" would work with a woman. As I grew older, my understanding of "technique" broadened to include ways to maintain an erection and to better satisfy women. While this may sound more liberated, it was still tied to the old culture: if a woman reached an orgasm, it reflected on my mastery of technique. My polio merely complicated these issues. In dating, the question of "seriousness" seemed to arise earlier for me than for my peers. Sometimes after the first date and certainly after the second, most mothers began cautioning their daughters not to get too involved, "for after all he might not be able to . . ." Bewildered and hurt, I eventually evolved a defensive strategy. I would date someone until we reached a fairly intense level of seriousness and intimacy, and at that point I would break off the relationship and start all over again with someone else.* As an adolescent, I needed a way to show the outside world evidence of my sexual capacity or at least attractiveness. Talking about "conquests" to my male friends was not satisfactory, if only because they were not the audience I was trying to convince. Dating a lot of women seriously, going steady, and eventually marrying were the symbolic and visible proofs of my capacity.

It was my initial introductions to the Villagers that made me realize what I had long been doing. More than in any situation in which I've participated, marital status was the essential, if not the first, piece of information that people shared about themselves, often followed by a casual comment on how long they'd been married and the age, sex, and number of children. If single, they would mention their future possibilities. Eventually the frequency and intensity of these remarks, as well as the feelings they evoked in me, forced me to see that more than demographic data was being conveyed. To be engaged or married, and even more so to have children was a proof against their being "a less-than." It made them a someone, a someone who despite his or her handicap had the ability to love and to be loved.†

*I more or less continued this pattern until I married. In fact, I never really resolved or understood what I was doing. At best I knew that there was something wrong with this pattern. What I did was choose a structural remedy—marriage.

†In a less sexually repressed society than the one we now live in, marriage as symbolic proof of sexual capacity will become less important. To the degree that such information must still be shared, it will be done in less formal and more open ways, such as living together or simply talking about sex.

But the expression of sexuality was not confined to indirect discussions of marriage. Whether it was the many incidents of touching, all the dirty jokes, or the stimulation at the Gala, sex seemed a large part of the atmosphere of daily living. At first I thought that this "playing-at-sex" was evidence that we were all overreacting to deprivation. But the night at Jacob Veere's (see Chapter 6) convinced me that something deeper was at stake.

After my conversation with Jacob I returned to my room more agitated than at any time since my arrival. As I prepared for my first shower, I tried to ignore my churning stomach and lose myself in the necessary details of showering. After undressing and getting used to the cold steel and hard leather of the wheelchair against my skin, I wheeled into the bathroom. The tilted mirror prompted me to look at myself fully naked for perhaps the first time in twenty years. I had, of course, seen myself naked before, but my unsteadiness without braces or canes for support had always made this visual encounter a brief one. But here I was, seated comfortably, with myself in full view. The hours with Jacob Veere, our conversations about the importance of physical movement had all made me acutely aware of my body. So instead of turning away, I placed myself squarely in front of the mirror. Though supposedly an unmasculine thing to do, I continued to stare at myself. Taking advantage of this sudden burst of narcissism, I locked the wheelchair and pushed myself to a standing position. Turning around but always leaning on its armrests, I tried to see myself first in profile and then from behind. I was struck then by something I had always known intellectually but had never acknowledged emotionally. I had always been aware that my braces, cane, and limp made me look different. But I also harbored the fantasy that without my braces and canes, on the beach or in bed, I would appear the same as anyone else. What self-deception! I am broad through the shoulders and chest, with a bit of a paunch, and then I have thin, almost spindly, legs. The adjective "wasted" stuck in my throat. Overdeveloped from the waist up, underdeveloped from the waist down. No wonder so many people worried how far this "below-the-waist" underdevelop-

ment went. The word "underdeveloped" also bothered me—
like some nation with few resources, or more humiliatingly, like
an evolutionarily underdeveloped creature.* Still looking at
myself in the mirror I backed into my wheelchair and sat. In a
sense I felt even more animal-like in this posture. On the wall of
our dining room at Het Dorp were pictures of chimpanzees,
large torsos with thin legs and long arms. And that was me, too!
Sitting in my wheelchair, I was shrunken. Stockily built from the
waist up but with my arms dangling by my side, almost touching
the ground, I *did* look like an ape. Gazing fixedly at my reflected
image, I began to touch myself. First my face, then my chest,
and then still not fully aware I started to masturbate. Neither
sexual stimulation nor frustration drove me. If anything, I was
combatting an emptiness. I felt a kind of tactile deprivation, a
numbness that I sought to relieve by stroking. My body tingled.
It and I *were* alive. And the satisfaction I felt on climax was not a
sexual relief but a reaffirmation of self.†

Only once before had I made even the glimmerings of such
a connection between sex and selfhood. At sixteen, hospitalized
with polio, and for several months impotent, I awoke one morning with an erection. I wanted to shout, "Look at this!" to my
friend in the next bed but was too embarrassed. The erection,
however, was not enough. Barely able to sit unaided, and still
feeling weak through the rest of my body, I tried to masturbate.
Not until about a week later did I finally succeed. When I did, I
felt no relief of tension, but a re-experiencing of myself. And yet
I was embarrassed by the accomplishment. It seemed appropriate to masturbate because of sexual frustration but to do it out of
"identity" frustration was beyond my ken, so much so that I

*For the first time I also understood how young women must feel when, if "flat-chested"
or "small-breasted," they are referred to as "underdeveloped."

†Thomas Szasz has put forth similar thoughts in his book, *Pain and Pleasure* (New York:
Basic Books, 1957). François Truffaut in his film, *Stolen Kisses* gives one of his charac-
ters the following lines. "After the funeral we went to bed. To make love after death, is
to reaffirm the existence of life."

suppressed the incident, as well as the psychological connection, for some twenty years.*

It seems that the existence of sexuality is either denied or, if recognized, is located entirely in the genitals—and the male genitals at that. What society in general and the rehabilitation literature in particular seem to have focussed on is sex as capacity and technique. If the researchers are not counting the marriage and divorce rates, or the number of children, they are compiling the number, frequency, and type of orgasm. And where the chronically disabled are concerned, the research and clinical efforts are on compensatory techniques, ways to stimulate or simulate erections and ejaculations, ways to reclaim some lost or weakened ability. And while I agree that sex involves many skills, it seems to me limited and foolish to focus on *one* organ, *one* ability, *one* sensation, to the neglect and exclusion of all others.† Sex and loving can surely involve the genitals and what is euphemistically called penetration. But we can also touch, show, and experience love in our fingers, hands, feet, tongues, lips, eyes, and ears, and in our words.

The loss of bodily sensation and function associated with many disorders, and its replacement with a physical as well as psychological numbness has made sexuality a natural place to begin the process of reclaiming some of one's selfhood. But as the self is located in no single place, neither is sexuality.

On Getting Angry   While sex was everywhere in the Village, anger was almost completely absent. In my life, too, I have been

*While some might argue that I was really trying to see if I could do it and, thus, it was ability more than identity that was at stake, I think not. As with other returning functions, I knew that once the process started, it was but a matter of time. I think here the stakes were higher and I was trying to reclaim my sexuality, my sense of control, and with it part of my selfhood.

†Sigmund Freud, *Beyond the Pleasure Principle*, trans. J. Strachey (New York: Liveright, 1950), was perhaps the first to explore the multiple aspects of sexuality.

much more sensitive to the issues surrounding sex than to those surrounding anger. The presence of my sexuality was to me as much a virtue as was the absence of my anger. I'm not exactly sure when this started but I connect it with my long confinement with polio. After several months' hospitalization, it became clear that there were many ways I was going to be dependent on others. Somehow I had to adapt if I wanted to "deserve" their help or at least make it easy for them to give it. I wanted people to do things for me because they liked me rather than because they pitied me. I'm not sure whether my mother repeated one of her favorite clichés at this time but I know I often thought of it, "If you can't say something nice about someone, don't say anything at all." For me it became a key to survival. Nice as I was, I would just have to be nicer. A friend recently put this "decision" into clearer terms. "Now that I've got this problem [a degenerative disease], I just can't afford to be angry with anyone. I need them too much."*

In the years since the visit to Het Dorp, I have facilitated several encounter-type groups for people with chronic disabilities, and the depth of anger (my own included) that was uncovered was amazing. In large part it was a simple accumulation of all the occasions when we feared to express our resentment, whether it was at fate or God's will, at the doctor's broken promises or society's patronizing attitudes, or at the simultaneous overprotection and distancing experienced from friends and strangers alike. Of course, outbursts had occurred, but they were regarded as "out of keeping" with our usual style of calm reticence in the face of frustration. And the guilt, embarrassment, even chastisement, that followed our tirades transformed what might have been justified rage into something to regret. We were socialized out of our anger.

---

*This has been hinted at in *A Life Apart: A Study of Residential Institutions for the Physically Handicapped and the Young Chronic Sick* by E. S. Miller and G. V. Gynne, (London: Tavistock Publications, 1972). There the authors note that the dependence on staff is so great as to stifle certain demands as well as emotions. It makes sense that the same was true of Het Dorp. I know that during my hospitalizations I certainly did not want the nurses or doctors angry at me.

In a sense we were taught that we had no right to complain. Everything that could be done was being done, everyone was busy and overworked, and, besides, "Weren't we grateful?" This gratitude has been our curse. In the first place, being sick made us by definition so dependent that any expression of anger or dissatisfaction became a threat to the continued care which we could not easily get elsewhere and in some sense (see Chapter 10) did not really deserve. In the second place, our anger was regarded as demeaning because it indicated we weren't sufficiently grateful for all that *was* being done for us. And yet the act of being grateful can in itself be both humiliating and invalidating. It has always been puzzling to me that students are "grateful" for the time that I, as a professor, give them in my office, or that patients should be "grateful" for the care given them by medical personnel. To me it meant that the time and care which constitute the jobs we have chosen were regarded as favors, special gifts given to the undeserving.

"Be grateful for what you've got. Look at all those who are worse off than you." From speaking with others about their experiences with consolations like these I, discovered an interesting pattern. They typically occurred when someone was feeling down about his condition and expressed this rather depressingly to someone who did not have any obvious physical defect. The inevitable reply was intended to have a reassuring effect, but it was, in fact, far more effective as a "silencer." Passed off as an attempt to prevent us from wallowing in self-pity, its real function may have been to protect the listener. Making us look at those worse-off than us rather than those better-off, prevented us from being envious and even resentful of our able-bodied friends. For they were the ones we wanted to shout at for having what we didn't have and being so smug about it, for not knowing what it's like and not letting us explain.

Some of the more common expressions of anger are not open to us. Often we do not have the physical strength to hit a pillow or kick a chair. And when we use what we have at our disposal, we are either condemned or run unusual risks. When a friend became so frustrated at this wife's behavior that he rammed his wheelchair into a wall, the hospital staff labelled him self-destructive. The one time I angrily lashed out, I lost my balance and fell. As a result I wrenched my knee and sprained my thumb, the sprain making it very difficult to use my cane. Other examples abound. Someone with the complications of diabetic retinopathy cannot swing their arms for fear of hemorrhaging. To these can be added the countless other people who because of their disorder have been warned by their physician *not* to exert themselves, *not* to worry too much, or *not* to get too excited. In short, they are instructed not to feel anything too intensely, especially anger.*

Thus, with virtually no acceptable avenues for expression, those with a chronic disability are forced either to turn their anger in on themselves or to blunt it. To the degree that we succeed in the latter we become increasingly unfeeling, and often so distanced from ourselves that virtually nothing can touch us. In this way we provide the basis for the stereotype in the professional literature which describes us as "difficult to reach." If on the other hand, we turn the anger inward, it is likely to take the form of depression. Is it any wonder that study after study documents the high degree of depression among those with a chronic disability? This depressed state is not merely a primary reaction to our losses, our dependency, our sickness, and thus something for us "to realistically come to grips with," it is every bit as much a socially induced defense, the result of our enforced inability to express anger. Society's gain by this process is obvious. Since depression is considered the result of one's inadequate adaptation and resources, it can be more easily ignored as the individual's problem. Anger, whatever its cause, has outward expression and direction. As such, it demands involvement if not response.

For those with a disability, the issue of anger, however, goes beyond the ability to express it. While it may be more

---

*The only accepted outlet for anger that is shared by the handicapped and the normal is sports. Perhaps overcynically, I've occasionally wondered if all the admiration expressed for such achievements as playing wheelchair basketball is not buttressed with a certain relief at the "venting-place" the activity provides.

blessed to give than to receive, where anger is concerned the two go hand in hand. If we are to be encouraged to be angry at things that bother us, then we must also be prepared to receive anger if *we* bother someone else. Though such a statement seems perfectly obvious, its daily application is not. And through the years I have grown aware that people are very wary about being openly angry or critical of someone with a chronic disease or physical handicap.

Once I attended a conference where a man in a wheelchair gave a rather controversial paper. While criticism was rife at this workshop, none was aimed at him. I was puzzled until I realized that often I also "enjoyed" a similar reception. In intellectual situations I rationalized that it was because my complex ideas often required more time for thoughtful criticism. In social situations I believed that I was simply too nice for anyone to get angry at. It took a student-friend to finally shatter this delusion.

After we had been working together on a thorny issue, where she obviously disagreed with my position, I confronted her. "Look, you're being evasive. If you disagree with what I've been saying, please say so. I won't get angry."

"That's not what I was worried about," she blurted out. "It's just that I didn't want to hurt you." And then, thinking she'd made a faux pas, she began to apologize.

I was shocked. Prevailing upon our relationship, I pressed her. "Where does this come from? What have I done to make you think this? After all," I joked, "most people, including myself, feel I'm a pillar of strength."

After much hesitation and prefaced with a list of my virtues, she went on, "All that's true, and you know how much I admire you, but I guess deep down I feel there's some flaw and that I could inadvertently destroy you."

All the remarks I'd heard through the years about how difficult it was to get angry with me, now took on another dimension. For all my perceived niceness and strength of character, somewhere beneath the surface was seen to lurk a sense of fragility easily wakened by criticism. The fact that I sensed no such fragility was irrelevant. Others saw it, or chose to see it. I realized how protected I'd been from the implications of such an attitude. For one of the greatest put-downs one person can inflict on another (as the feminist movement has pointed out) is contained in the phrase, "I'm afraid that you won't be able to take it." Since all of us have done things to upset others, to be denied their resentment is to be taken unseriously and to be deemed unworthy of response, to make the provoking action almost unreal.

It is thus that a full circle of anger-denial is completed. On the one hand, those of us with a chronic disability are unable to express our anger, and on the other, we are protected from seeing why anyone might be angry at us. What was originally fostered by our physical and medical dependency has been translated into a *modus vivendi* for our social dependency.

On Feeling Vulnerable   If the expression of anger was a loaded issue for Dorp residents, the expression of vulnerability was even more thorny. It involved admitting that being hurt was a real possibility. For those of us with a chronic difficulty the issue is most often seen in regard to our physical well-being. Long before my first visit to the Village I suspected that confronting their vulnerability would be an especially "heavy" process for the inhabitants. In fact, it seemed that a denial of this issue was perhaps unwittingly fostered by the criteria for entry into Het Dorp.

The admission requirements clearly stated certain minimal physical and psychological standards (see Chapter 1) which were to be met and maintained. As a result, deeply ingrained in the minds of the Villagers was the fear that, if their physical or psychological condition deteriorated, they might be forced to leave. Though the rule had never been invoked, and though the Administration seemed loath to exercise it, the written threat was always there.* The regulation embodies the threat that

---

*From a series of internal memoranda, it is apparent that the Village Administration, quite conscious of this issue, is evolving alternative measures. Under consideration for a

faces all with a chronic condition, that if they weaken they may be forced to leave their homes, their jobs, their relationships, their world.

This was the uncomfortable message that was communicated to me in the first days at the Village (see chapter 4) when my new friends disabused me of "visitor" status and reminded me that it was in the world of the normal where my stay was temporary. What this did for me was to name something that I'd often felt but never expressed. I clearly went to great lengths to retain my resident status in the normal world. Though I experienced the usual colds and flus, in the preceding decade I had never missed a day's work. I seemed to give into my cold, my flu, my injury only in the evening, on weekends, or on vacations. While I seemed to be able to cope with almost any major threat to my status, minor mishaps like slipping on ice or getting pressure sores from my brace would infuriate me. First, they were reminders of how such little things could put me out of action. Aside from whatever pain they caused, they inevitably forced me to alter the way I walked, causing further aches and strains. Second, these minor problems always stimulated the fear that this time it would really be serious—the fall would break my hip or the pressure sore would develop into an untreatable ulcer. Somehow I never seemed to be careful enough. In fact, I was really in a double bind because I had a certain stake (see Chapter 10) in not being so careful about what I regarded as little things.

This issue of vulnerability was also something that my Dorp friends touched on whenever they asked me what I intended to do *when* (never *if*) I got worse. Never having thought systematically of that likelihood, I began to realize how much I had invested in my own "invulnerability." Common to the perception of anyone with a disability is the assumption that there is a very wide range of impaired activities. More often than not, complete immobility and weakness are assumed rather

---

while was a special "nursing street" where more intensive care would be given, but what seems to be the most likely approach is the hiring of more skilled personnel to nurse "progressively worsening" residents within their current homes.

than partial or periodic difficulty. What is more subtle is the reverse, where because one is able to do a certain activity, the assumption is made that one should do it, perhaps even that it is good for you. I have experienced this both publicly and privately. Many times I have lifted objects beyond my ability, walked when I could have driven, climbed stairs when I could have used an elevator. The dynamic is seen more clearly in the privacy of my home. Regardless of the heat or length of time I'd been up and around, I would wear my braces, both leg and back, until shortly before bed. The reason was simple, to remove them made it more difficult to walk and almost impossible to carry anything or engage in any activity that required standing or sitting upright for a sustained period of time. In short, all the tasks I could ordinarily do, would without my braces require considerable effort and this was always difficult to admit to someone.* Even now when I'm much more comfortable with myself, I still feel guilty. Asking for help has always been difficult, perhaps a little more so for me, whose ordinary physical appearance (my braces are not immediately visible) does not continually confront the onlooker with a request for help. But hardest of all was to ask for something that I knew I *could* do. In fact, if I could do it, there was a moral imperative *to* do it, no matter how tired I was or what risk it demanded.

Only recently have I seen the complexity of these continual provings of myself. I did not want to be put in the position of always asking favors and thus having to feel obligated. This was especially upsetting in physical tasks, when I knew I would never be able to repay them in kind. But more disquieting was how tenuous I felt my identity was in the eyes of others. For the key was what *not doing* something communicated about me. It confessed to all a weakness, or more threatening, a worsening of my condition, since people might be aware that "once I could do it."

*I have recently been reminded that one of the ways in which I handled this situation was to omit social niceties like "please" and either demand something with my tone or sort of grunt out my need and point, "That pen . . ." or with a gesture, "Napkins . . ."—all without really asking.

Several years ago, this fear became a reality. I fractured my right heel and true to form, I managed not to miss a single class or appointment. On the other hand, I was, at least in my own eyes, suddenly transformed. From someone who had used but one cane, I now showed up at work (this was in my tenth year at Brandeis) with crutches. While I used to walk fairly briskly, now because of the pain, I limped along rather slowly. Where once I needed no special arrangements, now I had to sit with my leg elevated. And most of all, where before I had never asked for help carrying materials, now I did so all the time. And yet not a single colleague or student inquired as to what had happened! For nearly a week I said nothing, though I seethed. Finally, I confronted one of my closer friends and asked about this ignoring of my difficulty. His reply stunned me, "Well, Irv, I really didn't want to upset you. I didn't exactly remember what you had, but I thought it was some kind of chronic disease and that you now were in some kind of downward phase." It was then that I realized how alienated I had become from my own physical condition. Not only did my friends reinforce this separation ("I never think of you as physically handicapped") but so did I ("I never really get sick"). The separation was so great that only a few friends knew the facts of my auto accident and polio and fewer still, the history that went with them.* They never asked and I never told them.

There is another equally depressing outcome of this stance of invulnerability. How does one ask for help when one really needs it? I felt that for so long I had given signals of "I'd rather do it myself," that I could not hint like an ordinary person when I needed something. It seemed to me that I had to cry twice as loud for anyone to hear me, and this reinforced the desire not to cry at all. Again, a specific incident brought home the dilemma of succeeding too well. Like many large institutions, Brandeis University, my main work place, has procedures for assigning parking spaces. With my HP (handicapped driver) plates and

---

*I found out once that some students and colleagues had created an image of me as a heroic casualty of World War II. Arithmetic would have revealed that I was six years old when Pearl Harbor was attacked!

visible disability, I thought I'd have little difficulty obtaining a technically illegal space directly in front of my office. (Before the new rules, it was where I'd always parked.) Much to my surprise, my request and subsequent appeal were denied and I found myself calling the person in charge, a fellow senior faculty member with whom I had served on university committees. His reply, which he communicated to secretaries as well as myself, stunned me, "Just who do you think you are to be treated so special!" I was confronted with having to convince someone that I was sufficiently handicapped to deserve his special consideration. I tried to be indirect, "C'mon, you know me," meaning, "You've seen me with my cane . . ." But this was not enough for him, "You seem to be able to walk to faculty meetings all right." I was at a loss for what to say. Only when I converted my humiliation to anger, threatening resignation from the university and a legal charge of discrimination, did I feel again any sense of self. As I hung up, the victory at gaining the parking space felt empty. It was threats, not justice, which had prevailed, and the incident made me conscious of what happens to others in less powerful positions.* Having little to threaten, they do as I have done often in the past and learn that asking for certain kinds of help is just not worth the trouble.

No matter who one is or what the situation, the need to ask for help is perceived ambivalently by all parties involved. It's not that help is refused, but that it often has to be justified in demeaning ways. That so many of our aged have found it too humiliating to even apply for Medicare speaks eloquently to this issue. To be sure, the United States has many mutual aid organizations and ways in which people can acknowledge a certain mutual interdependence, but dependency is another matter altogether. Children are rewarded for doing something "all by

---

*Recently a student found herself in the same position of needing special parking privileges. Getting in touch with her anger was to no avail. When she presented a detailed medical excuse, documented by two letters, she was told that if she was "that sick" (i.e., needed such "special" privileges), maybe she shouldn't be at school. Only after I made a formal protest, complete with arguments and threats, was the decision reversed. Once more the "visitor" status of those with a chronic disability in a healthist society was reinforced.

themselves." Adults are reminded that "The Lord helps those who help themselves" or "Ask not what your country can do for you but what you can do for your country." During the Bicentennial, there was the refrain that "our spirit of independence and self-reliance has made America great." All this has created a situation where help cannot be asked for by those who need it. Instead American society has created many avenues for *some* people to determine what *other* people need, but few channels for those in need to easily ask for what *they* need. As the sixties showed, when such dependent or oppressed groups ultimately express these needs, they are called demands. And demands are something the society hesitates to acknowledge or legitimate. And so a final truism sums it up, "It is far better to give than to receive." What an enormous burden this places on anyone who needs! We can then never request anything as a right but can only come as a supplicant, dependent on others for even the opportunities and tools "to help ourselves."

Of all the emotional qualities I have dealt with, vulnerability is perhaps the hardest for which to find some path between denial and narcissistic self-indulgence or what is more commonly called self-pity. There is an almost instinctual drive toward narcissism in all of us which is, in many ways, repressed by society.* For the sick and the disabled, this drive is difficult to resist. In the physiological state of being sick, our body cries out for attention.† In the social position of being sick, we are deprived of all our usual sources of action, distraction, and entertainment. Both situations force us more into ourselves. The usual sterile environment of the long-term care institution further exacerbates this tendency. All of these features might seem to demand strictures against the focussing on one's weaknesses. And yet I suspect that these tendencies become problems pre-

---

*Sigmund Freud, *Group Psychology and the Analysis of the Ego*, trans. J. Strachey (London: Hogarth, 1949). Philip Slater, "On Social Regression," *American Sociological Review* 28 (June 1963): 331–364.

†David Bakan, *Disease, Pain and Sacrifice* (Chicago: University of Chicago Press, 1968).

cisely because society allows for little if any admission of vulnerability. The strictures against crying, particularly for males, is a
prime example. The fear is that once started, it, like self-pity,
will never stop. My own observation is that those people with an
over supply of tears are ones who have been unable to mourn
their losses fully, especially when they first occurred. As a result
they "leak" and mourn a little bit all of the time.

Most of us are shut off from our losses prematurely. We are
pushed to get on with the future and forget what is past or left
behind.* To mark the generally recognized losses and transi-
tions, there are, however, at least ceremonial rituals—from
divorce proceedings to retirement parties, from funerals to
wakes. Moreover, specific mourning periods are set aside—
from specified times during which one cannot remarry after a
divorce or death to the daily ritual *kaddish* said for a year by the
orthodox Jewish male. A chronic disease or physical handicap,
whatever else it may mean, also constitutes a loss—of time, of
capacity, of function, of appearance—and as such it has to be
acknowledged and mourned before it too can be put aside. The
mourning may not be a once and forever thing, for unlike the
departure of a person whose loss we may only occasionally be
reminded of, the physical loss of a function or bodily part is with
us all the time. Our braces, limps, drugs, and weaknesses are a
constant reminder. From this perspective it may be remarkable
that we are not crying all the time.

On Having Possibilities   The issue of potentiality epitomizes the
"damned if you do, damned if you don't" dilemmas facing those
with chronic conditions. In trying to plan our lives, we are either
pushed to regard our physical difficulty as the all-encompassing
touchstone *or* to claim that we are just like everyone else,
needing and wanting no special consideration. These alterna-

*Erich Lindeman, "Symptomatology and Management of Acute Grief," *American
Journal of Psychiatry* 101 (1944): 141–148.

tives are paralleled by two social-defense mechanisms, what Miller and Gynne in *A Life Apart* have called the "warehousing" and "horticultural" modes. The "warehousing" perspective, where the individual is seen as permanently in need of help, is the prevalent mode in most institutional and interpersonal arrangements the disabled encounter. The "horticultural" model of unlimited possibilities is the standard by which people are measured *before* society gives up and "warehouses" them. Though one may appear conservative and one liberal, both have been detrimental to the chronically disabled.

The "warehousing" perspective develops out of the view that the lives of the disabled are entirely determined by their physical condition. Much of this view is rooted in a certain reality. Our early lives as "chronically disabled" are spent under medical supervision if not medical dominion. For the most part our conditions are known and our physical dependence, be it on medicines, prostheses, or people, obvious. This is a reality so overpowering, so visible, so continually confronting, that it is difficult to resist. Still weakened by our physical condition, we then find ourselves the recipients of rehabilitation programs where further assumptions are perpetuated about our abilities and our best interests. This trend is exacerbated by the fact that most programs operate within a medical perspective, a perspective in which the givers of help and the recipients are most distant from one another and where the latter must unquestioningly place themselves completely in the hands of the former. Finally, medicine, drawing on basic American values, is a very pragmatic applied science focussing heavily on practicalities. Is there any other country where the statement, "Let's be practical," is the hallmark of so much thinking? As a result, there is a push to focus more on the practical possibilities of our limitations than the unknown potentialities of our strengths.*

But even in the purely physical realm, there is more potentiality than is often granted. On the morning of my first day at

---

*The most uncomfortable example of this is seen in all the "busy work" one finds in rehabilitation centers and sheltered workshops. My detailed reaction to this is found in Chapter 4.

the Village (Chapter 4) I was told that no rehabilitation took place at Het Dorp and that the residents had gone about as far as they could go. Yet I found this to be true in only a limited sense. While no resident's prognosis was altered, the conditions of many did reach a plateau. Even more striking was a subtle improvement in physical well-being. Through learning new ways to do things, they found themselves and their bodies less strained and in that sense healthier. While some of this was due to sheer electronic ingenuity, several of my friends ascribed it to a situation which not only pushed their capacities but at the same time allowed them to experiment and, within limits, to fail. It may well be that this unwittingly also created an environment for social experimentation. With so many physical needs attended to, time and energy were freed for social concerns. There was, for many, a social awakening—the first chance to be more mobile, more social, to learn or develop a trade, to have friendships, to create a home or even a family. For a few it succeeded so well that with their new-found strengths and resources (personal and social) they found it possible to leave.*

While freedom from a "warehousing" or "physicalist" perspective is not easy,† the seductiveness of the everything-is-possible "horticultural" mode can be equally entrapping. The documentary of the 1976 Summer Olympics which I described in the previous chapter provides an apt illustration. One could not help but admire or envy the athletes, but one should not endorse the message that with effort there is no physical problem that cannot be overcome. This is not the curse I seek when I ask for possibilities. Just because an individual *can* do something physical does not mean that he *should*. While for some people it might be important, if not essential, to their self-image, to spend two hours dressing by themselves or two hours writing a single-

---

*From my circle of companions, two have left the Village and one is planning to. Though the most common exit is through marriage or forming a group, I have heard of people who have left to "go it alone."

†Like those in the Women's Movement, we too find ourselves railing against the assumption that "anatomy is destiny" and the consequent perspective which traps us into some roles and excludes us from others. See Boston Women's Health Book Collective, *Our Bodies Ourselves*, 2nd ed. (New York: Simon and Schuster, 1976).

page letter, many would just as soon spend their time and energy elsewhere. By spending so much time and energy on basic tasks, we eliminate the possibility of realizing other possibilities. Most tritely, we find ourselves too tired to think and, thus, in a sense too tired to live more fully. What is often misunderstood is that this is by no means an individual decision, but one again where many of us feel we are living up to someone else's ideals. No matter that for many an external monitor is absent, the socialization process has taken, the message has been internalized.

The assumptions underlying the "success" of some with severe physical disabilities is also worth examining. Though I do not know the personal histories of the Olympic heroes cited, it's clear that their medical conditions did not rule out their ability to perform. On the other hand, the physical residuals of most chronic conditions are simply not things that can be overcome by endurance and hard work. It is, however, the exclusive emphasis in most "success stories" on the individual's personal qualities which I find most disturbing. Since I know no one else's history as well as my own, my "success" will serve as part of the data. For me, social barriers always outweighed physical ones, and for me, a network of friends and relatives proved far more important than my individual intelligence and personality. My overcoming began shortly after my discharge from the hospital for polio. Authorities at Children's Hospital recommended full leg-bracing and my transfer to the local residential crippled children's center. Not to do this, my family was warned, would impede my rehabilitation and lead to medical complications. To us, it sounded a bit like circular reasoning. For it was the bracing not my condition which would necessitate my leaving home. Since we lived in a third-floor walk-up the medical men simply reasoned that the ascent would be impractical.* On the other hand, I was sixteen, about to enter my senior year at Boston

*In a limited sense their physical assessment was right. In the first few months at home it took as much as three hours without braces and taking the last flight on my buttocks to reach my apartment. On the other hand, neither I nor my family was in any hurry and we arranged for rest stops (I'd stop off for coffee with my aunt half way up) and special handles to assist me in lifting myself.

Latin School, and already felt deprived of a year of my life. I wanted my adolescence, and with my parents' concurrence, I followed the more liberal orientation of Massachusetts Memorial Hospital, which did not prescribe early bracing. Neither institution, however, offered any suggestions to make our lives easier. My family and friends created all the solutions. My father and his brothers raised money for an exercise bike. My grandfather lent us money to buy a car. My uncle braced the bannisters and created supports to help me raise myself. My brother, only eight at the time, ran all my errands and fetched anything I couldn't reach. My mother was the general coordinator and chauffeur and my aunt was my most constant source of encouragement and support.

Getting back to school after nearly a year's absence had its own problems. Boston Latin School had no facilities to deal with disabled children nor any precedent to deal with a student who'd missed his junior year, tutored only sporadically by a retired school teacher. Boston Latin School was willing to let me take placement exams but my tutor shrewdly argued that this would prove too much of a burden and would interfere with my rehabilitation program. She argued that I be placed on probation during the opening months of my senior year and that if I passed, then I be given retroactive credit for my missed year. At school itself we had to pressure the Administration to let me use the private elevator and the teachers to let me arrive at class late and leave early. My friends took turns carrying my books and occasionally even me. In the social realm, my friends loomed especially large. They chauffeured me around, made sure I missed little, and even arranged my first date. Awkward enough as an adolescent, awkwarder still because of my crutches and appearance, I shudder to think what would have happened if the girl had refused the date and later my "advances"! The story could go on with other illustrations from my life and career* but

---

*A similar network of friends and relatives came to my aid in 1954 when I was a junior at Harvard and had the car accident. Though I was confined to a bed for the entire school year, we all created a system that enabled me to attend Harvard *in absentia*.

the point would be the same. To the degree that I was a success, it was because there were always possibilities and a group of people who were willing to keep them open as well as make them happen.

Thus, to emphasize individual personal qualities as the reason for success in overcoming difficulties (and the reason for failure if the barriers prove insurmountable) is self-serving for the individual and the society. For individuals who have lost so much, it rewards them at a cost of making them ignore what they owe to some and what they share with others who didn't make it* To the society this emphasis merely allows the further disavowal of any responsibility, and more important, any accountability, for the process which makes a chronically disabled person's entry or re-entry into life so difficult. Had my family been poorer and less assertive, my friends fewer and less caring, my champions less willing to fight the system, then all my personal strengths would have been for naught. On the other hand, if we lived in a less healthist, capitalist, and hierarchical society, which spent less time finding ways to exclude and disenfranchise people and more time finding ways to include and enhance the potentialities of everyone, then there wouldn't have been so much for me to overcome.

Two words summarize what faces an individual with a physical handicap or chronic disease: infantilization and invalidation. Infantilization is the process, invalidation the result. Being sick calls forth in feelings, behavior, and even treatment, a state of dependency most characteristic of children. When the temporary acute state becomes permanent, then, too, unfortunately, do the child-like qualities inherent in the role. But even more than the necessities of being dependent do this. In a society

*It's a trip I've been on too many times, one that I'm easily seduced into when someone flatteringly says, "I've always admired you and wondered how *you* really were able to overcome so much. . . ." My answer as well as others' answers negate the development of any patient consciousness.

which frowns not only on being dependent but also on being nurturant to one's peers, the able-bodied have only one model for making both themselves and the person needing help psychologically comfortable—the model of the "well parent" and the "sick child." Only children can continually demand help, and only parents can be continually expected to give it. Thus, in recognizing our needs for dependence and nurturance we take the only roles open to us.

The process of infantilization is, however, not only in the roles but in the content. Parents usually set limits on both their children's physical activity and their emotional expression. In particular, parents deny children their sexuality, anger, and vulnerability (i.e., we tell them not to be cry-babies) and put limits on their potentiality (i.e., the parents and the society determine when they are ready to engage in certain activities). But for children there is, theoretically, a time limit. When society engages in the same process with adults, the infantilization inevitably leads to invalidation.

I am led to a final dilemma by all I have written; I have had to give up my romantic notion of people's ability to *make* anyone happy. In today's language "making" puts one in the role of doer and one in the role of recipient. And whatever happiness this brings, it leads the recipients to be more rather than less dependent, and less capable of being happy on their own in their own way. To the extent that the recipients are aware of this, they cannot help but be less grateful than the givers of that happiness think they should be. This, of course, does not mean that a person cannot have a role in the happiness of another. At the very least, an able-bodied person can help work on the elimination of the barriers, work on the "building blocks," as did the founders of the Dorp. But then we all—founder, teacher, parent, lover—must "let go." In fact, the earlier the "letting-go" process starts, the easier it will be for all concerned.

By now the reader realizes that all of the "lacks" I have delineated are of the same piece. They all seem to reflect on the same issue, one's validity as a full human being. As I have written, and my Dorp friends here have spoken, they and I have often been confronted with being seen as less than human. This is inevitable as long as *different than* continues to be translated as *less than,* but then maybe that's the underlying purpose. Perhaps, as in the previous chapter, all I have been doing here is delineating some of the ways society denies full status to those it wishes to ignore, its minorities, its youth, its women, its elderly. Society diminishes them as persons, and having placed them in this diminished status, can more safely deal with them as helpless. For if blacks are too dumb to know, children too young to understand, women too emotional to cope, the elderly too old to care, and the chronically ill simply unable, then it's *their* problem, not the society's.

Epilogue

Some Concluding but Hardly Final Thoughts on Integration, Personal and Social

Another man may be sick too, and sick to death and this affliction may lie in his bowels as gold in a mine and be of no use to him; but this bell that tells me of his affliction digs out and applies that gold to me, if by this consideration of another's danger I take mine own into contemplation . . . .

Any man's death diminishes me because I am involved in mankind and therefore never send to know for whom the bell tolls: it tolls for thee.

John Donne

I have visited Het Dorp only four times but the place and the people feel as much a part of my life as anything I have ever experienced. While the sharing of this experience is the substance of this book, neither the story of the Village, nor of myself, is in any sense complete. At best I have written a progress report. By interweaving the accounts and reflections of my fellow residents with my own, I have tried to describe what it's like for someone with a chronic disease or physical handicap to live in a healthist society, a society which, at its worst, denigrates, stigmatizes, and distances not only those with disabilities but also any reminders of them within itself.

There are no simple answers to the undoing of this process, but the experience of the Village and the writing of this book have led me to a simple truth. Anything that separates and negates those with a chronic condition will ultimately invalidate not only them but everyone else.

With this guiding principle let me conclude with some thoughts on the notion of integration. Again it is easier for me to begin with a personal reference point and build to the social.

As described in these pages, I received very little encouragement to integrate my "disabled self" into the rest of my
life. Any attempt was interpreted as giving in or giving up the
struggle to be normal. Perhaps the road I have been travelling
may be seen through an incident that occurred in January 1975
when I was participating in a weekend devoted to a therapeutic
technique called "psychosynthesis." One of the exercises was a
guided fantasy where, with instructions from a leader, we pic-
tured ourselves, after an arduous climb, in front of a small
crowded house from which emanated familiar voices. We were
told that those voices represented parts of ourselves and that we
were to take two of them out for a visit. Here my story begins.

Two heads attached themselves to the voices and
peeked out the door. The first voice was forceful and was a
role; I called him Jean Spencer after my two favorite male
actors, Jean Gabin and Spencer Tracy. The second, less
clear in tone and shape, represented something more glob-
al, the handicapped side of me, and one I didn't like very
much. I called him Gollum, after a not-so-nice and occasionally pitiable character in the Tolkien trilogy.
While Jean immediately leaped forward almost
knocking me over, Gollum snarled and had to be pulled
out. As we walked along, Jean and I were like old friends
and he told me of the many times he popped out—while I
was teaching a class or telling a story. From what seemed
like far behind, Gollum merely snickered, "I'm there too
but you don't want to see me." His churlishness bothered
me and I snapped back, "I saw you once and I didn't like
you." Almost sadly he answered, "You didn't give me a
chance. I'm not really so bad." But I didn't believe him.
When we reached a small stream, Gollum refused to cross.
Jean and I had to pick him up and toss him over. He landed
on his feet, as I somehow knew he would, but he didn't
thank us. The day continued to be a fine one and we
wandered aimlessly. Gollum played hide and seek and

Jean and I tried to ignore him. I, at least, didn't succeed, and after a while I gave him a grudging smile. As I did, he began to change. His face softened and the snarl became a grin. For a moment I wondered who was in charge of this dream. Did I change him or was he really like that all the time? By the time we reached the next wide stream, we couldn't cross separately, so somehow Jean and I formed a bridge so that Gollum, who was now much larger, could pass over. It was strange; despite his increase in size, he seemed lighter as he climed over our backs. We soon realized that the house from where we had started now loomed on a hill in front of us. But instead of rushing towards it, we ran around in circles, stretching out the time. Not far from the top I lost my balance, and Gollum, much to my surprise, caught me. Jean looked on and winked back. At the cabin, the parting with Jean was easy. He said, "Don't worry, if not now, later . . . Besides, we know each other too well. Some people think I even come out too often." With Gollum it was harder. I was afraid that I'd lose something that I'd just gained. And so we just stared, absorbing each other through our eyes, and left, not exactly friends, but no longer real strangers.

As in fantasy, so too in real life. I am continually trying to sort out the Gollum parts. And while the most common way this surfaces is in my desire to understand what part of me, my life, my personality, is due to having a handicap and what is not,* there is another aspect of my new-found integration which has profoundly shocked me. For letting Gollum surface as a real, and not necessarily bad part of me, has allowed me to shed some of my super-strong, "I-can-do-it-myself" aspects, and, at the same time be more demanding of what I need. It is only within the last few years, in fact, that I thought I might even have "the right" to ask (later demand' certain "accommodations." For

---

*In an attempt to delineate a piece of this I once wrote a personal memo to myself entitled, "A Sexual Fragment: Reflections on Being Competent and in Control."

nearly a decade I went through channels—for example, an endless series of requests to the building and grounds department of my university to get a railing installed in front of my building. Neither justice nor charity finally prevailed, only a changed consciousness and power. Upon receipt of a lucrative offer from another university, the Administration asked what would make me happy enough to stay at Brandeis. I replied, "A railing so that I could more easily enter my building would be a fine start." Soon after I began to make similar requests. The first was to refuse speaking engagements in places where there were no bannisters or elevators. No longer did I automatically reply, "No bother at all," when asked if I minded climbing three flights of stairs to an office or lecture hall. And yet while all this was an important step in my own consciousness-raising, it also represented a certain co-optation into the American way. It reinforced the idea that the problem as well as the solution to the issues of disability was an individualistic one. Thus, while I was letting in a certain identification with my own disability, I was at the same time still separating myself from other disabled people.

I honestly don't know why the next expansion in my consciousness took place. Working more and more with people who had disabilities, one day I finally recognized that the pain I often felt was not merely empathy for their situation, but was really part of my own. All I really know is that as a new academic year opened in the fall of 1977, I changed my handling of invitations. When asked, as usual, if I had any special needs, I answered that I would only speak in a fully accessible facility. My host would be initially flustered and apologize for not knowing that I was in a wheelchair. When I told him I was not, his embarrassment would turn to confusion until I explained that accessibility was an issue for the audience as well as the speaker.*

*In recent months, my awareness of the meaning of "accessibility" has been further expanded. Thanks largely to my colleagues at the Boston Self-Help Center, I've realized that it pertains not merely to physical barriers, but to communication ones as well. Thus, I have begun to request at my public appearances the attendance of interpreters for those with hearing impairments.

As with me in my life, so too with society in general. Even with the greater attention to problems of chronic disease and disability, there is a way we speak of it which perpetuates a separation and a distancing. It seems that to justify rising health costs as well as the costs of moving current architectural and programmatic barriers, we must specifically define of whom we are speaking and quantify them. And yet in so doing we distort an important reality. By trying to find strict measures of disability or focussing on "severe" "visible" handicaps we draw dividing lines and make distinctions where matters are very blurry and constantly changing. By agreeing that there are 20 million disabled or 36 million, or even that half the population are in some way affected by disability, we delude ourselves into thinking there is some finite, no matter how large, number of people. In this way, both in the defining and in the measuring, we try to make the reality of disease, disability, and death problematic, and in this way make it at least potentially someone else's problem. But it is not, and can never be. Any person reading the words on this page is at best momentarily able-bodied. But nearly everyone reading them will, at some point, suffer from one or more chronic diseases and be disabled, temporarily or permanently, for a significant portion of their lives.*

---

*I am struck by the irony that nearly two decades ago I knew that there was something dysfunctional in the way that illness was conceptualized, measured, and even counted. One paper summed up my argument: "In most epidemiological studies, the definition of disease is taken for granted. Yet today's chronic disorders do not lend themselves to such easy conceptualization and measurement as did the contagious disorders of yesteryear. That we have long assumed that what constitutes disease *is* a settled matter is due to the tremendous medical and surgical advances of the past half-century. After the current battles against cancer, heart disease, cystic fibrosis and the like have been won, Utopia, a world without disease, would seem right around the next corner. Yet after each battle a new enemy seems to emerge. So often has this been the pattern, that some have wondered whether life without disease is attainable.

"Usually the issue of life without disease has been dismissed as a philosophical problem—a dismissal made considerably easier by our general assumptions about the statistical distribution of disorder. For though there is a grudging recognition that each of us must go sometime, illness is generally assumed to be a relatively infrequent, unusual, or abnormal phenomenon. Moreover, the general kinds of statistics used to describe illness support such an assumption. Specifically diagnosed conditions, days out of work, and doctor's visits do occur for each of us relatively infrequently. Though such

That we persist in this denial means that the necessary steps to undo this process are likely to be difficult to acknowledge as well as to undertake. But at least three steps suggest themselves to me. First of all, we with handicaps and chronic disabilities must see to our own interests. We must free ourselves from the "physicality" of our conditions and the dominance of our life by the medical world.* In particular, I refer to the number of times we think of ourselves and are thought of by others in terms of our specific chronic conditions. We are polios, cancers, paras, deaf, blind, lame, amputees, and strokes. Whatever else this does, it blinds us to our common social disenfranchisement. Our forms of loss may be different, but the resulting invalidity is the same. While organizing around specific diseases may be good for raising research money, it has divided our strength and pitted one disease group against another. Not only has this led to an overspecialization of services but to an underdevelopment of our consciousness. It has made us feel so dependent on others (the medical world for treatment, the general public for money) and so personally accountable that it has made us feel that we have no rights. We, patients all, perhaps the last and potentially

---

statistics represent only treated illness, we rarely question whether such data give a true picture. Implicit is the further notion that people who do not consult doctors and other medical agencies (and thus do not appear in the 'illness' statistics) may be regarded as healthy.

"Yet studies have increasingly appeared which note the large number of disorders escaping detection. Whether based on physicians' estimates or on the recall of lay populations, the proportion of untreated disorders amounted to two-thirds or three-fourths of all existing conditions. . . .

"Such data as these give an unexpected statistical picture of illness. Instead of its being a relatively infrequent or abnormal phenomenon, the empirical reality may be that illness, defined as the presence of clinically serious symptoms, is the statistical norm. . . . ("Culture and Symptoms: An Analysis of Patients' Presenting Complaints," *American Sociological Review* 31, no. 5 (October 1966): 615–616.)

Thus, I was fully aware that one could make a case for the omnipresence of illness. Yet while I have delineated systematically here and elsewhere what the medical, the research, and the sociological implications of such statements might be, it took nearly a generation for me to fully let in the social, the political, and the personal implications.

*Ivan Illich, *Medical Nenesis* (New York: Pantheon, 1976), is worth reading for any who claim that our only salvation lies in medical advances.

the largest of America's disenfranchised, must organize on our own behalf.* Cutting across specific disease entities, we must create advocacy, conciousness-raising, counseling, resource groups. And wherever and whenever possible, staff and members alike must have a chronic disease or physical handicap. I am not claiming that no one else can help or understand, but that, as with women and blacks, we are at a point in history, where having been there is essential to knowing where to go.

The self-help movement is, however, but one part of the struggle. It's a prerequisite for change, but not sufficient. We must deal as much with social arrangements as with self-conceptions. One in fact reinforces the other. Thus, the problems of those with a chronic disability should be stated not in terms of the individual defects and incapacities affecting our physical functioning, but in terms of the limitations and obstacles placed in the way of our daily social functioning. What should be asked is not how much it will cost to make a society completely accessible to all with physical difficulty, but rather why a society has been created and perpetuated which has excluded so many of its members.

There is a growing awareness that this exclusion is not an accidental by-product of industrial society. There is an ideological compatibility between capitalism and certain Western religions; they have continually justified the hierarchical arrangements of people through "hard work" or "the grace of God." When the notions of religion and law were beginning to lose their power as absolute arbiters of social values, Darwin, perhaps unwittingly, ushered in the age of biological determinism. One critic of the times realized the social import of his work by exclaiming with surprise, "Sir, you are preaching scientific Calvinism with biological determinism replacing religious predestination." The fixity of the universe and of hierarchical relations once attributed to God was now being attributed to the inevitability of science. In the ensuing hundred years, there has

*John Gleidman, "The Wheelchair Rebellion," *Psychology Today* 12 (August 1979): 58–64, and John Gleidman and William Roth, *The Unexpected Minority* (New York: Harcourt-Brace Jovanovich, 1980).

been an expansion of the influence of science and in particular medical science until medicine has in some ways replaced religion and law. Where once social rhetoric made reference to good and evil, legal and illicit, now it refers to "healthy" and "sick." We are experiencing a medicalization of society and with it the growth of medicine as an institution and instrument of social control.* And while some have argued that this is a more humane and liberal way to deal with social problems, the notions of health and illness still locate the source of trouble and treatment in individual capacities, not social arrangements.† To have a portion of our population declared physically unfit serves an important social function. It is important to recognize that in this country health occupations are the fastest growing category of employment, doctors are in the highest income brackets, and health-related industries are among the ones that make most profits.‡ Crassly put, "Some people are making money off the sufferings of others." In these ways the economic and political motives of the society have come to reinforce one another. And until the day that no one benefits economically, socially, or psychologically from someone's being beneath them, there will always be categories of exclusion.

The question of invalidity with which this book began is a question which faces all of us. What happens in the medical arena is the example par excellence of today's identity crisis, "What will become of the self?" This is the battleground not because there are visible oppressors but because they are almost invisible; not because the perspective, tools, and practitioners of medicine and the other helping professions are evil, but because they are not. The elements of the banality of evil

---

*Irving Kenneth Zola, "Medicine as an Institution of Social Control," *Sociological Review* 20, no. 4 (November 1972): 487–504.

†Peter Conrad and Joseph W. Schneider, *Deviance and Medicalization: From Badness to Sickness* (St. Louis: C. V. Mosby, 1980) and Robert Crawford, "You Are Dangerous to Your Health: The Ideology of the Politics of Victim Blaming," *International Journal of Health Services* 7, no. 4 (1977): 603–680.

‡Health Policy Advisory Committee, editors, *American Health Empire: Power, Profits, Politics* (New York: Vintage, 1971).

described by Hannah Arendt can be found here.* But here the danger is greater, for not only is the process masked as a technical, scientific, and objective one, but as one done for our own good.

Finally, regardless of whether we join activist groups, support those that do, or seek in other ways to change the social-political-economic structure of America, we must at the very least look into ourselves. For if morality or justice are not sufficient motivating forces, perhaps personal survival will be. All of us must contend with our continuing and inevitable vulnerability. Not to do so, can only make us further unprepared for the exigencies of life. For when we grow old, and with today's technology survive, and are sick and disabled for longer periods of time, we will experience a triple sense of powerlessness. First, because of our conditions, we will indeed be more physically and socially dependent. Second, through our previous denial, we will have deprived ourselves of the knowledge and resources to cope. And third, from the realization of what we have done to those that have aged before us, we will feel that we have lost our right to protest.† Is it any wonder that study after study reports many of the elderly feeling that their lives have been worthless? A sour ending to any story cannot help but result in a depreciation of not only the present but the past.

This book began with a quotation from Erik Erikson. It is worthwhile ending with it.

> Any span of the [life] cycle lived without vigorous meaning at the beginning, in the middle, or at the end, endangers the sense of life, and meaning of death in all whose life stages are intertwined.‡

*Hannah Arendt, *Eichmann in Jerusalem* (New York: Viking Press, 1963).

†To the extent that we at all feel we are receiving our "just deserts," it's very hard to demand any redress of the situation—we are left to the largesse of others to forgive, pardon and help us.

‡Erik H. Erikson, *Insight and Responsibility* (New York: W. W. Norton, 1964), p. 133.